Lake Marie

A. J. LeBergé

PAGE PUBLISHING, INC.
Conneaut Lake, PA

First originally published by Page Publishing 2021

Second Edition

ISBN 978-1-6624-4185-1 (pbk)
ISBN 978-1-6624-7994-6 (hc)
ISBN 978-1-6624-4186-8 (digital)

Printed in the United States of America

Chapter 1

Janet sat upon the whitewashed wooden swing hanging from her porch as she gazed, dreaming upon the glistening ripples of Lake Marie. For Janet, this was her dream come true. Having grown up closer to the city in the suburbs, her parents, Wes and Peggy, had owned this particular vacation property since Janet was born. Now Janet was twenty-one and had purchased the fixer-upper from her aging parents who had felt the maintenance had become too much of a bother. For Janet, it was a challenge she gratefully accepted and a future she was sure she'd warm up to quickly and humbly. It was an environment familiar to her, and the best times of her life had been spent vacationing with her family in this very home. Since the death of her grandparents, Janet inherited quite a sum of money and had now acquired the home from Wes and Peggy officially only yesterday. Such grand plans Janet envisioned for the lake house. Most excitingly, her own personal possessions would be delivered in just one day.

As the sun set upon Lake Marie, Janet grew more alert. An orange cast illuminated the surface of the water as the wake ripples made by earlier boaters had smoothed the liquid into what was now an apparition of calm glass. The air began to chill with evening breeze, and Janet shivered as an unseasonal coldness seemed to reach into the depths of her and touched the bone. If the cold didn't disturb Janet, the bugs coming out in the evening would. Mosquitoes were plentiful in the summer when evening triggered their voracious feeding frenzy.

"Time to retire indoors for a warm libation," Janet spoke aloud. She could not help but notice how her own voice seemed inaudible over chirping crickets and croaking frogs. They, like the mosquitoes, accrued in abundance in the woods surrounding the lake and countryside vicinity.

Scurrying inside and quickly preparing a soul-warming adult cocktail, Janet suddenly stopped and realized the fast-paced world she had come from had been left behind. This was the countryside. Antioch was a small town. A quiet and unhurried place to settle. Few people lived here year-round. *It might take some time*, Janet thought, *to become fully accustomed.* Here, neighbors were friendly, and everyone knew everyone. At least the locals knew one another. Doors were often frequently left unlocked, and it wasn't uncommon for neighbors and friends to enter homes unannounced. It was a place where many thought time had stood still through the decades. Janet knew her parents had entrusted the half dozen of the residents surrounding this end of the lake with keys to the home over the years to help with maintenance. She did not care at all and hadn't ever given it any real thought. After all, she had grown up with all the folks surrounding the lake and even knew most all the people from town, which was just a five-minute-or-so drive away. Perhaps she'd need to change the locks when she could get around to it. For now, her thoughts just wandered from one thing to another as she admired her new abode. That was what mattered most to Janet. It was her home now.

People Janet knew in town never seemed to be a problem. It was the tourists who always caused trouble. Many were campers from the campgrounds on the opposite side of the lake. Boaters accessed Lake Marie through the connecting waterway channels, churning any trash they littered into what was once crystal-clear water. They made noise on the lake with their powerboats and boisterous yelling. They often made trouble searching out any home looking vacated to loot, vandalize, or party around. In some cases, they would break in and party inside. If not the homes being at risk, clearings in lakefront woods served nicely for rave partygoers who had been known to let their campfires get out of control, including talks of cults holding rituals in the forest preserves from time to time. Sometimes, they would even graffiti the trees and damage natural surroundings. As Janet often wondered, who would bring spray paint with them to the middle of the countryside? Despite the bad tourists coming, Janet knew and appreciated that the season for them visiting was short. With so much to be accomplished this summer in particular, autumn would soon arrive, and the autumn air would keep them away for quite some time after.

In the four-season room with glass walls, one wall attached to the porch overlooking the lake, Janet sat facing the lake. Falling darkness quickly hindered her view of the lake only a mere one hundred feet from the front porch. Her thoughts were still rambling but mostly centered on all the work she wanted to accomplish this summer. The house was in need of a major cleaning, and Janet wasn't sure as though it ever really had a thorough cleaning. Janet wanted to remodel, but the house had an unusual layout in a functional way with a versatile floor plan so rooms could be utilized as she saw fit. Yet there was even more to ponder. The unfinished basement needed a serious cleaning. Dampness had created a mold, and that moldiness could be a health hazard. The gardens and lawn needed much care and probably should be replanted altogether. A motorboat docked in a private boat slip extending off her property needed maintenance as did the pier the slip was affixed to. The two-car garage, plus boat storage, was loaded with cracks and peeling paint, and the floor was covered in oil. Above the garage perched a one-bedroom apartment. It had never been used, as Janet could recall, but would make a great studio for Janet to create her canvas artwork. Contemplating, Janet did not know if she was better off cleaning before remodeling or performing a major cleaning after any remodeling mess was over with. "One thing at a time." Janet focused on perspective. Tomorrow, her things would arrive, and the movers would haul away what remaining household possessions her parents would be keeping for themselves.

Sleepiness and alcohol took over her alertness as the antique grandfather-clock hands spun and a ticking from the swinging pendulum within it hypnotized her. Unaware, tired, and relaxed, Janet fell into a deep-sleep dream state. She was smiling and very contented.

Chapter 2

From the inside doorway, entering the porch from the living room was a man in the dark shadow watching Janet as she slept. The smile on Janet pleased him. It excited him, and he was glad she was there. He stared longingly at her for the longest time as she slept, unaware of his presence. Considering the length of time he watched, he barely flinched an inch as he stood motionless. Just staring. Just watching. Just fantasizing a twisted scenario in his own mind.

With a kink in her neck, Janet arose to greet a new dawn from the chair she had fallen asleep in. The sun was rising in a bright manner over the water while tiny whitecaps sparkled like diamonds in its rays. It was a frequent morning view of the lake Janet had always appreciated. On second thought, she considered how she liked any view on the lake. All that remained of the chilly night air from the night prior was a slight coolness in a breeze, which rustled the leaves on nearby trees. Reportedly, temperatures were expected near eighty degrees, and the breeze was welcome. Last drops of dew nestling atop the green grass blades brought joy to the awaking eyes of Janet, while aromas of lavender and honeysuckle brought joy to her breaths. This was a most-appreciated time of day when the last few early fishermen left the lake with their quiet rowboats and just before the speedboats would start turning out in quantity. On a day like this, water enthusiasts would most certainly be out in force. Much more so than years ago when she had been a child, positioned in this very spot looking out at the same lake, same sun, and same view. Only now the trees were bigger and structures much older.

For Janet, there was much to be done today, and her daydreaming had taken too much time. Having allowed little time to get ready on this morning, the moving truck would be arriving shortly, and she wanted to be prepared. Her parents would be show-ing up too. Janet hustled. Removing clothes from an overnight bag she had brought and tossing them onto the bed, which she now claimed as her own master bed, she stripped off the clothes she had slept in and hurriedly sprinted into the shower.

Water ran in the bathroom as the dark shadow of the man who had admired Janet from the previ-ous night emerged from her bedroom-closet louvered doors. He headed to the bed where the clothes Janet had worn only last night were strewn about. Picking up her panties, he held them to his face. With hasty rhythm, he repeatedly inhaled their musk-like scent. From between his lips, his tongue extended and stroked the crotch. It was exciting, and he was excited. Not just excited over the silk-like fabric he held in his hand and pressed to his face but also over the imagery he had witnessed of Janet undressing through the closet-door slats. It wasn't the first time he had seen her naked over the years. He was certain this would not be the last.

Making his way down the hallway and passing the open bathroom door, the man could see the nubile form of Janet through the steamy glass shower doors. Wanting to stay and admire the vision, he avoided his desires and pressed onward out the back door. Away he went—at least for now.

Janet was sure she had heard the back door as she rushed to get out of the shower and into a towel. Shouting, she repeatedly called for anyone who might answer. "Mom? Dad? Is there anyone there?" She wondered if the moving company had arrived already. Nobody responded, and nobody was there at least now. But Janet didn't know that. Comprehending her own imagination, Janet convinced herself the noise she thought she had heard was just one of many an old house might make and she'd eventually grow accustomed to them.

Just as Janet completed dressing, a moving company van pulled up. It was pure coincidence that her parents pulled up at the same time in their land yacht, which had followed the moving van in from the main thoroughfare. Out the back door and down the few steps leading up to it, Janet headed to greet everyone. First, she approached the moving men. There were three of them who stood with their backs against the truck while talking. All of their eyes fixed upon Janet's perfect, jiggling breasts as she hustled toward them, not wearing a bra under her tank top. What any one of the men wouldn't give to see her breasts and nipples. Wes distracted their obsessed fixation with a greeting, yelling out from his car window.

Peggy quickly became her usual take-charge self and began bellowing instructions for everyone to follow as she stepped out of the car. "You men, I want you to start with Wes inside the garage while I speak to my daughter about details." After barely inhaling a breath between commands, she said, "Janet dear, I brought a cake, snacks, and lunch for all of us. Be a sweetie and please come help me get the grocery items inside before they bake in the heat inside this car." Before Janet could utter a word, Peggy continued speaking about another new topic, "You know your father. It's hot as hell out today, and he would not turn on the air conditioning in the car. As if the heat wasn't bad enough, we had to smell the putrid stench from those horrid dairy-cow pastures most of the way here." While Peggy was a take-charge kind of woman who could talk up a storm, nobody could ever say that anyone would go hungry while she was around. From the looks of it, Peggy had brought plenty of food to feed a small infantry.

Janet quickly realized she'd have no personal say so in how this moving coordination would transpire. Instead, she took a deep breath and let out a sigh. Putting a big smile on her face, Janet rushed to her mother. Peggy handed Janet the cake and was speaking rapidly, covering one subject and another and then another. By the time Janet got into the house with Peggy, Peggy had described the entire morning she and Wes had getting up to the lake. Yet Janet thought to herself, it wasn't any different from any of the hundreds of trips to the lake they had made over her lifetime.

Meanwhile, Janet's father had opened all the garage doors and was instructing each of the moving men. Everyone seemed to be scurrying about outside, and items were going into and out of the garage. Within minutes, one of the moving men came to the back door. "First casualty. I've got a cut on my hand," he explained to Janet and Peggy. "Cut it on a saw blade. Good thing it wasn't one of the old rusty ones." While not particularly nasty, it was best to treat the wound appropriately. Taking charge as she always managed to do, Peggy led him into the bathroom while Janet sat at the kitchen table, feeling useless in her own home. Peggy and Wes appeared to have everything under control as always. As one should say, under *their* control. As always, they meant well. Longing for being away from their control was most likely the best feeling Janet couldn't wait to experience by being on her own.

By 4:00 p.m., the moving truck had departed, which later led to a quiet evening indoors. Wes and Peggy decided to spend the night and take it easy. While it was impossible for Wes and Peggy to ever run out of conversation, the moving event had exhausted them. It seemed wise that they make a fresh start of it in the morning as the moving truck would not be delivering to them until then. Despite exhaustion, her parents seemed quieter than usual. That did not bother her. It was just an observation.

Wes broke the silence. "You'll need to change the locks on the doors. Now that you will be living here alone, I mean. Your mother and I worry about you."

"The thought crossed my mind," Janet replied. "So much to do. I'll be able to pick up new locks in town tomorrow, I guess. If I have any trouble installing them, will you come back one day and put them on for me?"

"Ask Armani Mirelli next door if you have any trouble," answered Wes. "The guy is amazing. He can do most anything you'll need done around here. He might charge you, but he's worth it. Maybe you can do what you can by yourself and pitch a few bucks his direction to help when you are in a pinch. It's probably cheaper to ask him for help by the time I'd put gas in the tank. I'd like you to get that done ASAP." Then Wes changed topics and said, "I'm going to turn in early now with your mother. It's been a long day, and your mother and I aren't accustomed to all this excitement. We'll have a lot to do tomorrow when the moving men deliver all of our stuff they hauled off today. They said they'll be there bright and early. Your mother and I will need to hit the road by 6:00 a.m. if we expect to be home by 7:00 a.m. Though 5:30 a.m. might be best." To which Peggy was nodding in agreement.

"I'll be up on my own by the time you leave if you don't wake me before." Janet was certain. "Don't leave without seeing me." As much as Janet longed for her freedom under what she always felt was controlling on her parents' behalf, Janet knew she'd miss them. "I love you!" She concluded by blowing them a kiss as they parted ways to their bedroom.

Peggy blew a kiss back. "Good night, Janet dear. Sleep tight."

Chapter 3

As always, with a new dawn came the early hours of a fresh morning. Janet awakened from her sleep and slipped into a bikini bathing-suit top covered by a short-sleeved shirt and short shorts before sitting down by a cup of tea Peggy had waiting.

"I anticipated you might desire a cup of tea," Peggy said to Janet. "Not much in the house this morning. At least nothing healthy for a breakfast. I hadn't planned on us staying the night. You get yourself to the grocery store today. I don't want you withering away just because your mother isn't here to cook for you and wait on you hand and foot. There is some leftover cake, which can tide you through until lunch, if you desire. I know you'll be missing my baking, but I don't want you existing on junk food either just because you are too lazy to cook healthy meals. Hear what I'm saying, young lady? Besides, you are a pretty, single girl and too young to get fat like your mother is." Peggy was only joking and not fat. She only lacked the youthful, girlish physique Janet possessed. "I'm glad your father and I stayed the night. I know we'll be back, but this was like the end of a chapter in our lives. Enjoy your new home, dear. We love you."

Janet appreciated the kind words but didn't want things to get mushy before they left. "The grocery store is already on my list of things to do today along with visiting other shops in town." Janet spoke as Wes entered the room.

"Locks!"

"I promise I will not forget new locks for all the doors. I'll stop by the hardware store in town as well."

"And Janet," her father said, "I want you to get the boat to the Baskin Boating Shop on the river channel for some oil and gas in it. Maybe they can look it over and tell you if it's been kept up properly since we last had it checked out. Armani has been taking care of the upkeep on it for us, but he doesn't know everything about watercraft. He's no expert. Any small oversight can become a costly repair. Maybe you'll want the mechanics to do a total overhaul on it after season when the boat is pulled from the water."

"Sure thing," Janet replied with a hint of frustration in her voice. Her parents often spoke as though Janet had never discussed things with them before. Having the boat examined was a topic that came up at least once or twice every year with the start and end of boating season. The topic had been discussed recently with the sale of the house. Janet knew her parents meant well, but now she could hardly wait for them to leave her be in peace. She loved them very much, but they easily frustrated her.

"We will be leaving now, Janet," her mother spoke immediately upon a lull in voices. "I'm leaving the morning newspaper on the table for you in case you want it. Save it when you are done to wrap things in. You'll find it comes in handy around here, I promise you. The subscription will stop coming any day now. I forget the date I told them to stop delivery, but you may want to continue it in your name." A quick kiss on the cheek from her mom and dad, and they departed.

Janet returned to sipping her tea, which had already cooled off too much for her liking. With a sour look upon her face, Janet put the cup down and reached for the thin newspaper coiled tightly in a rubber band. Her sour look turned to one of disgust. Janet found the headlines to be unsettling. They were especially unsettling as it was local Antioch news. There it was, *ANTIOCH*. All in capital letters in the headline. Antioch, where a young woman named Kim Kinski had gone missing from The Come On Inn almost a week ago and still hadn't been heard from. She was just one of many people missing over time. The family of Kim poured their hearts out in the article, asking anyone with information to please contact the local authorities. Not much ever usually happened around Antioch that Janet was ever informed of. Maybe a lot did happen, and Janet was ignorantly uninformed. The news weighed heavy on Janet's mind; and no matter how much more of the paper Janet attempted reading, her mind kept focusing on Kim, and she expressed no interest in the other stories.

Throwing the paper down on the table, Janet leaped up from her chair, leaving her tea and paper behind. "I've got too much on my mind without being concerned over newspaper articles," Janet reassured herself aloud. "I moved here to get away, and that is what I am going to do." It was then that Janet realized she had been talking to herself as of late. It was not something she had recalled doing in the near past. Something else for Janet to now ponder. "I know I am thinking aloud to organize my thoughts because there is so much I should be doing right now." Again, that was spoken aloud.

Going over to a stylish, antique 1960s telephone table bench, Janet sat down and picked up a pad of paper and pen to start making lists. So many lists she should be making; chores, groceries, hardware, and work supplies were included. Once she compiled as many items on the lists that she could think of, her mind wandered again. Her eyes were fixated upon a powder-blue landline phone, which Peggy had left behind. Janet's parents were never into modern technology, but the blue rotary-dial landline seemed so archaic. Picking up the receiver, it was evident that the phone company had already cut off service at the request of her mother. Why Peggy had left the phone behind, Janet did not know. Perhaps it was a subtle way of reminding her to stay in touch regularly. How appropriate it seemed to Janet that her mother rushed to tend to that detail. Peggy always kept everything so organized in life, and now Janet was discovering just how unorganized she herself was. *THINGS TO DO TODAY*, Janet wrote and underlined in capital letters on another sheet of paper.

1. Continue cleaning and unpacking.
2. See neighbors and inform them I have moved in.
3. Check the boat over and take it to Baskin's Boating Shop Gas Dock.
4. Go to town and shop like crazy.
5. Figure out what I want to do about newspaper delivery.
6. Introduce myself again to Armani.

So much for her to do, and where to start? Janet decided it best to clean for awhile while she put her things away. Not that she owned much. Just what she had brought from the bedroom she'd grown up in, stuff from attic storage, her painting supplies, and items she needed for her work. More importantly, now was the time to see what her parents had taken back home with them and what they had left for her. It would not hurt, she thought, to pack up items like the blue telephone to give back to her parents at a later time. Janet started in the kitchen with the refrigerator and freezer as it was the first thing she saw as she lifted her head from the writing pad. That task soon led her into the basement where a spare freezer was running. Best to see if her parents left any frozen foods down there before she shopped for more and overstocked. While overstocking was a great idea during winter seasons when roads might be impassible, there was no need for that during summer months.

Basements normally didn't bother Janet, but this one did. As a child, her older brother had once played a prank on her. When the freezer had been delivered when Janet was four years old, her brother, Steven—or Steve, as he was sometimes referred to—had been playing with her in the basement. They made a fort out of the box the freezer had come in. While Janet was inside of it, Steven duct-taped the box shut. Trapped inside the box, Janet retained the incident in her mind as having lasted an eternity. In reality, Steven had let Janet out rather quickly; but the basement always left Janet feeling trapped ever since. The only doors in the basement were vertical cellar doors leading outside, which Wes had always kept a lock on and the interior door to the basement from the hallway. That interior door was up a long, steep climb of now-aging wooden steps. It seemed as if it hadn't been but a handful of times Janet went down those stairs since Steven had taped her in the box. The basement was just storage and no place for her to need to venture into. It was rarely used storage because it was musty and, on rare occasion, prone to ankle-deep water if the sump pump gave out. Everything in it was raised off the ground in case of such rising waters. Janet predominantly had no interest in ever going down there. There was little to store down there anyway as this had been only a vacation home and not much was ever left behind to accumulate. Janet's father occasionally went down there to putter, and she did not even know what he puttered with since the garage was his main puttering domain. Mostly, it was used by Janet's mother to access the freezer during larger family gatherings and to do laundry. Besides her parents, anyone else rarely had reason to go down there. As a matter of fact, she had been down there with her parents only recently with the home inspector. It was just before the sale of the house. That seemed different at the time. She was older now, and she had not been alone. Today, alone, upon opening the basement door and peering down the steps to the cement floor below, Janet felt like the scared child she once was. It was dimly lit down there, and she felt as if she was walking into a trap.

Step-by-step, the feet of Janet treaded until they stood firmly on the cement floor of the basement. "Not so bad," she said aloud, hoping it would calm her nerves. Whether she believed that or whether it actually did calm her was another story. Her father and the movers had cleared it nicely, leaving nothing but the washer, dryer, freezer, a lawn game in the corner, a few empty mousetraps on the floor, and a small box of trash she'd need to dispose of. Some light streamed through a glass block window, and the overhead light bulbs were shining adequately despite one being burned out. "Guess I'll be down here a lot more now that I will be doing my own laundry," Janet concluded.

The freezer downstairs was empty and already had been cleaned. Janet's parents used it frequently when the extended family would visit, but that had been some time ago. As of late, her parents seemed less enthusiastic about visiting the lake and entertaining there. Maybe the family just grew older and grew apart. Maybe the house was just becoming too much work and a burden.

Her brother, Steven, had used the place frequently with some of his friends until her parents learned he was inviting his friends there for drugs and underage drinking, which made Steven immediately end up in rehab. It wasn't the only time Steven was in rehab and would end up in there over and over again until he eventually moved to Palm Springs. Supposedly, the CA desert had a renowned rehab clinic, and they were evidently able to keep him clean. Living too far away in recent years for Steven to visit the lake, he never came around anymore. For that matter, Steven never came to Illinois to visit the family. That did not please Janet and the rest of the family, as anyone who knew her and her family would understand.

With nothing left to do downstairs at the moment, Janet picked up the box of garbage off the floor and headed back up. Clouded by thoughts of Steven, Janet didn't even notice that her fear of the basement had subsided and left her mind completely. Out the back door and to the trash can by the garage she headed with box in tote.

"Hello, Janet," a man's deep, sexy voice bellowed out from the garden of the house next door to hers to the north. It was Armani. Armani was a man five years her senior and no longer the boy Janet had grown up around. He had been a boy Janet always admired and dreamed about, but age seemed to hinder anything serious between them. He was a friend of Steven's when Steven was in town and was younger, but Janet was too young to be included in activities between the boys. Now he was a man and a man Janet still found very appealing.

"Hi!" Janet was quick to reply with almost a blush. "How are you and Marissa?" Marissa was Armani's ex-girlfriend, which made Armani single and even more appealing to Janet.

"I'm just great, Janet," Armani answered. "Although Marissa and I stopped dating about four months ago. She didn't like that I live the lake life, and she wanted to see the world. I wasn't enough for her, I guess. She split." Armani didn't seem to still be grieving over the fact and volunteered more information than she had asked him for. "I saw a truck here yesterday and things coming and going. Are your parents redecorating?" Armani questioned.

"No!" Janet said proudly, but with some sorrow. "My grandparents passed away and left me some money. I bought the house from my parents and will be living up here full-time now. Everything happened so quickly. I assumed my parents would have already told you that much. You know how on top of everything they usually are. Now that my parents probably will not be around as much because of that, my dad had asked me to call upon you to help me out with some tasks—maybe. That is, if you can and are willing?"

"Wow! That's some news," Armani commented with a surprised look upon his face. "Not often we get a new full-time resident around these parts. Not even an old one."

"So much to do," said Janet. "I was just about to take the boat to gas it up and looked at by the boat shop. Then I need to head into town for a few things. I'll let you know after I go to the hardware store if I'll need any help shortly."

"Well, Janet, I'd not mind coming along with you for the day if you don't mind? I need to pick up a few things myself," Armani asked coolly, hoping she'd not object. "I'll even buy you lunch to celebrate your move."

"An offer I can't refuse," Janet accepted. "How about giving me thirty minutes to freshen up and we can go?"

"Sounds great! I'll meet you out at your pier in, say, thirty minutes?" Armani questioned with a sexy smile that melted her heart. Perhaps it was his voice, but the smile and his good, rugged looks only added to his masculine appeal.

As Armani walked away, Janet noticed how much work he had invested in his gardens and lawn. Everything was so lush and maintained while her yard looked an absolute mess. The only flowers growing around her were apparently weeds, and it only went to remind Janet how much work she had in store for herself. Her view quickly changed from weeds to that of the shifting of Armani's firm, sexy ass as his muscular buttocks moved back and forth in his perfectly fitted jeans while he walked away from her.

Chapter 4

Thirty minutes later to the very second, Armani was waiting on the pier as promised. Only now he had changed into boxer-style swimsuit trunks with a tight T-shirt, which Janet found very appealing. Janet continued wearing her bikini top and shorts she donned earlier but had removed her shirt, which concealed her shapely, ample breasts. More now than ever before, Armani saw Janet in a mature form. For the first time, he was seeing the young woman she had developed into. He had seen her grow up but still always viewed her as just a child.

Their boat left the pier slip and sped up rapidly toward Baskin's with Janet at the controls. Armani quickly took over driving when they reached the channel so Janet could inspect the boat for any supplies she may desire to pick up at the boat shop. The boat ride was a very short distance across the lake and down a connecting channel to the next lake where Baskin's set perched lakeside. Along the way, Armani occasionally glanced behind to admire Janet as she bent over to inspect the storage crevices within the vessel.

Janet loved Baskin's. It was more than a gas pump for boats. There was a huge warehouse for storing beautiful marine vessels not in use. Some boats were for sale. More excitingly, there was a store with marine necessities, fishing supplies, groceries, and gifts. Attached was a casual grill restaurant with a dining patio overlooking the water. It wasn't a large place to shop and dine; but there were always interesting finds, and the food was great for what it was. There, Armani and Janet dined for lunch that day while a mechanic performed a basic inspection on Janet's boat.

Conversation between Janet and Armani flowed. It was as though they had known each other forever and never had been apart during off seasons. Technically, Armani had known Janet her whole life. So much to discuss, and time went quickly.

At first, their conversation centered around the headline Janet read earlier that day. Armani didn't have any comment pertaining to Kim Kinski's case and hadn't read the paper recently. He mentioned that he did not have television in his home either and that he'd been too busy to watch news or anything on one even if he had. He relied upon his clients to fill him in on any news stories, but they had not said anything to him recently. People wanting to be isolated from the world were commonplace in Antioch. Armani was evidently one of them. To keep his part of the conversation flowing on morbid subjects, Armani began discussing all the awful events on Lake Marie that had made headlines years ago. Some Janet had not heard of, and others she may have just been too young to recall.

For one, a drunk fisherman had fallen off his rowboat and drowned. Authorities had to comb the water before pulling his corpse out. A gash on his head indicated he must have struck his head in a fall from his aluminum rowboat.

Second, a water-skier fell down, and a motorboat speeding by decapitated the skier. The head was never recovered. Very recently, a group of campers disappeared from the campgrounds across the lake. And there were others he mentioned.

None was more disturbing to Janet than the incident involving the girl who had lived next door to the south of Janet. Her name was May, and May was a few years older than Janet; but they still played together often. May was her best friend in the area, and there weren't many girls to associate with. Janet had been there the day May wandered onto the pier during her own birthday party. Seemingly, nobody noticed that May had fallen down, struck her head on the dock, and had fallen into the lake where she drowned. It was an event Janet had almost totally wiped from her adult memory because Janet chose not to think about it. Yet it had been a lesson for Janet to always be alert when near the water alone. As Janet grew up, Janet handled the water alone superbly. She respected it. She respected the rules of driving a boat, fishing regulations, and sun safety as best she could. The thought of safety reminded her of the new locks she needed to purchase and might need Armani's help to install.

With that thought, Janet rushed Armani through the rest of lunch and suggested they be on their way soon. She still wanted to look quickly through the boat shop store and talk for a moment with anyone in there she may know and had not seen in a while. Then they would still need additional time to head home and change clothes in order to drive downtown.

Conversation never seemed to dwindle while Armani and Janet were together. On their trip to town, Janet realized how much Armani had done for Janet and her parents over the years. He always had their backs. Even when the other boys laughed at her or played pranks, he was never a part of any of it. Now the age difference seemed to not matter so much. It had mattered when she was four and he was nine. It mattered when she was nine and he was fourteen. It even mattered when she was fourteen and he was nineteen. By the time she was eighteen, Armani was otherwise involved. Now that she was twenty-one and he was twenty-six, the age difference didn't seem to matter one bit to Janet. More importantly, Armani didn't seem to mind. He appeared to be treating her as his equal. His conversation even became flirtatious at times. Detailed talk had become mature in nature, and subject matter was intimate at particular points in time. Not that any topic was approached blatantly, but Janet felt that her childhood dreams of coupling with Armani could become a real possibility now.

As the wonderful day they spent together wore on until early evening, they found themselves about to part ways. Shopping had been rushed and exhausting, but they did get what they had gone for. It wasn't what Janet had imagined her day would be because she originally thought she'd be alone and have time to stop in and visit with shop owners and employees she was familiar with. Instead, she had spent it in almost its entirety with Armani, and only they were able to accomplish what was needed. Not that Janet minded that in the least. Time had gone very quickly. Not wanting Armani to leave as of yet, Janet spoke up and invited him in for a cocktail using the excuse she wanted to thank him for lunch, helping her carry store bought goods in, and for showing her a wonderful day—to which Armani accepted the invite. He hadn't failed to notice she said she'd had a wonderful day with him.

Both seated upon the living-room sofa with cocktails in hand. Janet made a bold move and discussed her lifelong feelings toward Armani, exposing her vulnerabilities. Without responding with a word, he grabbed her face, placed his hands upon each side of her beautiful cheeks, and drew her in closely for a passionate kiss. Without words, he gazed into her eyes and kissed her again and again. Janet was so dazed by the experience that she noticed nothing except the passion he lavished upon her. Never in her richest dreams would she have thought her evening would be ending like this. Until that morning, she was sure Armani and Marissa would be getting married, and she'd never stand a chance. Her own home, Armani, and freedom from her parents… It seemed she was being blessed with all she could have ever wished for.

From the living room, he led her to her bedroom and laid her upon the bed where he ravaged her with immense passion. Seducing her, he kissed her body all over from top to bottom while pulling off what few clothes she had on. When he was ready, his swollen manhood penetrated her mound of *love pudding* and thrusted in and out of her over and over until they both climaxed at the same time. Over and over, he ravaged her though the dark night until they both laid exhausted and spent. Janet did not know what even happened come the very end. Perhaps she passed out or was just lost in some type of a dream state? Her head was spinning, and when she somewhat regained her composure, Armani was done and lying beside her. On the sheets was the blood of her virginity. Armani was surprised Janet had remained a virgin, and he had taken that from her. It seemed so uncommon for a woman of her age these days, he thought, given his past experiences with women.

Later in the morning, Janet awoke alone. She was uncertain at first if what had transpired had not been all but a dream. *Perhaps it had been*, she wondered. The virgin bloodstains told another story. It had not been a dream by any stretch of the imagination. Why had he left? Why had she not been awakened to see him off? Her head still seemed to be spinning somewhat, and her thoughts reeling. This confusion was starting to become a feeling she was experiencing more frequently, and the possibility of a potential medical issue had to be considered.

Chapter 5

Janet wandered over to Armani's house, but he didn't answer the door. She peered in his garage window, which was caked with filth, but could see there was no car in there. How strange he had left without saying anything, she felt. Not even a note left behind. Now he evidently wasn't at home at all. Maybe he had an early job she did not know about? Maybe he'd have called if he had her phone number? Maybe hooking up with the guy next door was a mistake? Maybe their night had been imagined and never happened at all? She knew it happened, but why was she thinking crazy thoughts like that? It had to have happened because she knew she had never imagined anything like it in her whole life. Yet it all seemed so surreal to her. Having lost her virginity was a big deal to her even if Armani was accustomed to screwing women. Waking up the morning after alone in a bed was not the way she pictured the experience would end. Not that she knew what to expect, but that was definitely not it.

Walking as she wondered, Janet headed over to her other next-door neighbor's house, a friend of her parents, Gertrude. Gertrude lived in the house to the south of Janet's, and it was in rather close proximity given all the vacant land around. People did not see Gertrude often, and Gertrude tended to keep to herself. In the past, Peggy went over to visit with Gertrude, and then Peggy relayed any gossip they discussed over family dinner. Gertrude was a loner who led a sad life, in Janet's opinion. As May's mother, Gertrude never got over the death of her only daughter and child. Gertrude drank to cope with the incident, and her husband eventually left her for a much younger woman. That only apparently made Gertrude drink even more. She never seemed to leave the house and relied upon Armani to run her errands and tend to the outside of her home, as far as Janet knew. Janet never seemed to see her around at all. Few people would ever know she was there at all.

With a knock on Gertrude's door, Janet was surprised that Gertrude appeared at the door instantaneously after the first tap. Without opening the door, Gertrude yelled, "I don't know you! What do you want?" She was a feisty old lady, and her voice suited her. Quick to reply, Janet announced herself. Gertrude flung open the door with haste and was thrilled to see Janet standing there. "My, how you have grown, my dear sweet girl!" Janet stood on the porch, speaking casually for a couple of minutes and telling Gertrude about her move into the house and how they were now full-fledged neighbors. Gertrude reciprocated with small talk. Janet was surprised at how cleaned up Gertrude was and not intoxicated at all. In fact, Gertrude looked heavenly and not at all like Janet's mother had been describing her. Instead of continuing their conversation at the door, Janet invited Gertrude over for cake and tea. Gertrude eagerly accepted and walked outside, locking the door behind her. It seemed quirky to Janet. Not so much as quirky that Gertrude locked her door but that she had her keys attached to her wrist with an elastic band as if she'd been expecting to go out or was worried she'd lose them.

At Janet's house, Gertrude ate the cake Peggy had left behind with a voraciousness in her appetite. Janet conducted much of the initial conversation while Gertrude had her mouth full of the sweet goodness. Janet complimented Gertrude on how nice she looked and also how nice her home appeared from what she observed. "It's thanks to Armani," Gertrude paid a compliment to him. "He takes care of all my household needs and has taken care of me since… well, since I wasn't well." Janet thought that was very kind of Armani. The more Gertrude spoke, the more she seemed to speak of Armani as if he were her own son. While it seemed odd, Janet was understanding of the old woman. Gertrude was obviously a lonely person, and Armani helped her out frequently.

"On the subject of Armani, do you know where he might be?" Janet inquired, hoping to get some information out of Gertrude. "I need some new locks installed on my house as soon as possible and was hoping he could help me with that. There are other things I need as well. He supposedly has tools—all the tools I haven't yet acquired for myself. I mentioned it to him yesterday, and now I haven't been able to find him yet today. I had just come from his place before coming to your home."

Gertrude hadn't a clue where Armani might be. However, the issue of locks seemed of most importance to Gertrude. "You keep your house safe. One can't be too careful, you know, especially a pretty, young girl like yourself alone around here. When you get to be my age and get to be looking like me, you won't need to worry as much."

Janet got the sense that Gertrude was providing her with warnings, and Janet felt the need to ask for details. "Why is security such a concern around here now after all these years? Growing up here, I never recall any problems."

"Why, Janet," Gertrude told her, "you probably wouldn't know. People around here like to keep their secret lives to themselves. I know what goes on though. I've been around here long enough to see and hear things. You can't keep anything from old Gertrude for too long. If you knew, you'd worry. Then again, I'm not one to gossip."

Gertrude's answer did not satisfy the curiosity Janet had. "Do tell?" Janet questioned with the desire to hear all the gossip.

"Well, Janet... You know the big house a few doors down? The one that has been abandoned and in disrepair since the original owners committed suicide? Why they'd leave the house to their only son who is in a facility for special needs is beyond me. He can't use it. About seven years ago, they found two young girls in there drained of their blood. I know because I found them. One day, I went outside and saw a coyote walking with a human hand in its mouth. I came right back inside my house, I tell you, and called the sheriff. Might I say, I don't think he believed me. He arrived, and we looked around the area. Well, he didn't know I was walking where I was, but I walked in that house right behind him. And there they were, dead and naked too. Shameful and so sad. It was a horrible sight to behold! I thought my ticker was going to give out on me right there and then. It skipped a few beats, I'm sure."

"Gertrude, I can't fathom it all. Who pays the taxes on the property? Who takes care of the property? Why didn't I hear about this?" Many questions were raised by Janet.

Gertrude seemed to have all the answers. "A trust fund belonging to their son pays the bills. Armani keeps the outside grounds maintained minimally. Armani is really hired by an old coot, Irwin. You may know him? The old man who lives up the road? Irwin knew the family and was their son's godfather. While looking out for their son, Irwin looks after the property as well. He is the caretaker. These days, Irwin is too feeble to look after anything, if you ask me. Know what I mean? As you can see, he doesn't do a great good job with his own home nor at the estate I'm speaking of. I'm surprised that the house is still standing given its disrepair, and it hasn't been vacant all that long. You'd swear nobody has lived in it for a hundred years. That day, the back door was open when Sheriff and I entered the house. I thought I was going to see Irwin ripped apart in there by a pack of coyotes. Instead, there were two girls. I was asked not to say anything because it is an ongoing investigation, but those never go anywhere around here. If somethin' isn't solved right then and there around here, it doesn't get solved. That doesn't mean the nice sheriff and police don't try hard. Their staff has been cut clean to the bone with budget cuts. Nobody around here wants to pay higher taxes. Nobody's got the money. Say, Janet, have you got a nip of gin around the house? This tea you served up just isn't my bag. Get it? Tea? Bag? Tea bag? Forgive me. I just spend too much time alone humoring myself," Gertrude apologized.

Janet had stocked her bar from her trip into town and was quick to jump up to get some. Conversation with the old woman was intriguing, and Janet could see why her mother spent time speaking with her. As Janet poured a generous glassful of alcohol for her guest and a shot for herself, Gertrude kept right on talking. Alcohol this time of the day was not a habit Janet usually would indulge in, but it may have seemed rude to make her guest drink alone.

"You know, Janet, when my little girl died, that was a so-called ongoing investigation. It never went anywhere. Those people missing from the campsite haven't been found. Pretty teen girls spending nights with young men in the woods doing nasty things. They are a so-called ongoing investigation as well. Those girls could have run off with the boys to God-knows-where, but all their stuff was left behind. I mean, purses with identification and such just left behind. People just don't run off and leave that kind of stuff behind. Know what I mean? I ask you... What young girl goes off into the woods with young men? Maybe they got what was coming to them? Of course, I only know what I know from local gossip. Every time something happens around here, Sheriff Dean comes a knocking on my door. The sheriff is like a son to me too. All these boys around here are like real sons I never had. Some good, and some not so good." Suddenly, Gertrude's voice became somber. "Except for your brother. He never bothered with me much, and I don't think he liked me a whole lot."

Janet felt a need to defend her brother. "I am sure that is not the case. Steven has always gone his own way and been a loner. You know what that's like? You are a bit of one yourself. He lives in Palm Springs, California, now. I don't even hear from him as much as I would like, and I know my mom and dad don't hear from him much either. Our family was only here during the summers and occasional holidays. In general, I don't think Steven liked leaving our main home to come here much. He missed his friends back home, and Dad always kept him so busy with chores around here. Even when we were very small, there was always so much to keep us occupied. I know Steven appreciated the good times though.

"You know, Gertrude, my mom always said not to bother the neighbors, and that included us bothering you. Being a young girl and boy as we were, my mom felt you didn't want us coming to the neighborhood and disrupting your peacefulness. It's bad enough our motorboat would make noise. Then we were often outside hammering loose boards and working or running around, whooping it up as kids do. Dad would get so mad at us if he could hear us. If he could hear us, that meant our voices were echoing and other people could hear. That wasn't permissible. My mom and dad wanted us to be prim and proper when other people were about. That's all different now. Times have changed. We've grown up. I'm here now, and I'd like to be your friend. Your adult friend. You can call upon me if you need something. Anything, anytime."

"To friends!" Gertrude toasted with her glass in the air after having helped herself to another serving of gin. In a flash, Gertrude's persona seemed happily normal again. Maybe a bit more sloshed, but happy and normal. "Janet, there is a lot going on around the lake and in town, so be safe out in the world. You can't trust the tourists. They are outsiders, and you don't know them like I do. They come from all over and leave their world behind. They become different when they are here. Things they would not do at home, they feel are acceptable here and without consequence. Carefree, they are, like a bunch of wild animals. You gotta show extra care and caution for they don't watch out for the ignorant actions of others. You get what I'm saying, girl? You don't know people here like I do, but you'll soon learn."

Janet listened to Gertrude's warnings and eventually noticed the clock on the wall. "Gertrude, would you look at the time? I should get on with my day. So much to do and so little time. It's already noon, and I have yet to do anything much productive. I need to go see if Armani is home. I so appreciated our talk."

Gertrude arose from the table, and they headed out the door. "You keep those doors locked," Gertrude stated with warning. "I'd hate have anything happen to my new friend who is probably my only woman friend in this world," Gertrude said that with a chuckle, while Janet knew that wasn't the case.

Her mother liked her very much and considered Gertrude to be a friend. That was not the same being as though her mother would not always be around to rely upon as Janet would now be. This was something Janet was proud of, and it happened totally unexpectedly. Never had she thought Gertrude would be so welcoming in allowing her into her life. Gertrude was not an old hag and useless drunkard as Janet may have imagined her to be or was led to believe from others talking about Gertrude. Now they were friends. That was an accomplishment for one day. A disturbing accomplishment, Janet thought, being she was now befriending her mother's friends; but an accomplishment nonetheless.

Chapter 6

Armani pulled onto the dirt-and-gravel road adjoining his garage just as Janet approached. "Hello! I have a lock installation job for you. That is, if you are up for it?" Janet asked modestly the moment Armani stepped out of a new, elite white sports car. "Nice car!"

"That's how you greet the man who took you to heaven just hours ago? 'I have work for you,' and you compliment his car? What about something like 'There's that stud of a man'?" Armani jokingly complimented himself.

"I did not want to swell his head too much!" Janet joked back.

"I'll give you something to swell," Armani continued the joking.

He grabbed Janet tightly and planted a wet kiss on her lips. His tongue penetrated her mouth forcefully even though she wasn't sure if she liked French kissing much. It was new to her. Not wanting to offend him, she let him do as he pleased. His tongue was thick, firm, and wet in her dainty mouth. It slid in and out, taking her breath away. His kisses made her head whirl, and her oxygen level depleted within his suffocating liberties.

She had never been kissed in such a way, and she never imagined it would be like this with any man. This was nothing like the makeout sessions she'd experienced with younger boys in high school. While in college, Janet had stayed focused on her studies, friends, and family. That didn't mean guys did not try to get with her. Guys she may have considered never expressed interest in her or were not available. The two male friends she had through college turned out to be gay. They introduced her to other gay men whom she associated with and to other straight males but whom were on a more intellectual basis than love interest. However, single, straight men never played a major role in her life otherwise. Perhaps the gay men she associated with may have kept the straight ones away, Janet briefly thought then chuckled.

Never had she been in the arms of a man like Armani. The last thing she wanted was for him to think she could not handle him physically, emotionally, or intellectually. It was almost embarrassing enough for her to have been a virgin. That alone was an obvious indication she had never fully experienced any man. She knew Armani had experience with women. Her virginity was not something they had talked about. Neither before nor after she had bled. It meant a lot to her. Was he pleased she had saved herself for him? Was he surprised? Did he not know what to say about it? Had he been grossed out by her blood? Was there any need for him to say anything about it at all? She so wanted to be inside of his head to know all of what he was thinking. Perhaps the right moment would come along when they could discuss it sometime…someday. That time was not now as Armani slipped his tongue into her mouth and probed deeply.

She wondered, had she greeted him inappropriately, making her come across as too easy? Should she question where he went and why he never told her he was leaving come morning? Had she sounded too nagging by presenting him with a chore? Did she lack passion and would she need to step up her game to keep an experienced man such as Armani interested in a plain, average girl she felt she was? Janet was far from average. She basically just simply never gave herself credit nor had she lavishly displayed herself for the benefit of others nor had she even cared. Now she found herself caring. That meant something to her, which he, as a man, may not be comprehending. It would require discussion. This was not the time for such words.

When the kissing came to a halt, they gazed into the eyes of each other… She with her sparkling blue blues, and him with his deep, rich Italian brown irises. "I feel so surprised by you, Armani. I was a little girl, and now here we both are. Both all grown up. I was a virgin, and now here we are doing this. I didn't know where you went to this morning, and now you are here. I do know that last night wasn't just a dream, and I'm so happy. By the lump in your pants, I think you're happy too." Suddenly, the questions Janet had been wondering and the feelings she held inside spewed with ease as words from her lips. They almost flowed without any thought at all.

Janet's body twirled around as Armani grabbed hold of her. His 220-pound muscular frame was so large compared to her delicate, girlish figure of 98 pounds. Before she could comprehend what was happening, Armani unbuttoned the button on her shorts, slid down the zipper, and dropped her clothes to her ankles. They hit the garage floor. Compressing her against his car, Armani slid his thick, dripping, and oozing Italian penis inside her and thrust gently. Janet was surprised how easily his cock entered. Armani had a gentleness about his movements. His uncut tool had a large foreskin, and the outer layer of skin was loose enough to soften the firmness of his thick muscle. Janet moaned in ecstasy while Armani grunted and groaned with delight. Anyone nearby would have clearly heard the sounds of mating, but Janet was too lost in pleasure to think about it. She did not even mind that the overhead garage door was still ajar, facing the paved pebble-rock country road. Janet didn't even mind that she felt she had never said a word of consent to being taken in the exposed garage. It all happened so naturally for her. Janet didn't even mind that they had not been using protection and Armani's tool had just shot a huge amount of semen onto her. As he continued with gentle thrusts, his liquid oozed out and splattered the inside of her panties and then ran onto the cement garage floor beneath them. Any thoughts aside from complete satisfaction had totally escaped Janet's mind.

Armani pulled off and shoved his man parts back into his pants, while Janet rested momentarily against the car. "Is that why you chose a white car? So it doesn't show the stains?" Janet joked, not knowing what else to say. Armani didn't verbally respond to her. He headed to his trunk and popped it open before heading around the vehicle to fiddle with something while Janet composed herself. "About those locks I came to speak to you about..." Janet felt the need to speak while noting that Armani tended to be quiet after sex. It seemed most comfortable for Janet to say something off the topic, not knowing if it was appropriate to discuss the intimacy or change the subject matter altogether. The discussion of locks seemed to just slip out.

Armani finished what he was doing and then closed his trunk without seeming to Janet that he had actually tended to anything inside of it. He was perhaps sidetracked by Janet's conversation. "Let's do that now. I have the tools right here in my garage," Armani suggested.

Perhaps he had done something in his trunk, and Janet was just too preoccupied pulling up her shorts to have noticed. It seemed to her he had not, but it mattered not. With a wet ooze in her panties and a cum-dripping crotch, she was more concentrated upon herself and her own actions. However, something was eating at Janet, and she was wondering about Armani's actions and how he had avoided her earlier questions. It would now be awkward to bring them up again and sound like a nag. He seemed to always be doing things and speaking or not speaking in manners that made her wonder. Generally, Janet didn't like surprises unless it was a box of candy or flowers. Although getting banged in the garage was sure a nice surprise, and one she had totally unexpected. The act made her feel trashy, but she had very much enjoyed it. Janet realized again that her wondering seemed to be preventing her from being appropriately responsive in situations. Maybe Armani was going to surprise her with flowers or candy from his trunk and she had blown the moment? Asking Armani to do chores after sex… What was she thinking? Maybe she was making a bad impression? She'd need to make it up to him somehow.

Less than an hour later, the locks had been easily installed, and other chores tended to. The whole time doing chores, Janet wanted to speak to Armani again about the questions she'd had and things on her mind, but words didn't seem to come out. Trying to make some sort of an effort to address life in a way she did not know how to do properly, Janet offered Armani a spare key by dangling it in front of his face. "This isn't to say, 'Here is a key to my house because we are lovers now and I have expectations,'" Janet felt it necessary to explain. "You know… In case I lock myself out or there is an emergency. It would be nice if you had a spare. Anything else you want it to mean is up to you." The gesture of entrusting him with the key was the greatest compliment she felt she could pay him. Armani shook his head and reached for the key before putting it into his shirt pocket. Analyzing his every move and expression, Janet didn't know how to read him. He didn't joke about it. He didn't smile extensively. Conversation was void, and his expression was rather empty. Janet did not know what she did expect him to say or how he'd react, but she expected something. His void reaction was almost uneasy for her. Maybe it was uneasy for him? If he would only talk to her about his thoughts and feelings. However, Janet knew that men did not like to speak their mind about passion in the way women do. They think differently and feel differently about these things, and she knew that much about men from psychology courses and female conversations. Some things, it seemed, Armani could talk about for hours so easily; while other topics he obviously avoided entirely. Still, she was happy he took the key. Taking it was an indication of trust and respect. He accepted it. Whatever it meant to him, she knew what it meant to her, and that's what she believed counted.

Breaking the uneasiness, Janet asked if she could pay him or offer him dinner perhaps. "Please accept something. I insist."

Then he finally joked again, "Pay for the sexual services or the lock install?"

It was, again, not a response Janet expected from him; but she was happy that the uneasy feeling had passed and he was smiling and jesting. "Either," Janet offered with a straight face. *Two can play this game and joke with empty expressions*, she thought. "But I'm afraid I'd never be able to afford such a high-priced, experienced gigolo of your caliber," she stated eloquently as though she were acting in a play.

"Didn't I tell you, madam? The first time is always a free-trial offer. It's the ones after that you must pay dearly for," Armani spoke in a disguised voice. Reaching for her hand, Armani cupped it firmly with his own and kissed each of her fingers delicately.

Now Janet began to understand a bit of Armani she never knew. He could be a joker and seemed to have an appreciation for playacting and extreme actions. With that now in mind, Janet changed her voice and said, "But we've gone beyond that, and now I owe you? Please, sir, allow me to prepare a gourmet feast for you. I can cook some exquisite wieners on the grill and a pot of baked beans to die for. You'll be needing your nourishment. I'm a woman requiring 24/7 gratification."

Armani liked her playfulness. "It's a date," Armani accepted. "I need to go home and clean up and tend to things in my trunk. I'll be back in, say, oh, an hour?"

That suited Janet fine. Having given Armani the key, she'd have plenty of time to boat over to Baskin's and get spare keys made. How many keys? Janet pondered. How long before her parents would ask for one? Should they have one? Should she keep a spare in a secret hiding place? Always so much to think about. Unfortunately, making final decisions wasn't in her nature. She had always just done whatever had come to mind and then dealt with the aftermath. With changes happening in her life, she wanted to make more rational decisions. That, she found, was more effort than she expected.

Before she'd leave, she'd best call her parents, she thought. On one hand, her mother was likely worried that so much time had passed since she had called them. On the other hand, the phone works two ways, and they had not called. No news was usually good news. An answering machine picked up the call at her parents' home, and she was relieved in a way. Best to leave a quick message instead of talking to her mother directly as she could easily talk for an hour or more. Once on the phone, there was no getting her mother off the phone when she was in a talkative mood. Janet didn't have that much time to waste. "Hi, Mom and Dad. All is fine, and I will call you again soon. Sorry you aren't there to take my call. Armani did put new locks on the house and did some other little jobs for me. He's coming over for a late supper barbecue shortly so I can thank him for what he has done. I have lots to tell you. I've been so very busy. I will call you later. Don't worry about me. I'm doing great. Love you both so much!"

Chapter 7

Baskin's came into view as her boat pulled up dock-side. Eli Charter stood outside, pumping gas into one of his boats. Eli was a fun character. His last name was Charter, and he ran a charter boat service around the local lakes. Charter's Charters, he called his service. Not a bad-looking dude, but Janet never gave him a look. "Good afternoon, Eli!" Janet's voice rang out as her motorboat slowly died off and the boat scooted alongside the dock nearest him. Eli was quick to assist and grabbed Janet's boat ropes, tying them to the dock. His golden hair glistened on his head and arms in the soon-to-be-setting late after-noon sun. Sunlight in Janet's eyes prevented her from seeing many details on him up close. "Thank you for helping," Janet stated. "It's great to see you again. It's always nice to see a friendly, familiar face." Janet reached out her hand, expecting Eli to be a gentle-man and help her off her rocking boat.

Eli unexpectedly declined. "Sorry, Janet. I've got fish guts all over my hands from cleaning out my craft. Had a fishing group today. They caught quite a catch they hauled home with them. One man caught a northern pike. It was the biggest I have ever seen in these waters. You don't want fish guts on you. Janet, was that Armani you were here with the other day? I thought I saw you two leaving in this boat."

"Yes. It was," she answered the question. This time, she wasn't going to psychoanalyze the conversation and wonder why he'd ask. Eli was probably just making small talk.

"I have not seen much of him around this summer. Not like I usually do. I was wondering how he's been doing and why he's been so scarce around here. Come to think of it, Janet, I haven't seen you much this summer. I thought your family might be avoiding us this year." Eli seemed saddened as if any avoidance of him had been intentional.

"Well, Eli, I am now here full-time year-round. Bought the old place and boat from my parents, and I'll be living here. It's not my business to know what Armani does. I've not been around much because of so much going on elsewhere. I am sorry to say that I can't talk now, and I am in a big hurry today. I'm still getting situated moving in. Dinner company is coming by, and I just ran here to get a key made. Don't want you thinking I am antisocial or anything. I just need to get this key inside to be copied so I don't run late for my guest. Nice to see you, Eli."

Eli could relate. "Dan is working inside today, and I'm sure he'll be happy to help you with the key," Eli stated. "He'll be happy to see ya too. Don't mind if I stop by your place sometime and officially welcome you. People around here are going to do a dance of joy when they hear you've moved in. It's probably the best news any local 'round this lake has to share right now. Don't see many locals 'round much. It's all about the tourists for my business this time of year. Except for the sheriff. Sheriff Dean always makes time for me. He's always coming by and asking questions. That man is always snooping for something. He's like a bloodhound on the trail for a scent. I don't think the scent ever leads him anywhere. He does speak to me though. I give him credit for being the only local who has interesting stories to share when he comes 'round. Just listen to me talking your ear off when I know you're in a hurry. Nice chatting with you, Ms. Janet."

"Stop by when you can," Janet offered. "I'm in and out a lot though. I'll leave my number with Dan. I'm sure I will have plenty of time to stay in when winter comes. Anyway, glad you find my moving here to be exciting news. It's exciting for me to be here, and I'm open to accepting any housewarming gifts when you do stop in," Janet spoke in jest and waved a goodbye to Eli with her fingers as she headed toward the shop's door. Eli studied her fine figure silhouetted within a glow of a sunshine ray aura as she strutted away from him. Never would she have thought Eli would be looking at her from behind, but as was typical of her, she was oblivious to the effect she could have on men. It would shock her if she knew what men were thinking as she crossed their paths.

The shop door had brass bells, which tinkled as Janet opened the screen door. Inside, it was much cooler from many fans, which circulated air. Her nose was quick to pick up on many aromas she was quite familiar with. Some smells were from age and the lake-moistened air. Other smells were from food and products. The combined aroma was special to Baskin's, and its aroma was distinct. It never seemed to change with time. Blindfolded and led in unknowingly, anyone who had visited before would know immediately that they had been led into Baskin's. It was that unique and memorable.

"Hi, Dan!" Janet had known Dan as long as she was old enough to know anyone. One could bet that if Dan was around, Eli was likely there, too, or somewhere nearby. The two men had been best friends since as long as Janet could recall, and they just happened to be her own age thereabout. That did not mean Janet knew the two fondly as they were distanced from the house of Janet's family. Yet she knew them well enough from the boat shop to be well acquainted and, on rare occasion, unexpectedly ran into them at a function or shopping in town. Eli could often be seen running his charter-boat passes around the lake. Dan, of course, could regularly be found working at Baskin's. Dan had helped his parents out around Baskin's ever since he was a small boy, being that his family owned the place for generations. "Eli said you were working. I need a few keys made if you have time, but I'm in a hurry. Three copies should do me just fine. That Eli character talked for the longest time even though I told him I had to hurry. I'm afraid he held me up a bit, and I can't be late. Can you help me right away?"

"Eli?" Dan reiterated with a question. "Stay away from that one. He's trouble. Me, on the other hand, I'm one you should get to know." Dan winked as he took the key from Janet.

"No trouble. I'm on it." Janet laughed. "No wonder there seems to be a shortage of single men in the world. They are all around this lake." Janet caught her words and rescinded them. "Oh no! I'm not flirting. I didn't mean to imply anything. I was just trying to joke around. That doesn't mean you are not handsome, but don't get any ideas."

Dan chuckled. "I got it." He continued after a moment of concentrating on the key matter, "If you ever were to be interested, you know where to find me. If that's not being flirtatious, I don't know what is!"

Janet giggled back, but her attention was broken by a bulletin-board posting by the door that advertised missing and wanted people. "All these people missing around here?" Janet inquired with amazement.

"Ya. I guess so. Maybe the police are just looking for some of them for some other reasons. I don't recognize any of them, so it doesn't interest me. Too many visitors come by here once and then never return. It has to be someone very special for me to pay any mind." Dan turned away to make the keys.

"Seems they are," Eli's voice answered as the screen door to enter the shop opened with him entering inside. "Sheriff thinks so, at least. He's always asking questions. From the way he drills us, he must think one of us is responsible. He's always pushing us around. Just like that Armani neighbor you were having lunch with. Both were once good friends of ours even though they were older than Dan and I. Then they started to always pick on us, and we grew apart more and more. Now the sheriff thinks he is someone special in that uniform."

"Don't mind Eli," Dan interjected. "Sheriff is just doing his job. Eli is still sore about those incidents when we were younger."

"What are you talking about? What incidents? I don't understand," Janet was inquiring. She wanted to know everything about everyone now that she was a regular around town.

"Never mind," said Eli. "No need for details all the time, Dan."

"You know I love telling these stories as much as people enjoy a good laugh, Eli." Dan continued speaking despite protests from Eli, "The older guys picked on us a lot, but we're just having fun. Eli always got the worst of it. I think they liked me better because my parents had this shop here. They loved getting him good. There was a water-skier who had been decapitated one year. The head was never found. Get this… One year, all the guys went fishing. The older guys, especially Armani and Sheriff Dean, decided to play a joke on us. They put a realistic latex head on the fishing line of one of the poles. Get this… Dean said he had to pee and entrusted Eli with the pole. When Eli looked away for a moment, Armani told him the bobber moved and he best set the hook. There was Eli setting the hook and reeling the fishing line in for what he thought was going to be the biggest fish catch of the day. The guys had Eli going and were cheering him on and crap like that. Eli gets the line reeled in, and this latex head came floating up. Eli started screaming like a little girl, and we all could have sworn he pooped and peed himself. That head became a prop to prank Eli with every chance the older guys could. He's still sore about it."

"Except that once, Dan," Eli said with raised voice. "It was a real head that I saw. I swear it. I saw it, Janet, and nobody will ever believe me," Eli said, seemingly serious about it.

"That was cruel, Eli. I'm sorry. But there is some humor in it. A real head? Come on. I've seen some strange things in my life, but even I haven't been seeing no severed heads." Janet let out her girlish giggle. "They all still play these pranks?"

"No," said Eli. "They stopped." Eli began to tell a story about a boy named Mark. "We were out diving off the rocks one summer. Mark, one of the kids from school, was with us. He missed the water, and his head hit a rock. He was bleeding and disoriented. It happened only moments after joking around, and the older guys thought Mark was playacting, just getting even with them for gags they had played on us. We were not goofing around, and we were not joking. Mark was really badly injured. By the time we got him help, it was too late. He had lost consciousness and then died shortly after. The guys said they'd not prank anyone anymore. After that, the dynamics seemed to change between all of us. Dean and Armani stopped hanging around us. Sad how people come and go in life. There was a time we thought we'd all be friends forever. That was combined with us growing up and becoming more mature." Eli made a crazy face, hoping to get a laugh. "We went to different schools after that year and made new friends. Except for Dan and me. We still hang together. Obviously."

"So much has been happening around here."

Dan jumped back into the conversation. "Dean treats us like suspects each time something happens. Sometimes, he accuses us of having played a prank to make him look bad at the police department. As if we'd ever do anything like that to him. Eli and I don't even know what he's talking about much of the time when he's angry over something. Except look at those people on the board right there. Those people on the bulletin board you see probably had bad things happen to them, and nobody reports knowing anything. Yet everyone on the lake becomes a suspect in their disappearances when Dean is around. He must figure everyone does their shopping here. Seems he's the only one, though whoever wants to acknowledge something may have really happened to them. It also seems other people around these parts still like to joke and play pranks at times. Must be difficult for the police to know when something is to be taken serious and when it's not. Guess they need to take everything seriously, huh? I'll give you an example while I finish up your keys here…

"Eli was the butt of another prank recently. You see those four missing campers in the pictures there? They were charter riders with Eli while camping here. The day they were reported as missing people, someone had thrown buckets of cow blood all over Eli's boat and left bloody handprints. A joke? Who makes a joke out of something sick like that? Our dear Sheriff Dean and his crew were here running all sorts of tests on the blood and questioning us. Some prank! Dean still thinks we messed up the boat to make him look bad in front of his department as some sort of gag. He reprimanded us for possibly being the types to make a mockery of the police department. You know, that kind of publicity doesn't make Baskin's nor Charter's Charters look good either. The person or persons who perform these stupid pranks are likely tourists or kids from town looking for kicks. One would think people would have better things to do with their time. It takes up a lot of people's time and makes a lot of people look bad. There are also the incidents of cults performing rituals at the far end of the lake and forest, but that is another discussion for another time."

"That's terrible!" Janet truly thought it was. "Playing childish pranks like that when people seriously need help is cruel. Shame on them! I won't ask about the cult incidents as that is too much for me to take in right now." Janet accepted her keys and left exact bills and change on the counter. "I'll see you men around. No pranks from me. No joke!" Janet departed with the pun in hopes of lightening a dank mood.

As she left, both men, and another who had entered the store during their conversation, noticed her feminine physique sway as her lengthy legs carried her off. "Not often we get new blood on the lake," Dan said as the guys continued speaking among themselves out of Janet's earshot.

"And not one so perfect," Eli responded.

Chapter 8

Dinner of beans and franks accompanied with a couple of store-bought side dishes Janet was serving were quickly prepared and nearly ready to eat when Armani arrived. Letting himself in, he greeted Janet in the kitchen with a big bouquet of roses he'd home-grown in his yard. "I hope I didn't startle you when I came in. Since I had put new locks on and your door was open and screen door unlocked, I assumed you wanted me to come right in. No?" Armani asked.

"I did," Janet said, happy to greet him. "The flowers you brought are beautiful, Armani. Thank you! I thought we'd sit outside. I've been back and forth to the grill and would not have heard the bell if you had arrived while I was barbecuing. The doors were left open for you, and your timing is impeccable. Dinner is almost done. I guess it really is done, and we can warm it back up on the barbecue and eat anytime you desire. Are you hungry right away?"

"Sure," Armani said without care in his voice. "We can eat now. Any plans for after dinner?" Armani asked, not having any in mind.

"Not really," Janet thought about it then spoke. She wasn't sure if that was what he wanted to hear. "I

60

don't know. Why? Should I have planned something kinky and exciting for you?"

"I wasn't implying that at all." Armani thought for a moment. "It would just be nice to spend some relaxation time together. That's unless you want to be alone and get settled. You've only been here three days, and I'm sure you have so much to do."

"I don't mind if you hang around," she said, hoping he'd stick around awhile. "Nothing special is going on around here tonight without you." Janet led Armani outside to a picnic table by the grill and set things up for dinner while continuing their conversation. "I was just going to start thinking about what I can do to make this place feel more like my home. That doesn't need to be tonight. I should have plenty of time to do that. However, I do value your input. I'll likely be asking you to help with most renovations if you are capable. Besides, if you hang around and play your cards right, it may someday be your home too. You are not ready to make it your home too, are you?" They both knew Janet was not serious.

"That was my implication," Armani was quick to say. "I think we should sit down right now and discuss plans for later. How much later are we talking, hours or years? You know, we'll need to add on at least five more bedrooms to this house for all the kids you'll be bearing and raising. I'll just continue to live at my place. I don't think I could handle living with children and a nagging woman." Janet knew Armani was getting in the festive, jovial spirit of the conversation.

"Speaking of joking, Armani dear, I was talking to Eli and Dan. They were telling me about your sense of humor and pranks you've played on people." Janet motioned shame with her fingers… "Shame on you."

"I figured what you didn't know, someone would someday be telling you," Armani suspected. He didn't seem uncomfortable, but he obviously had things to say about it. "That was a long time ago. Pranks ended with Steven as far as I was ever involved. He made me look at life more seriously. Most of us around didn't really know Steven was feeling seriously hurt at first. We were always just guys having a good time. Our camaraderie sure changed after that. Poor guy."

Janet did not know what Armani was speaking of. She was referring to the death of Mark, and Armani was discussing her brother. Her curiosity at this point was most certainly piqued. Not wanting to let Armani know that she knew nothing about her brother as far as this conversation was concerned, she chose her words carefully. "I don't like secondhand stories from people I barely know across the lake. Why don't you tell me your side of it?"

Armani thought for a bit and composed his words. "We were in high school when I found out your brother was gay. I found some old pictures he had of local naked guys hidden under his mattress in the bedroom here. Your parents had hired me to flip the mattresses after they left for season, and there the pictures were. What I never told anyone else was that he had naked photographs of boys and men he knew in the area, which had been, from the looks of them, taken through bedroom windows at night. It seemed obvious the subjects in the photographs didn't know the pictures had been taken. I told Steven I would not tell on him but I would not give the photos back. I did not want anyone to see who they were of, and it would probably be an embarrassment if certain people knew those pictures existed. Please don't talk of it again, Janet. What people do know is that matters got a bit out of hand afterward. Taking pictures through widows wasn't just a hobby of Steven's at Lake Marie. Seems he was doing that at your parents' Prospect Heights home, and they found out. Your mom found some pictures that Steven had apparently taken at other locations too. When I later spoke to Steven, I blamed myself. He had initially assured me there were no other pictures. Apparently, there were other pictures, and I found out about them. Never mind the details, but he had been lying to me. I don't even know the full story, but one photo was really questionable. Apparently, the person in it was later of great interest to the police. Had I turned Steven in when I first learned of his perverted hobby, maybe, just maybe, I could have spared him from getting into further trouble.

"To make matters worse, Dean learned through his father who worked at the police department that there was more to this story than expected. Word was getting around. I pleaded with Dean not to say anything to anyone else when Dean had told me. As it turned out, Dean had already told some other guys around Antioch. Your brother got beat up badly just shortly after that. It may have been someone from here, but I never found out who had beaten him up so badly. People talked around town until the subject seemed to no longer be of interest to anyone. You know how gossip runs its course. It seems I never saw Steven around here much after that. Then I heard from your parents that Steven had moved to California. Funny thing though, I tried to locate Steven to try and perhaps comfort him and tell him things could still be okay between him and me, but I never could reach him. Maybe he wasn't up to talking with me. Do you know where he is?"

She did not. Janet stared quietly for a moment and then said, "I'm so embarrassed for my family. What must people think of us? It explains a lot of things I often wondered about and could never rationalize." A tear rolled down Janet's cheek. "I hear from Steven so rarely and only when he calls me. I never can reach him at any number he ever gives me. Seems Steven hasn't been up to talking to me either. I know word got to him about my grandparents passing on, and he received his inheritance. I'm not even certain who reached him. I think it was the family attorney. I never knew why he distanced himself from the family and Illinois."

"Janet, nobody blames you," Armani assured her. "They don't blame your parents either. It's best you just not speak of this stuff at all and just forget about it. There are parts of this story I don't even know. I only know what I just told you." Armani was as comforting as he could be to her and could see she was saddened. For Janet, her world seemed shattered at the moment. Steven's behaviors seemed to be an embarrassment to her. How naive she was and how uninformed. Now every person she sees will be a curiosity. She'll wonder if this person or that person was someone involved or knew it. She'll wonder what they think of *her*. How could Steven had done this to her or their parents? Who knew of this, and who was in the photographs? "People knew he was gay, you know," Armani assured her. "It was hard not to notice from his mannerisms. Other guys sometimes would pick on him a lot. I protected him all I could, but at times, it was rough on me as well. Any guy getting too chummy with your brother also became the subject of ridicule. Other kids played pranks on Steven, and I felt sorry for him. I changed my ways and stopped joking around so much," Armani spoke sincerely. Not once had he mentioned Mark's death. "I realized harmless jokes were a form of bullying, and I stopped after that."

Managing to compose herself through the evening, Janet tactfully sent Armani home. She stood at the sink, waiting to hear the back door close to assure herself Armani had left before her sobs audibly mingled with the running dishwater. While washing dinner dishes, Janet tried to piece information together. How could she have not known what her brother had been involved with? They had seemed to be so close growing up. Now all she could really think about was her own embarrassment. In just one conversation with a neighbor, her own inquiry would forever change the way she'd view her home, family, and the world around her. As so frequently common, Janet was so involved in her own ego and thought process that she failed to be even the least bit aware that she was not alone in the house.

It almost seemed like deja vu. Janet, once again, sat upon the whitewashed porch swing with a cocktail in hand. The scene was just as she had been in the night she arrived at the house as the new owner. Just as she had done that night too, she fell asleep where she sat. Again, she was unaware that a shadowy figure lurked behind her. Lurking. Just in the inside doorway to the next room. Observing her as with some intention, but without actually acting upon any specific intention. The figure stood almost motionless for the longest time.

Chapter 9

Rain clouds formed over the lake come morning, and a sprinkle began gently tapping. Several fishermen were out in their boats, pointing at fish jumping clear out of the lake into the air. Janet appreciated fly casting and reeling in caught fish. The tougher the fight they put up, the more she enjoyed the challenge. She had no problem skinning them for cooking preparation. It was a task she'd learned to do at an early age. "Soon," she spoke aloud. "Soon, I hope to be out there enjoying myself fishing with the rest of them." So many lake activities to appreciate, and Janet had made no time for any of them recently. Then her cell phone rang and interrupted her thinking.

The screen on her phone indicated it was *Mom and Dad.* Janet was not looking forward to this call. She realized she had not been calling her parents as often as she knew they would have liked. Four times a day would not even be enough to please her mother. During this call, Janet did not know how to address the conversation she would want to have regarding her brother and his problems. Today was maybe not the time to discuss Steven? Maybe it was? Still, her parents had withheld information pertaining to the issue from her, and she was mad. Just before the call would have gone to voice mail, Janet answered, "Hello. Good morning. I'm just waking up. Give me a moment."

Janet placed the phone against her chest and let out a sigh before clearing her throat. "Ya. I'm here." After Janet listened for a moment, she endured an uneasy feeling of being watched. Considering that the four-seasons room she was in was glass on three sides, it was not unlikely. There may have even been someone watching her through a telescope from across the lake. With so many people on the lake at times, privacy was not something a person often thought of. As many trips to the vacation home in the past had included an entourage of guests, again, privacy wasn't often something considered. Janet opened her blouse in a seductive manner and shook her breasts about in a playful display, which lacked concern. Then she smiled. She needed that smile. Feeling silly helped her chill.

Her mother started speaking. Janet would have liked to chill over the conversation as well. "Yes, Mom. It's just starting to rain here. I know I haven't called and should have. I know you worry. Really, you have got to stop worrying so much. I'm an adult and can take care of myself here. Neighbors are taking really good care of me and watching out for me. I've spent a morning with Gertrude, and she was delightful. She's become my new friend. Imagine that! We have a common friend. Armani changed all the locks just like Dad had suggested. Eli from the charter service said he'll stop by one day when he is on the lake and has time. I've just been so busy, and time gets away from me. I promise I will call often enough."

After she and her mother spoke of trivial matters for a long time, Janet decided to bring up the topic of Steven. "Mom… I heard things about Steven that disturb me. You know what I'm talking about. Just bits and pieces from everyone, but enough to put the whole story together. The story isn't a good one. You know I love my brother, but I'm concerned. It's embarrassing. It's about things the family never mentioned to me. It all caught me off guard. I know I can't help what Steven is or what he did or does. I'm now just not sure how other people might react toward me being here. I'll be wondering who knows and what they think."

Her mother cut Janet off and spoke up loudly, "Don't act differently now that you know things you didn't know before. It's got nothing personally to do with you. You can't take responsibility for other people's actions. Believe me when I say that most people around there have enough to be embarrassed about themselves. You are a sweet, innocent, young lady, and people know that. Most of what people think they know about your brother is just hearsay anyway. Your father and I are the only two people besides your brother who know the whole story. It's not your business, and best you just forget it. Not everything other people do involves you. I don't want to hear another word about it." Janet seemed comforted even though she felt she had just been apparently scolded.

However, her mother had a way of sweeping things under the carpet to avoid any white elephant in the room. Peggy also had a way for making Janet feel she'd been unexpectedly reprimanded. While the words from her mother were wise ones, this was an issue Janet would just need to work through herself without her mom or dad involved. Apparently, this was simply another aspect of being on her own and becoming her own person. Her mother spoke again before Janet concluded their conversation pertaining to the topic. This time, she was calming. "Nobody has ever said anything to you about it before. Honey, if they haven't said anything before, I don't see any reason they will treat you or think any differently of you now. And everyone there has always been so nice to you. Haven't they? Your father and I never would have sold the house to you and let you move there if we thought you'd have any problems. And, Honey, if you ever do hear from Steven, have him give your father and me a call. We have not heard from him on the phone in quite some time, and I'm still disturbed that he did not attend the funerals of his own grandparents. All we got was a note in the mail saying that he could not attend. We love him too. Your father and I worry."

Upon hanging up, Janet had sworn she'd seen a shadow move in the next room. She thought about it but hesitated to react. It eventually got the better of her imagination, and she went to inspect. Looking into the room from the doorway, she saw nothing in particular. A cool breeze wafted through the house from a few open windows, which were all blocked with security screens, and Janet assumed she may have just seen a shadow cast from wind-moved curtains. With an "oh, brother" shake of her head and motion of her hands, no further inspection was carried out.

One chore led to another until Janet realized how time-consuming each task could be. Changing the light bulb in the basement had been one task Janet forgot to have Armani tend to when he had been there changing locks. It was nothing she could not manage. Just the time it took to locate a step stool, locate where she had set the new light bulbs she had purchased in town, install the new light bulb, throw the old one away, and put the step stool back seemed to have taken an eternity. Janet had no concept of time and had not been looking at a clock. For curiosity's sake, she checked the time she'd ended the call with Peggy and then calculated how much time had lapsed tending to the simple project. Almost twenty minutes, and it was now eight thirty. Flicking the switch on and off to the new basement light bulb, Janet was proud of having accomplished even such a minuscule task. Not knowing if it was the conversation she'd had with her mother or the task she had completed, Janet was feeling better about herself and life, in general.

After dressing herself, Janet headed out the back door to take a walk in the light drizzle just so she could clear her mind and appreciate how blessed she was. The day was beautiful even if an occasional drop of warm water from the sky landed upon her. Even a downpour would not have spoiled her contentment at this time. As a youth, she often appreciated walking the pebbled road as far as it led until the more-developed blacktopped streets replaced and intersected it. She was in awe of the surrounding natural beauty. Every bit of it. From the rippling lake of ever-changing water color to the trees of leaves that changed colors in the fall and became completely bare in the winter until decked with white snow, Janet admired every inch of it all. That included Armani's home, which she'd pass by.

Armani yelled over his picket fence before she got far beyond it. "Well, hello, hot stuff!" he yelled to her. "Passing by without stopping in?"

"It's nice to see you, Armani. About last evening, I'm sorry. The conversation about Steven sort of got to me, and I did not want to admit it. I'm over it now. All is good as far as I'm concerned. Is all good with you and me?" She hoped so.

"Of course, it is," he replied. "I'm glad you're okay. I just did not want any secrets between you and me. I've always looked out for you, and I don't want you to worry. Don't want your beautiful locks turning prematurely gray now. Do you? Stress will easily do that to a person." He laughed, exhibiting the humorous side of him, which she appreciated.

"No worries, my sweet man," she said in a comforting tone. "I was just going to take a walk. Care to join me?" Janet extended an offer.

Armani graciously declined. "I have a lot to do here in the garden, and it looks like a heavy rain may hit before I accomplish them. Another time?" Janet nodded.

Heading happily on her way, Janet found that she had actually changed directions from the way she had been heading before Armani stopped her to talk. Instead of heading north as she had been, she was now turned around and heading south. It wasn't a concern. It was just then she noticed how she really was walking aimlessly and without care. Carefree was how she wanted to feel, and that was how she was feeling. It was a true sense of freedom. She could smell a perfume of nature's blend of lilac and roses in the air. The aroma was intoxicating. She realized how every plot of land had a different floral fragrance emitting from it depending which flowers were growing in that area. The air was warm, but a mild breeze was comforting.

South she headed until she found herself at the gate to Gertrude's property. One step led to another until she stopped directly in front of Gertrude's door. It had not been her intent to visit her neighbor while walking. But there she was. She assumed there must have been some reason she led herself there? But there really wasn't. She'd just been entranced in a world of mindlessness and had been lost in an appreciation of the beautiful surroundings and intoxicating, aromatic splendor.

Ring. Ring. The doorbell alongside a spotlessly white metal door rang out loudly. Gertrude was slow answering but eventually opened the door to greet Janet. "I'm sorry it took me awhile. I was just taking cupcakes out of the oven. There will be some for you later on. I could have given them to you right now if they were cool enough to frost. Wild berry cupcakes they are, with a fresh whipped cream topping and just-picked berries on top. I'm not much at being fancy, but the taste of them is enough to knock anyone's knickers off."

Janet smiled and was happy that Gertrude would think enough of her to share her baked goods. "I don't even know why I'm here," Janet stated to Gertrude. "I was just taking a walk, and your house was along my path. Such a pretty time for a walk and to appreciate life before a storm comes rolling in. I do believe I detect an advancing storm. One can smell it in the air and see the change in the color of the sky. The weather app on my phone even anticipated a storm would be brewing for our area. A significant storm at that. I love storms. Don't you?"

"I love storms too," Gertrude agreed. "Care for company on your walk?" Gertrude hoped. "I have time to let my cupcakes cool, and I need to check in on Irwin's place. He was going to visit his sister, and I told him I'd check in on his place while he's away." Gertrude never seemed at a loss for words, and it was one of her more admirable qualities.

"Sure thing," Janet said, accepting the company. "I had asked Armani to walk with me. He was too busy in the garden to come along." Janet wanted the old woman to know that. She wanted Gertty to know that she had considered wanting a walking partner to go along with her and it would be no invasion of her alone time.

"I don't like walking much these days." Gertrude was speaking as her tiny feet shuffled beneath her pear-shaped body. "Lord knows I need the exercise. The rocky road is uneven, and my balance isn't the best. Neither is my eyesight. Who am I kidding? Nothing on me is at its best any longer. It all seemed to go downhill over the last few years after turning, eh, forty something. If you believe that, I have some swampland in Florida to sell you." Gertrude laughed at her own jovial wit, taking Janet's arm while continuing to talk as their walk continued. "Speaking of selling you swampland, you could probably afford it. How much did your grandparents leave you?"

Janet was taken back by Gertrude's lack of social etiquette and outright brazenness. Not knowing how to respond, Janet cracked a joke. "Oh! So much that I haven't had time to count it all. You know, millions and millions. Isn't that evident by my estate crawling with hired help and the limo, which I keep parked out front? On the topic of the almighty dollar, Armani must be doing pretty well for himself," Janet said, hiding her question within a statement. "The outside of his home is so nice, and that car of his is really something. Isn't it?"

"If you think a beater work truck is something special, well then, I can't say much for your choice in rides," Gertrude said curiously. "And I can't say much for the inside of his home. The man does have a knack for landscaping. I'll give him that much credit."

"Work truck? No!" Janet quickly interjected as soon as she could speak. "Armani drove up in a new sports car. There's been no work truck around that I've seen. I seem to recall him having had a truck at one time. It would make sense that he has a truck for work. I haven't seen one around though. And what were you saying about the inside of his home?" Janet inquired.

"Well, child, I don't know anything about a new car," Gertrude proclaimed. "If he has one, I'm sure I helped him buy it. He nickel-and-dimes me each week over chores and other stuff. As for his home, I have never been in it. I just can't say much about something I haven't seen before."

"You haven't been in it?" Janet was surprised to hear that.

"Nope. Honey, I only know the house needed major work when he inherited it," Gertrude was certain. "You know, his mother died some time ago. It was just he and his father after that. He took care of his father well. Now and then, caregivers would come and go and said the house was a disgusting cockroach motel inside. Apparently, Armani did a great job at taking care of the landscape and people. He just isn't much of a homemaker type from what I've heard. There is something not quite right about that boy. You'd be best to watch yourself around him. He'd take your last penny along with the shirt right off your back and leave you flat-out buck naked in the middle of that lake." Gertrude seemed adamant she knew what she was talking about. How strange when she had seemed to speak so fondly of him before. Fondly, as though she thought of him as her own son. Now her interpretation of him was not the same. It was confusing.

"Gertrude? Do you hear what you are saying? Are you serious? I have known Armani since forever, and that does not sound like the fine man I know. You are lucky he has been around all these years to look after you." Janet did not know how to respond without concern. Janet did not know if Gertrude was actually a delusional old woman or what to make of the change of heart. Why? Why, Janet wondered, that each time she spoke with someone recently, the conversation left her with a questionable concern. "I can't imagine Marissa would have stayed there as often as she had if the house had roaches."

"Gurrlll," Gertrude said with long, drawn-out syllables... "I should not have not said anything. I best have kept my mouth shut and minded my own business. You mind me though. I know that boy and you best be on your toes around him. Let's just leave it at that." Gertrude concluded her rant.

"Here we are," Janet pointed out an obvious fact. "Irwin's home, Gertrude. Can I call you Gert? I know my mother does." Janet had never noticed that Irwin's house was the same exterior layout as her own with a slightly different facade on the exterior. The lawn and garden looked only marginally better than her own.

"Gertty is fine to call me if I can call you Jan?" Janet nodded with approval and chuckled. Gertty had already called her by so many names and terms that it seemed best to permit Gertty to call her *Jan* before she came up with an onslaught of other less-pleasing nicknames that might stick. Gertty had a concerned look upon her face. "Uh-oh!"

"What's uh-oh?" Janet was unaware of any reason to say *uh-oh*.

"I don't know. Look at Irwin's back door. His back door is open. Do you think he never left? If Irwin did not leave, he will probably be upset with me that I haven't been by here sooner to check on his place. Jan honey, what will I say to him?"

"Gertty, I've been in this situation myself only recently. I didn't know how to say something. I found it best to just wing it and be honest. Don't admit guilt unless you must. Play it by ear and don't offer any extra reasoning." Jan felt that uncomfortable discussions had become a part of being neighborly. It's probably best to avoid them altogether. "You are worrying about a potential conversation with Irwin that is not even taking place yet. Keep quiet and play it cool."

Gertty knocked on the screen door and then rang the bell. She knocked and rang the bell again. "Irwin? You here?"

"Perhaps Irwin is outside, in the garage, or out on the lake?" Janet tried to think of places Irwin might be. "I'll take a look around while you stay here so you don't fall," Janet offered before starting to search around the house exterior on uneven patches of grass.

Irwin's vehicle was in the garage. At least there was someone's vehicle in the garage. Jan could not recall what kind of vehicle Irwin had, and the garage was dark. It looked like a truck. Jan yelled to Gertty, "There is a dark vehicle in the garage. I assume it's Irwin's. It's too dark in the garage to see much. He's not on this side of the house though. I'll go around the other side and then check out back by the lake." The lakeside of all the houses on the lake should actually be referred to as the *front side*, but Janet always referred to it as the backyard. They were the prettier side. It just seemed to her the front should be where the road and garages were. Some homes could be hard to determine since they faced sideways. No matter. She'd check it out. Janet searched and looked everywhere she could visually see. There were no signs of Irwin anywhere.

Upon her return to where she had left Gertty outside the door, Gertty was not there. "For heaven's sake," Janet mumbled. "Gertty? You inside?" Janet yelled at an audible tone she believed to be suitable before climbing the rickety, paint-peeling steps to the door and going inside uninvited.

Gertty was there, staring at what would be the basement door if one were to exist on its hinges. In Irwin's home, a preexisting door had been removed and was now an open void. Gertty was motionless and quiet.

"For heaven's sake, Gertty. I did not know you had come in," Janet exclaimed as she approached Gertty's side. "What are you up to?" As the question escaped her lips, Janet saw what was going on. Gertty continued to stare, motionless and silent, at the contorted corpse of Irwin twisted at the bottom of the basement stairs. A large pool of more-or-less dried blood encased his face down his head. The phobia Janet had of basements suddenly became all too real again. Now they both stared silently down the steps. It wasn't only his corpse loitering at the bottom of the stairs, Janet noticed. It was as if death was literally there and consuming the oxygen out of the air she was inhaling. Dead silence plagued the area, and Janet could say, time metaphorically took a break. Nothingness surrounded them until Gertty let out a hoarse, blood-curdling scream, and a look of utter terror overcame her wrinkled, aged face.

"Relax, Gertty. Try to compose yourself. I'll call for help." Janet attempted to compose herself and take charge of the situation that, in all actuality, had her stunned as well.

Janet then let out a scream of her own. Unaware as to why and assuming it was a delayed reaction to seeing Irwin, Gertty did not know that Janet made a startling discovery, which was terribly upsetting. Janet's phone already had the numbers *911* punched in, and her phone just needed the call to be activated. Janet couldn't help but wonder how the numbers were set on her phone when she had no recollection of dialing them in herself. Doing what had to be done, Janet placed the 911 call and did her best to carefully describe the situation at hand to the emergency operator.

Chapter 10

Thunder and lightning crashed about as a couple of police cars and an ambulance arrived. Gushing rain drenched Antioch with a torrential downpour. One by one, the officials entered the home with rainwater sloshing off of them. Sheriff Dave Dean was one of them.

Janet had already anticipated emergency crew would require dry towels and was in the hallway gathering them from a tiny linen closet while leaving Gertty to do the talking. Upon returning with the towels, Janet took over the answering of questions. Gertty was simply too shaken to discuss the situation diplomatically. "Look, Sheriff Dean, is it? This is Gertrude, and she lives next door. I know you know her pretty well. I'm Janet. You may recall who I am from way back? No reason in particular that you should. I just moved in full-time to the home my parents owned, which is just next door to Gertty's place. That way. I was going to take a peaceful walk today when Gertty here asked to come along. You see, Gertty doesn't like walking the gravel road alone and needed to check in on Irwin's home. Irwin was to be out of town. There's a luggage bag over by the door. He probably intended to take it with him. When we got here, the door was open. I went around the outside of the house to see if I could find Irwin. I couldn't. When I got back to the open door, Gertty wasn't outside there, waiting where I had left her. I came inside and could see Gertty standing by the basement stairs. She was looking down then. As I approached, I saw what Gertty had been staring at. The poor dear woman seemed to be in shock, and I would not doubt if she still is a bit. I guess we sort of both were and maybe still are. Then I called 911 immediately on my cell phone, and here we all are."

"Yes. Here we all are," Sheriff Dean repeated Janet's words. "There are still many questions to ask of both of you. Perhaps you'd like to answer them as best you can before we speak to Gertrude again?"

"Looks like an accident," an unfamiliar gentleman in plain clothes interjected in their conversation. "We won't know until we get the autopsy results and look around. Please don't touch anything else around here." While the man was eventually introduced to Janet and Gertty, neither would later recall his name and didn't care. It would later be difficult for Janet to recall any of the emergency staff's names with the exception of Sheriff Dean. More emergency crew had arrived since the original onslaught, and they were all actively buzzing about, in and out like a hive of buzzing bees. They were all talking at once. Janet and Gertty could not focus on much of what anyone was doing or saying.

"Irwin did have a weak heart," Gertrude tried to speak loudly enough for anyone to hear and take note of. "You may want to check him for a heart attack."

"I'm sure they'll do that, ma'am," Sheriff Dean assured her, addressing her in a professional tone despite knowing her well. "In the meantime, you ladies will be around the area in case we have any further questions?" Gertty and Janet both nodded and were free to leave the premises.

Janet walked Gertty home during a lucky break in the rainstorm. Gertty was happy to be out of Irwin's home and back in her own place. Given the course of the evening, Janet had forgotten all about their earlier conversation they'd had on the way to Irwin's home. It was now of no importance. Seeing death so close to home made Janet think more about the things that mattered in life and how unpredictable life can be. While Janet was only first getting to know Gertty, Janet was still very much deeply concerned with Gertty's well-being and what Gertty must be thinking of Irwin's death. Also, about how old and fragile Gertty was and of how a terrible fall could have just as easily have happened to her new friend or anyone for that matter. Gertty assured Janet that she'd be just fine. "In case of trouble, I have the handgun my late husband left me. It's all loaded and ready for use."

"What?" Janet was taken back. "You're suicidal?" Janet couldn't believe her ears.

"No! Silly girl! I mean, to protect myself with," Gertrude said with security and confidence.

"What are you saying, Gertty? Why are you talking about protection? What are you protecting yourself from?" Janet wondered.

Gertty's verbalization had concerned Janet. "I don't know what I'm saying. I'm just a silly old woman who is shaken up by the loss of a friend. Don't you worry yourself. I'll be just fine, Jan honey. If only I had checked on his place sooner." Gertty blamed herself. "I'm just worried about what I over-heard at Irwin's house. His death may not be an acci-dent, until an autopsy proves it as being one. It had me thinking. That's all."

"Don't beat yourself up, Gertty," Janet said as reassuringly as she could. "Unless you had been there when it happened, you'd likely not have been of any help. From the looks of it, I don't think you could have helped at all anyway. There was nothing you could have done. It was just his fate. Don't think of me as uncaring. But I'm sure it was a common house-hold accident and it happened all too fast for anyone to have been of help. You saw his neck and how out of shape it was. It was obviously snapped instantly during the fall." Janet thought of anything and every-thing she could say to comfort the depressed, con-cerned old woman. What more could she possibly do?

Gertty knew all that. She just wished she could have prevented the accident and been of any help at all. This had been a man, neighbor, and friend she'd known for many years. He'd been a great entrusted confidant for a long time when few other people had been around, and now he was gone forever from her life.

Janet stood on Gertty's covered porch until Gertty entered her home safely. With a flip of a couple switches, Gertty illuminated her foyer and also her yard with an array of multicolored spotlights. How nice it looked to Janet. How nice the moisture-cooled air felt this time of year. How nice the rain kept the bugs at bay. Too bad what could have been a nice day had been spoiled by the upsetting accident of their neighbor.

Janet arrived home for the night just as the storm broke loose with full intensity again. Timing the rain had been on her side all the way home, and she'd been fortunate. Lightning now lit up the night sky, and buckets of water pelted the lake vicinity in a steady downfall. Puddles in her yard turned to a pool, and mud ran every which way. Thunder crashed with rumbles vibrating the house, and loose contents rattled within. How safe she felt in the comfort of her own home and out from the storm. How lonely it now felt not to have her parents or anyone there. Perhaps it was a taste of the loneliness people like Gertty and Irwin may have felt at times. The feeling was rapidly fleeting for Janet at this time.

Slipping and sliding into her bedroom on the wooden floor wet with water she had carried in, Janet hastily removed her saturated clothes and applied a heavy robe, which had hung on a hook on the back of her bedroom door. From inside her closet, a man peered through the closet-door slats and observed every inch of her womanly nakedness as she changed into a robe. Turned on with excitement, he reached between his legs and began rubbing his throbbing member through the woven fabric of his trousers. For all the time the man had been lingering in the closet, hoping for a glimpse of her changing clothes, the anticipated show now quickly excited him... especially since he wanted the precious moments to last and knew they likely would not. As quickly as she undressed and dressed, he came while not making any sound she'd detect. The look on his face was that of a primal madman with one eye squinting through the closet-door louvers. Janet sensed someone was near. Just not enough sense to put her finger on what she exactly was sensing.

Outside a nearby window, flashing lights penetrated into the house and ricocheted off various walls. They appeared to be white lightning until colors of blue were intermingled in. Janet observed Sheriff Dean exit his vehicle and run to her house door. There, Janet shyly greeted him in her robe, slippers, and nothing more. Perhaps it was he she had sensed was coming?

"Sorry to bother you, Janet. I saw your lights on and was wondering if I could talk with you for a short while. There is a lot going on tonight, and I don't have much time to spend." The sheriff was cordial, and there was some sense of security she felt with him being there. It was more than enough to ease any final depression of being alone and feeling isolated.

Maybe it was the storm that just had Janet shaken? Odd, considering she usually loved storms. Maybe the events at Irwin's had her shaken? Whatever the case, Janet felt that the events of the last few days were more than she'd experienced in her whole life combined. It was a bit much in such a short time. She was happy to speak with Dean just as soon as she grabbed some fresh towels to cover her floors where he would walk and then allowed him to get comfortable out of his wet Private Eye-style trench coat and hat for whatever time he'd be there.

"I'm glad you moved in. Not many pretty faces grace the town year-round. Really, not any at all I can think of. Until now, I think Gertty was about the only one." The sheriff was obviously making a joke as he smiled. It was obvious to anyone with eyesight that Gertty was not exactly a pretty face. Janet smiled too. She noticed how firm Dean's chin looked when he smiled. Handsome. As handsome as Armani, but in a different way. More ruggedly mature and distinguished. Not the pretty-boy type Armani was. It was nice of the man to try to create some levity on such a disturbing night. It was of comfort. "Are you all right here, Janet?" Sheriff Dean would have asked that of anyone. Mostly because it is part of his job.

"Of course! Why would I not be all right?" Janet inquired of him, not knowing why he would ask the question in that manner.

"I didn't know how well you've known Irwin over the years, and it's always possible that Irwin's death wasn't an accident." The sheriff then alluded to the fact that an autopsy had not been performed yet. In one respect, he seemed to imply not to worry until an autopsy had been performed. In another respect, he seemed to imply she should worry until they ruled out any possibility it had not been.

"You are saying something to the effect that we should worry his death was no accident? Gertty seemed to imply something of the sort to me earlier. What exactly are you implying, Mr. Dean? Should I say *Sheriff*?" The sheriff had her interest piqued greatly.

"You can just call me Dean, if you'd like. Most people do. I don't mean anything in particular, Janet. I heard Gertty call you Jan. Is it okay if I call you Jan? What I'm saying is that sometimes, party people break into these homes looking for a good time. Maybe they didn't know Irwin was there, and things got out of hand. I'm not saying that in particular happened, but things are not always what they seem. A person learns that in my line of work. It's my job to get to the truth and discover what really happened. You know what I mean? I don't take things at face value. I just want to make sure you're okay here by yourself. I don't want any more accidents happening around this lake, in my jurisdiction, on my watch. Also, I was just making sure you are okay after stumbling upon such a horrific find. Not many witnesses walk away from a scene like that without some emotion. Since you mentioned it, what did Gertty exactly imply? You said she implied something of the sort? Just what sort is that?"

Now Janet believed she had opened a can of worms over what was probably nothing. "Gertty made a comment about her safety tonight. Everyone seems so up in arms over safety around here as of late. Nobody has ever said anything about it before. Look, Sheriff… Maybe I am just a bit analytical because me being here is a safety concern of my folks. They had me change the locks. I've only just arrived here recently, and so much is all so new to me. Life seems different. Then my folks speak of safety. Gertty speaks of safety. Eli and Dan speak of safety. Armani speaks of safety. You speak of safety. I've never felt I was in a safer place in my whole life while everyone else seems so overly concerned around here these days."

"Incidents have happened around here, Janet. Some business I'm not at liberty to discuss. Police confidentiality. You understand?" Dean asked, but as more of a statement.

"Understand?" Janet quipped. "I understand nothing, and now you're going to make me jumpy over what I don't understand, Sheriff Dean. I wish someone would help me understand anything! Anything at all!"

"Worrying you is not my intent, Jan. Nobody understands anything at all, and that is what I am trying to understand myself. What did you mean by Armani speaking of safety?"

"I don't know." Janet could not even really recall. She tried to justify her mentioning of it at all to Dean as best she could. "He's known me since I was little girl, and he looks out for me when he can.

He changed the locks for me, and I gave a key to him in case I need help. I don't recall all he has ever said to me. Not in exact words. There was some talk of safety and security, and he was in favor of me changing my locks. I guess that is all."

"You and Armani got something going on?" The sheriff's question was direct and brazen.

"People do not seem to mind getting too personal around here. Do they, Sheriff Dean?" Janet thought for a spell. When she had a question, nobody ever seemed to give a direct answer. With this question Dean had asked, Janet felt she'd play their game. No need to lie, but not answer directly. Rather, she'd answer it with a question of her own. "Whatever are you implying? He's known me since I was a little girl. I told you that."

"I know him very well too, Jan." The sheriff's discussion disguised itself as a warning. "Too well. He's a real lady-killer, and I'd hate to see you mixed up in any way with someone like that. Take me, for example. I'm a great guy. If you are looking for a man in your life, you may want to consider looking me up. You could do worse, and I'm very much available. Easily lovable too!"

That was more of a lighthearted, unprofessional conversation Janet had been waiting for with the sheriff. His words put her at ease. "I understand your name is Sheriff Dave Dean. Were you ever called Deputy Dave? Deputy Dean? It has more of a ring to it. Don't you think?" Janet said as she nodded.

"Never been called that by anyone who knew what was best for them. If it gets me a date with you,

I'll let you call me anything you want. What do you say? I can be a lot of fun despite business." Dean hoped for a favorable answer.

"I'm not looking for anyone right now. If the right guy comes along and something happens, well then, I might just consider pursuing something." Janet felt that was a good enough response to the sheriff's advances.

"Is something happening? It sure is for me," Dean stated kindly. "I could be the right guy for you, and here I am. Will you at least think about it, Jan? If I am making you uncomfortable, I'll go away."

Their conversation was interrupted by a ringing of the doorbell. "Saved by the bell," Janet smirked and said with gratefulness to have wormed her way out of making any rushed decision.

At the door soaking wet was her brother, Steven. "Steven! What are you doing here? I'm so happy to see you. I did not know you were coming, and you never called. I'm flabbergasted! How rude of me. You know the sheriff? This is Sheriff Dean. What brings you here of all places? Why didn't you let me know you were coming?"

"I know who he is." Steven grimaced. "Got some kind of trouble here, Sheriff Dean?" It was obvious Steven had some issue with the sheriff being there. His question was presented in a bullying tone.

"My business here is done, I think. That is, if Jan is done with our conversation for now?" Sheriff Dean seemed as surprised as Janet that Steven was there at the house, having seen the squad car outside. "Your being here seems to be a surprise to your sister."

"Am I being questioned?" Steven wanted to know. "I've been a part of this town since before my parents owned this property you are now standing on. You got a problem with that?" Steven's defensiveness surprised Janet. That wasn't his usual nature, and it had come off as an inappropriate response.

"No questions for you. Just an observation. I'll be leaving now." The sheriff put on his coat and hat. "Thanks for drying me off, Jan. Think about what I said, will you?" As the sheriff departed, he glared at Steven with a second look.

"Steven, I'm so glad you are here. My big Steven-Weavie came to see his little sister. What a surprise!" The visit was a sudden event of which she was caught totally off guard. It was wonderful that he had taken her mind off the events of the day with his unexpected arrival.

"I wanted to surprise my little sister," he said as a big smile came over his face. "I'm not an inconvenience if I stay a couple or few days, am I? I can get a room in town if I'll be in your way. Or maybe I can stay in the apartment above the garage if you don't want me around the main house?" Steven already knew Janet would never turn him away.

"You must stay here, I insist," said Janet. "I've taken your old room, and you'll need to use one of the other bedrooms. The apartment above the garage hasn't been completely cleaned out in years. It's a terrible mess up there. Spiders and cobwebs everywhere. Dead flies litter the floors and windowsills." Janet hadn't expected any overnight visitors so soon. "I've started doing some work up there in the apartment. Not nearly enough to make it usable yet. I was hoping to eventually turn it into a work studio. One day at a time."

"Would it be okay if I put some meat in the big freezer downstairs?" Steven asked. "You still have the freezer? A car hit a deer, and the person shot it to put it out of its misery. I had the opportunity to take the meat, and I couldn't pass up a deal like that. It needs to get frozen quickly. If you want, I can clean up the apartment up there. I'd like to help. I heard you were taking over the house and am so happy for you. So happy you are keeping it in the family." Steven's offer to help was gracious as he looked out the screen door at the window above the garage.

"Whatever you'd like. The freezer is still downstairs. You are welcome to do all the work you want around here for free. What brings you here? Why don't I hear from you often enough? Even Mom and Dad don't hear from you from what they tell people. I am so excited to see you." Janet was, in fact, excited, but still curious why he had come unannounced. So many thoughts were running through her head that the question of asking who had informed him of the home purchase totally slipped her mind before she got around to asking him.

"I just wanted to see you. We'll talk more later. We've got plenty of time." Steven did not seem too eager to speak in his wet clothes.

Janet had many questions for Steven but sensed he was not too anxious to make small talk. The storm seemed to have people rattled, and she should see to it that he got into some dry clothes. More importantly, she wanted to discuss his past behavior without upsetting him. *That would not be easy*, she thought. With people aware he was the town pervert, she did not know how a discussion like that would go over. Perhaps she should wait to discuss the matter after she had time to think about what she wanted to say to him. Janet loved her brother dearly, but his alleged past behavior had been a shock for her to discover.

After Steven became more settled, Janet informed him of Irwin's demise and told him of how she and Gertty had found him. That was why the sheriff had stopped over. She intentionally did not mention the sheriff's flirtatious statements. Janet did, however, explain that she had been overwhelmed by getting settled in the house. Never had she thought it would be an experience to become settled in a house, which had always been her home away from home. Had she had her druthers, Janet would have chosen to think of this house as her permanent full-time residence all her life. She'd never been fond of their other home in Prospect Heights. Prospect Heights was just basic, old, boring Midwest suburbia. Lake Marie, on the other hand, offered so many joyously fond memories. There were so many lake activities she enjoyed. Had anyone ever told her that she would have been there this time of year for days and had not yet fished, water-skied, suntanned, or enjoyed any other activity she was prone to participate in, Janet would have thought them to be out of their mind. Steven was now around even if only for a couple days, and just maybe, Janet could enjoy some family fun time with him. But their appreciation for the home still differed. Steven would rather have stayed in Prospect Heights, and his visits to the house were always bittersweet just as Janet had explained to Gertty.

"How long are you planning to stay for, Steven? Are you up for some fun activities while you are here? You still haven't told me what really brought you here or anything." Janet wanted some answers soon, or she thought she'd explode with inquisitiveness.

"We'll have plenty of time to talk. I drove here from CA, and it's been a long trip. Can we talk more in the morning?" Steven's voice cracked and seemed exhausted.

It was evident Steven was looking very worn and haggard, and Janet knew it was not all because of a trip from California to Illinois. With the money Steven inherited from their grandparents, he could have selected a better mode of travel instead of having driven the whole distance in a rental vehicle. Why not have flown first class? She could have picked him up at the airport. If he had wanted to drive, why had he not taken more time to stay at hotels along the way and get in some relaxation along the way? It seemed all things people were doing these days baffled Janet. There were even more questions Janet still had not yet asked Steven, and her curiosity was eating at her. It often did. "I'll bet you are tired? Remember when we were kids and we'd stay up all night here, talking? I miss those times." Janet reminisced momentarily of the good old days.

"We were kids then, Sis. This body has gone through a lot of changes since then," Steven said wearily. "Right now, I need sleep and lots of it."

"It looks like it," Janet said from an obvious observation. "Now get your beauty sleep. I can't be seen with you looking the way you do. In a few years, I'll be your age, and I don't want people thinking that haggard look runs in our family," Janet said that, knowing it would bring a big smile to his haggard, drawn face. Blowing him a kiss, Janet turned off the light. "One last question tonight. Who told you I bought the house? Mom and Dad said they haven't heard from you. Whom had you been speaking to?"

Steven answered, "The attorney who handled our inheritance. I don't know how he knew. I guess I just assumed he handled the legal aspects for the sale of the home."

"He did." It came as no surprise to Janet that the family attorney had mentioned it to Steven. Their attorney was a longtime friend of her father, and there had never been any family secrets when it came to legal matters. "I was just wondering if you had talked to anyone I'd be interested in. I don't speak to any other relatives directly. Mom always fills me in after she talks to them. You know what I mean. Good night, Steven."

While the storm continued to rage with fury outside, Janet turned off the remainder of the lights in the house. Steven had even left the basement lights on while putting away his venison in the freezer as Janet noticed from light illuminating through the bottom of the basement door. Opening the door to access the light switch, it was visibly apparent that the bulb Janet had just replaced had gone out again. Grabbing a chair from the kitchen, Janet took a fresh bulb and attempted the task of replacing the bulb she had only recently replaced. Janet grabbed for the bulb with a towel on her hand to prevent a burn in case it was hot and was surprised to find that the bulb was only very loose. It was cool to the touch and been barely screwed in at all. Janet was positive she had tightened that bulb appropriately when she put it in. She was sure of it. It had been working just fine earlier. Who would have climbed up to unscrew it? If Steven had done it while he was downstairs, how could he have reached it?

Preparing for sleep, Janet slipped into a comfy nightgown and just stepped out of her slippers when, to her surprise, her foot stepped in moisture somewhat near her bedroom closet. There was nothing on the floor she could see, but she was certain her foot had felt moisture. With so much going on, Janet hoped she'd have the best ever sleep that night. That was not likely to be. The storm made tremendous noise. Thunder boomed, and earplugs along with pillows over her head could not block the sound. Irwin's twisted body was imprinted in her mind with his pale, ghoulish face coated with crimson blood. His neck, snapped like a twig with bone protruding out his neck. And so much blood drying on the floor. Janet did not think the gruesome image would ever in her life leave her head. Tonight was a perfect night for a tranquilizer she had been prescribed a couple years ago but rarely ever took. And hopefully, thoughts of knowing Steven was there with her might help her calm down.

Dr. Artemis Paul had seen Janet periodically throughout her life for psychiatric purposes. Janet's parents had become concerned when Janet took up a habit of nightly sleepwalking at an early age. Dr. Paul never offered any confirmed reason for it. Hours and hours and countless dollars of counselling were of no benefit. Not even cognizance tests nor a brain MRI showed anything abnormal. The final explanation was that everyone thinks of stress differently, and Janet was likely, in her mind, under some stress other people did not understand. A calming medication had been prescribed. While Janet had not experienced sleepwalking in the last couple years or longer, the pills had only rarely been taken when Janet wanted a good rest. Under the circumstances, Janet knew she was feeling some variation in levels of stress. For tonight, a tranquilizer would definitely help take the edge off. Janet spoke aloud as she rationalized justification in taking the pill under given circumstances. It soon proved that the pill may really not have been needed by the fact Janet was asleep just minutes after hitting the pillow following having taken one.

The tranquilizers, however, always did cause Janet to have bizarre dreams. A dream scenario played over and over in her medicated mind. It was one of Irwin falling down the stairs. She was standing at the top of the stairs reaching out to him and trying to save him as he tumbled out of control. Irwin would tumble down stair after stair until his head cracked on the basement cement and bones protruded from his flesh. The blood would spray the walls near and pour out of the exit wounds from the protruding bones. It played out over and over and over until Janet's shifting and tossing awakened her into a half-alert, drugged stupor. As her eyes cracked open slightly, lightning jolted through the sky and gave Janet a glimpse into the real world before blinding her, and she passed back into a dreamy sleep once again. It was during that quick moment between sleep, waking, lightning, and sleep again that Janet was sure she briefly focused on a dark shadow of a person leaving her room. It didn't matter to Janet at this time. She was back asleep and on to some other twisted, nightmarish dreams she wouldn't recall when she'd eventually awaken.

Chapter 11

While walking the perimeter of her yard, Janet conceived a plan for cleaning up and planting the lawn and garden as best as she'd be able to for the remainder of the growing season. The outdoor walk made her feel refreshed and with a clear mind. She thought it would be nice if after her morning regiment of cleaning herself up, she should gather a pack of venison out of the basement and bring it upstairs to defrost. She'd surprise Steven with cooking dinner and was hoping he would plan to be around for it.

Within the next hour, Janet had prettied herself up and was entering the kitchen with the meat. Steven was already awake in the adjoining living room and had made himself comfortable with the newspaper and a cup of coffee. Not unusual for Steven in the morning, he was relaxing in his boxers with his feet up on the coffee table. It was a vision Janet had seen almost daily growing up with him. Steven was a nudist at heart and never liked to wear clothes when he was growing up. It was thanks to Janet's mother that Steven wasn't permitted to sit around the house completely naked, and it was nice for Janet to see that Steven hadn't abandoned the practice while in her home. Ever since he had been a baby, she was told Steven would pull off his diaper and refuse to wear it. Janet's parents could never get him to keep his clothes on, and Wes was not much of an inspiration. He, too, was either nude, in only underwear, or in a swimsuit whenever he was around the house; Steven was just like Wes. While Janet didn't dress up, she was always appropriately attired should anyone have unexpectedly dropped by. Funny, Janet thought, how her mother was always dressed up with her hair and nails done. Peggy always carried herself with social class and feminine style while the rest of the family were more lax in their outwardly appearance. Janet noticed her nails and thought, at first, she should get them done along with her hair. On second thought, why? Why get them done when she had so much work at the house ahead of her? Who would appreciate it anyway? Someday.

"I made coffee, Janet!" Steven yelled with his voice carrying into the next room.

"Good morning, sunshine," Janet responded. "I hope your coffee is better than the sludge Mom brews. I swear she drinks her coffee so thick that she must fry it into a solid form. I think she calls it coffee cake!" Janet peeked in at Steven to see if he was paying attention to her pun.

Steven noticed her peeping through a break-fast-bar opening and smiled. "I got up early and thought I'd start cleaning the apartment before it gets too hot!" Steven yelled out. "Remember yesterday, I told you I'd help some while I am here? You know that apartment was always stifling this time of year during midday. Best to get started up there while it's early," Steven suggested. Janet knew that was best.

Janet peeked into the living room again quickly and informed him and made a request. "I know, but I had hoped we could talk some and spend some time together. You said you were only here for a couple days, and that's not much time. How about if I help you up there? We can talk and clean just like when Mom and Dad had us do our chores. It always made the time go by faster when we worked as a team." Janet missed those times with Steven even if they had been laboring doing chores. She missed any time with him. He had been the best big brother a girl could have ever wanted when she was growing up, and he could have done no wrong in her eyes in those days. Things were different now.

"Sounds great!" Steven yelled back to her as she turned to walk away. "I'll really get started as soon as I finish my coffee and paper. Just give me a few minutes, and I'll get dressed."

"Thank you for checking in on me last night, brother dear. And I brought up some venison for dinner. I'll cook. Hope you don't mind?" Janet wanted to get small talk off to a good start before she laid into heavier conversation later.

"I didn't look in on you. I slept soundly all night." Steven spoke but had not in a volume audible for Janet to hear in the other room. Then as Janet had entered the living room where Steven sat, Steven continued speaking, "Venison sounds wonderful. Where do I find your cleaning supplies for the apartment?"

"In the basement," Janet said as she curled up on the sofa next to him while sipping her beverage. "Under the stairs. Speaking of the basement, Steven, when I was down there, I noticed a light bulb I had just replaced had been unscrewed. It wasn't lighting. I tightened it last night, and it works now. Had you loosened it for any reason when you were down there last night?"

Steven asked, "Is it the one nearest the corner by the stairs? It was out when I went down there. I assumed you had known about that. Why would I loosen your bulb? You are just as screwy as always, Janet." Steven denied having tampered with it and added, "Maybe there is a ghost in the house who has a thing for bright lights?"

"Now you are being your usual silly self, Steven. Always trying to scare me. Well, it won't work. I'm too old for that now. You know as well as I do that there has never been a ghost in this house. It does remind me of the ghost stories you would frighten me with as a kid. Thanks to you, I slept with my lights on until I was eleven and had to inspect every inch of my bedroom before I went to sleep. I admit that I fell for your monster-in-the-closet and under-the-bed stories for many years. Not now. I refuse to check the closets and behind drapes because I will not let your stories and my imagination get the better of me. I'm too mature for that. Besides, you being here is enough to scare away anything. Even a ghost with light sensitivity!" Janet reciprocated conversation with humor.

"Could it be that Irwin is here haunting you? He's a fresh spirit and may have just arrived. He's coming to get you, Janet." Steven never did display sympathy, and no topic was free from joking about. "He's here. I can feel his presence. He's trying to communicate with you, Janet. He's saying that you are his type and he wants to be with you…forever!" The voice Steven spoke in changed to one of menace. He did the voice well, and it sounded exactly like what she recalled Irwin having talked like… If Irwin had been menacing.

Janet did appreciate humor and knew how weird her brother could be. What Steven had been saying had been meant in jest and was of quick wit. He'd never change and nor would he ever likely mature. She appreciated as much from him. Irwin's death had been a terrible event, but she and her brother always did make light of serious subjects. The weirder, grosser, more disgusting the topic, the more they'd find to kid about. When Janet was down, it was her brother who always lifted her spirits.

The day had progressed, and the weather outside had turned from intermittent storming into a slow but steady rain. The apartment did not seem as hot as when the sun beat down directly upon the poorly insulated shingled roof during hot summer days. There was no air conditioning up there. While not hot today, the apartment still had a very stifling, musty, locked-up smell. It always had a distinct moldy smell that would cling onto and pene-trate anything that had been up there for even the shortest length of time. Janet considered installing a window-unit air conditioner.

"Notice that smell?" Janet asked. "I would like to get that smell out of here. I want to remove the cupboards and carpet. Then paint the room when it's clean enough. When it's completed, I hope to use the room as an art studio to do my work. I don't know if anyone told you, but I'm a professional artist now. I design the ads for a few little shops. Some of my canvas art creations hang in a small gallery. It's not much for now, but I suspect my business will grow quickly once I invest more time in it. I know so little about your life these days. What have you been up to?" Janet was anxious to hear anything Steven would tell her.

Steven was not happy about what he wanted to say to Janet and felt it was as good of a time to talk. While working at his task, he'd not need to look Janet in the face if she reacted adversely. Seeing Janet unhappy always made him unhappy too. If there was anyone he ever cared about, it was Janet. "I've been sick a lot, Janet. Medical bills have added up. If not for Grandmama and Papa having left us money, I don't know what I'd be doing right now. I got Lyme disease here in the woods several years back. You may recall I had that tick on me one summer and Mom burned it off. It grossed you out. That was probably one of the only creatures I've ever known you to get grossed out over. I guess that was when I contracted it because it is the only means of transmission I can think of. It's been painful lately."

Janet felt terrible for Steven and told him such. The words seemed like little consolation. She was hoping he'd keep speaking because she did not know what more she could say to comfort him.

He did keep speaking… "You know my life-style. It's not been much of a secret. I met a guy, the only guy I had ever been serious about, and we both contracted hepatitis. The hep with the Lyme's combined has just run me down. Of course, I am on medications, but they only do so much. Each time I thought about coming to see the family, I was usually too broke from medical bills. Illness has made the concept of working a regular full-time difficult for me. I worked as much as I could at a local hotel. It paid the bills and gave me medical insurance. When I had the availability and ways to get here, I was usually too sick to make the trip. Just lucky I guess that I have good friends in CA who looked out for me, and charities helped out so much. Good news is that I feel good today and I am here. I'm not sure how the newly gained money will change my life. Can we leave it at that? To think about what I have been through is depressing."

"Sure we can," Janet replied with a sorrow in her voice. "Again, I'm so sorry. I'd like to help if I can," Janet sincerely offered. "I obviously can't make you better or ease your pain. There is something else I want to know about, Steven. It's hard for me to speak of. It involves some pictures that got you in trouble.

Is it true? I want to hear the truth directly from your mouth."

Steven composed his words carefully. "That's a part of why I'm here, Janet. To make things right, I mean. I need a little time to correct some wrongs. Can we talk about this another time, Sis? Soon, I mean really, really soon? There are some things I need to clear up while I'm in town, and then I can tell you the truth and the whole story." Steven seemed forthcoming.

"Okay, Steven. If I can be of help, you let me know. You know I love you. I just don't want you to think I grew up to be like Mom, sticking her nose in everyone's business. Yet there are things I need to know." Janet wanted to help in any way she could. "How long will you be here for, Steven? A while? You said it would just be a couple days, but I can't believe you drove here in ill health from California for only a couple days. Can't you stay longer?"

"I've already been gone from California for a while, Janet. I have a cat and roommate back in Palm Springs. My roommate is great about helping out, but only to a certain extent. I can't take advantage of his graciousness. He does so much for me. So far, he's happy I'm away and has the place to himself. My cat is probably not so happy and misses me. Then there is my job. I don't want to go back. The medical insurance makes it necessary. I've not decided what to do about that. Let's just say that I have things to do while I'm here and things to get back to in California. I'll stay around here as long as I can," Steven answered.

The answers Steven gave made Janet think of more questions. "So you have business here, Steven? You said you have things to accomplish?" Janet knew there was something going on but could not determine what he was dodging speaking of. "Is your roommate in CA the special guy you spoke of?" Janet concluded.

"Yes, he is," Steven admitted. "I'm not much comfortable with calling him more than a roommate. He is more than that. As for the other question, I meant I have people to see here. If I start feeling really sick again, I will need to get back to my doctors right away. I wasn't even sure family would want to see me here. I am not the best relative the family has."

Janet was in disagreement with her brother. "I, for one, am thrilled you are here. I know Mom and Dad will be happy to see you. They love you. Who else matters?" Janet couldn't figure and didn't care. Steven was here with her, and that allowed her to walk on sunshine even on such a dreary day.

"Ya, who else cares?" Steven figured most people would not be happy to see him. Some were very unhappy to see him. The family would be among the happiest—if he could call their reaction a happy one.

A clock ticked away time on the wall. It was a wonder, considering Janet didn't even think anyone had been in the apartment in ages to care about changing the batteries. The clock was an old cuckoo clock Janet had been enamored with since she was a child. A pretty little bird would pop its head out every half hour. Every hour, dancing Bavarian people came out to perform a little dance. Janet so admired that clock, and her mom had stuck it away up in the apartment where it could not be appreciated by anyone. Janet's mother said the noises it made disturbed her, but that was likely a fib since it did have an on-and-off sound switch, which Janet had not known until examining it now. That switch would not have stopped the ticking sound. Maybe that's what bothered her mom? The clock had been passed down from Wes's mother, and Peggy despised her mother-in-law. Grandmama and Mom never did get along at all. Janet and Steven's mother always joked that the clock was a nice remembrance of the minutes that could be counted until Grandmama would pass away. Now that she has passed, it's sort of ironic Janet would have that thought come into her head. Their mother kept the clock until Grandmama passed, and now their mother didn't need to count the minutes anymore. It had been passed down to her. Janet would keep it unlike the blue phone. Peggy's despise for Grandmama was a more likely reason Peggy had for placing it out of her sight in the isolated apartment.

Steven was aware of the lull in conversation between them but was glad for it. The hardest topic discussions he planned to have with Janet for the day were over, and she seemed temporarily at peace with his answers. A lot of time had passed since they started working that day, and Steven felt it was time for a break. "Should we knock off and go to town to get paint supplies for here?"

"I'll tell you what," Janet thought. "Would you mind going to get the paint supplies for us? I know just what I want and can give you a list. I've become an expert at making lists. I'll finish cleaning up here, and then you and I can start painting tomorrow after the rain. You know…when it's less humid and we have more energy. I know you don't mind being seen in public looking like a workman, but I'd rather die than be seen in town looking this way. I look worse than homeless people do. It would almost take me longer to wash myself up than it would take you to go and get back." Janet knew she could count on Steven to go alone even though she'd miss spending precious time with him. "I have a couple other personal things to do today anyway since I didn't know you were coming. While at the paint store, if you want to grab us an Italian beef at the restaurant on Main Street, my stomach would sure be appreciative. I'll get the deer steaks defrosted in the microwave for later and season them like you like for this evening." Janet thought that all seemed like a wonderfully laid-out plan.

Steven agreed and laughed. "You sure are our mother's daughter. Making organized lists, planning every detail with a schedule, talking one subject to another without so much as letting a person get a word in edgewise? Yup!"

Janet explained about the house keys and new locks. "A spare key to the main house is under the planter on the kitchen counter," she told him. "Take it in case I lock the doors or step next door."

111

Shortly thereafter, Steven returned from the main house to the apartment and was all cleaned up. "You really should be locking all the doors at all times. They were unlocked when I went to the house, and I left them unlocked now in case you didn't have the key. There is no key under a planter on your counter," Steven informed Janet. "I'll just take my car to town, and I'll still need a house key. That is, if you want me to take one?"

Janet was sure she had placed a spare key under the planter in her kitchen. She had spares and wanted one handy without it being out in the open at all times. Janet removed a house key from a key ring on her person and handed it over to Steven. "Just in case you need one while you're here. I have others."

Proud of all the work they had accomplished in the apartment, Steven left for town, and Janet wrapped things up. The cuckoo clock indicated Steven had been gone for approximately thirty minutes before Janet headed back to the main house. "I'm sure it will be another fifteen minutes to an hour before he gets back," Janet calculated aloud. "Not much time to get done with all I wanted to before he returns."

Inside the main house, Janet made a beeline right for the kitchen. There was no planter on the counter. There was no key where the planter had been. Janet searched around and found the planter on a spare bedroom armoire. "I am certain I didn't put it here. It's not the room I am using, and it's not even the room Steven is staying in. Why would I have put it in here? I'm sure I didn't put it in here. Who did put it here?" Janet pondered with no likely answer. "*Who put this here?*" Janet hollered at the top of her lungs. No answer. Only silence touched her ears except for the distant sound of motorboats on the lake. Under the planter on the armoire was no key. Janet wept. She cried because she momentarily believed she could not handle this life when she had been sure it would be so perfect. She cried because things like this hadn't happened to her in years until now. The thought of them happening again in her life made her terribly concerned. Would the tranquilizers help? Should she see the doctor again? Were the adult responsibilities she was experiencing in her new adult endeavors be more than she could ever handle on her own? One thing was for certain: she wasn't going to worry people. She could not tell her parents as she knew they would worry about her and start treating her like an incompetent child again. It had been their lack of confidence in her and their past treatment of her that caused her past unhappiness… their constant control and nagging. Knowing of her past stress issues and previously prescribed medication, her family would worry much if they thought she was having mental troubles again. And they had shown such faith in her by letting her buy the house from them. This was to be her escape and new start. This house was to be her freedom and the answer. But was it?

Janet returned the planter to the kitchen counter and watered the drying soil in it. She found her spare keys and placed one under the planter. She accounted for them. Two had come with the new lock for the main door, and she had three made at the boat shop. "Not too hard to figure that I had five keys total. I gave one to Armani and one to Steven from my key ring. One I am now putting under this planter. While I should have two left, I have only one. Where did I put the other key if not under this planter?" Janet talked to herself as no other explanation came to mind. Had she only intended to put the key under the planter and never got around to actually doing it? She was sure she had placed it under the planter initially, and nothing could convince her otherwise. She was sure she had never moved the planter, nor had she removed the key from under it. Who had been there? If nobody had been and Steven had not moved it, this was a clear sign she was having mental issues again even if she'd not face that reasoning. These were the types of things that had happened when she was sleepwalking. There was no reason anyone she knew would do this to her. She had already given Armani a key. She would have gladly given Steven one, and she did before he left the house. Had he wanted, he could be having a copy made without her knowing at this very minute. She trusted people. Janet's thinking was starting to be garbled. No matter how garbled it was getting, she'd refuse to believe that her own neurotic delusions were occurring again. Yet every time she seemed unhappy or stressed in life, these things would happen and then stop as soon as she felt in control again. Not being in control would certainly be the way to describe her own life right now. It was different from anything she'd ever grown up with or known. It would take the feeling of being in control again to understand what was happening.

It would not be long before Steven would be returning, and Janet had wasted a lot of time thinking about keys. Not only that, but she noticed an unreasonable amount of time had passed since she had returned to the house. "Where had the time gone?" She could not explain. After locking all the doors, Janet showered. She could not wait to wash off the rotting smell from the apartment, which had tarnished her usual lovely scent of peaches and cream. Not a natural scent, but a product line Janet had created from essential oils she very much appreciated. She knew her clothes would need to go right in the washer along with Steven's when he returned.

Upon stepping out of the shower, Janet sensed someone had been at the bathroom door. The door had never closed properly that Janet recalled, and it never sealed properly as it slid side to side to open and shut. The slider door was warped, and a small crack always remained. She often felt she was being spied upon because of the crack but also usually ignored any neurotic notions her mind created. If she didn't ignore them, her mind would be overwhelmed even more than it was. Throughout the years, her dad had refused to fix the door by arguing it wasn't bad enough to worry about. Janet would argue that it was. It was especially disturbing when extended family had come to visit, and extra privacy was of concern to her. Now it was her imperfection to repair if she desired to. To do so would require ripping part of the wall down to remove the old pocket door and insert a new one. It would be a lot of work, just as her father had been debating with her. "It's just us here," her father would say when Janet worried about using the bathroom. "Nobody here cares what you've got to see. We've all seen it since you were a baby. We were all there to change your dirty diapers, and who do think gave you your baths? You think because your chest added a few pounds and you grew a bush that we don't know what you've got?" Janet believed that her father didn't understand that she had been growing into a rather modest young woman by today's standards and wanted her privacy. While Steven and their father would walk back and forth from the bathroom to their bedrooms buck naked and sit around in underwear, Janet thought not respecting her desired privacy was disrespectful. They were also, however, men. Many men are not concerned with modesty, especially with Janet's father Wes being in the military. Now Janet could have all the privacy she wanted. But was obtaining real privacy now being replaced with delusions of monsters in the bedroom and ghosts peering through cracks going to haunt her? She certainly hoped not.

Janet's mother wasn't any help either when it came to this subject. On occasion, Peggy would say to Wes and Steven, "Janet is here!" as if that were some attempt to stop male genitalia exposure in front of her eyes. Wes would say to Janet regarding Peggy's comments, "Hi, honey! Glad you are with us." He could not have been that stupid not to know what Peggy was getting at. Perhaps that would have been an appropriate comment from Wes had Janet come back from anywhere. They could not seem to grasp there was an impressionable, young lady present. While Steven did have an exceptional body, Wes did not... Not that Janet was comparing nor was she interested in seeing any of her family running around the house stark naked. Any protest she had pertaining to the matter fell on deaf ears. The family had no sympathy for any modesty Janet had and thought she was strange for being so concerned. The family found humor in her complaining. The family guys never even closed bathroom doors at all when they were in there. While there was a second bathroom in the house, it required a lot of work, and the shower leaked too badly to run water in. The family had designated the use of that bathroom to the toilet-and-sink needs only. And so Janet was subjected to family male nudity around the house on a regular basis.

Closing the door today should be a gesture that she wanted privacy had she actually believed someone had been by the door. Maybe Steven was home and simply walked by it. Not that he'd have reason to go down the hall in that direction, but perhaps he was looking for her. Hearing the shower water should have been enough of an indication she was in there, Janet thought, until she came to her senses and realized she was only justifying made-up scenarios. Janet dried off quickly and dressed. Upon examination of the house, she noticed Steven was apparently first coming up the walkway with some bags, and the door was still locked.

Janet opened the door to greet Steven as he came in. "Were you in here a minute ago?"

"No," he said, appearing to be truthful. "I'm just getting in here. I tried the apartment thinking I'd put the bags and paint in there, but it's a different lock. Why? Did you see me? Seeing ghosts perhaps?" Steven began singing ominous musical notes.

"Would you knock it off about ghosts? I was in the shower and did not know if anyone was here. Then I saw you coming up the walkway and didn't know if this was your second load. Need help or just want the apartment key?" Janet offered options and hoped she didn't sound paranoid in any way.

"I'll just take the key," Steven reasoned. "You're clean and all. There's no need in getting all dirty and sweating carrying work supplies." Steven put some bags down on the kitchen table while Janet fetched the apartment key from a small box of spare keys. "I see there's now a planter on your counter."

Janet didn't answer. She did not want to explain to Steven that she was experiencing any additional weird happenings. He'd either worry or make fun of her if she told him.

"I stopped for a few groceries too. If I'm going to be eating food here, I may as well pitch in what I can. It was no bother. Help yourself to anything except my soda. Hands off! I bought more coffee. I know it's not your favorite drink. Mom and Dad will likely be drinking it when they come. The paint shop wanted to take a while to mix the paint color you requested. That gave me extra time to shop. I found a great bakery in town too. It's new since I've been around. I got us some treats. Just don't eat them all without me, or that womanly figure you have is going to become porky again like it was when you were little. You were the little porker! Did a hot man fuck the baby fat off you?" Steven bellowed off a hearty laugh.

Janet returned and provided him with the key. "Stop it! I wasn't a fat kid, and no, a man did not do that to me," trying to remain demure. It had been a long time since she had even been a pudgy baby and lost the baby fat quickly. "Yes, it is an incredible bakery. Just don't tell Gertty or Mom that it is anywhere near as good as their homemade baked goods. They are sensitive that way."

"That's not what the other boys were saying about my sister growing up!" Steven joked. "They said she is a chubster!" Steven had fun making up stories about people. "And I would never knock anyone's baked goods. They are always wonderful. Mom's is the best. I'm biased because I grew up with her cooking." Steven smiled.

Janet liked to see people smile even if it did involve some joking at her expense. "Well, they were wrong. I never heard any of them say any such thing about my figure." Janet knew Steven was just teasing her. "Mom's cooking is the best." Janet agreed to that. "Everything looks great, Steven. Thanks for picking it all up. I shopped the other day, but I had just come to town and had much to do that day that I rushed through the shopping. I had forgotten to get some of these groceries. That was with a list! I've come to realize that Mom has two abilities. The first is to make a list, and the second is to stick to them." She was about to add that Armani was with her and had distracted her while shopping but then thought it best not to volunteer that bit of information.

"I have the receipt here for the paint supplies, but don't worry about it." Steven was gracious.

Janet appreciated it but replied, "No. I won't worry about it today, but I'll make it up to you before you leave. Can we eat our sandwiches in the four-seasons room and watch the drizzling rain after you unload the supplies? Remember how Mom would bring us lunch in there while we played on rainy days? I miss those times."

Steven performed all the unloading and carried every last bit of the materials up to the apartment. Janet was appreciative of all the work he had saved her. She knew those five-gallon paint buckets weighed a lot had she been on her own. Steven was busy for awhile and then came back to the main house. Janet asked for his clothes to start washing, and he stripped down. No modesty on his behalf. He just stripped his clothes off right there where he had entered the main door. Janet turned her head the opposite direction and reached out her arm for him to drape his worn clothes upon. Steven cleaned up while Janet washed clothes. It took him awhile before he was done, and he walked out with a towel around his waist.

The two of them headed to the four-seasons room and devoured the late-lunch delicacies while reminiscing. Just about every subject was covered. The afternoon seemed so nice. No discussion seemed off the table.

Small talk began with Steven reminding Janet that the shower wasn't getting hot water to it with the washing machine filling. That was why it had taken him so long to wash up. Food was the next topic. Then Steven jumped into the more probing line of questioning. "What, no boyfriends? I'm surprised you didn't marry by this point of your life. All you ever talked about was getting married. Remember how you'd put a blanket on your head and pretend to be a bride? You had some imagination as child. You were always making up pretend scenarios and acting them out. I would hear you accept Armani to be your husband." Steven had a boy crush on Armani as well.

Janet felt she could somewhat confide in Steven. He had been answering her questions since he got there and had not been asking many in return. He wasn't the prying type and was more secretive about his life than she was. She had little to hide. Her life was boring in comparison. When she did discuss her life with family, they seemed to always cut her down for everything.

"I have seen Armani since I came here," Janet said admittedly. "Mom and Dad have always been fond of him, and Gertty next door seems to appreciate all he has done for her. Nobody knows though, and don't say anything to Mom and Dad yet." Janet wasn't sure if she was proud to make the announcement because something didn't feel quite right when the words came out.

"Not Armani!" Steven interjected. "Listen, Janet. I've known him too, too well. I know him a lot better than you do. He's no good. He's no good at all. He may have Mom and Dad fooled, but they don't know how two-faced he is. Besides, he treats women like trash. That's why Marissa left him." Steven's face turned beet red. Janet needed to diffuse Steven.

"Just a minute," Janet said. "I've only seen him on a social level since I moved here a few days ago. Scum or not, he lives next door and is my new neighbor. It's obvious that some people like him and some don't. But I am a woman and not your kid sister anymore. You haven't even been around me in years, and suddenly you are here telling me how to live my life and who to see? It sure looks like you haven't lived your life all that great. There are people who think you are scum, but I love you and am on talking terms to you. I don't know where you are heading with your words… But you had best select your next words to me very carefully in my home."

"I'm sorry, Janet!" Steven knew she was right. "I just want to look out for you when I'm around, and you need to be careful of certain guys. Just look at me and what you've learned about me recently. Nothing about me is what you think it is, and I need time to get that through to people. I'm hoping to do it while I am here, and that is why I am here. I'll fill you in as I can. I need to be careful what I say right now, or I could screw up my chances to set the records straight. It is very easy to gain a bad reputation. It's a bad thing when you don't deserve having one."

"Steven, you tell me I need to be careful. Mom and Dad tell me. The sheriff tells me. Gertty tells me. My doctor tells me. Even the last priest I saw told me to be careful in life in the last sermon I sat through. *But nobody will tell me what it is I am to be careful of!* I'm here, aren't I? I have done okay for myself into my adult life. Yet people around me seem to be a totally screwed-up hot mess on toast, and they are telling *me* to be careful. What gives, Bro?"

"You are right. They are right. And I am right too. I'm so proud of you, and I don't want you to be unhappy. There are things and people I just can't talk to you about at this given moment. I know some other people are in the same position that I am right now. I'm sure they would explain to you if they could. I'm sure they know things you don't. If you aren't careful, you will end up as screwed up as the rest of us," Steven said. "But seriously, I've got history with Armani. I wanted to clean up that history with him while I am here but haven't seen him yet. Not sure I want to see him yet. After I speak to him, I can probably speak to you. You understand what I'm saying?"

Janet could respect Steven for saying what he did. She had things she wanted to say to Armani too, and they were not things she'd share with Steven at this given moment. She wanted to know where Armani and she stood as a couple. It really wasn't Steven's business, but she could relate to what Steven was trying to say. Now she felt she had been rude for having barked at him. So what if Steven wanted to speak to Armani about something? What business was that of hers?

"You are absolutely right." Janet wanted to change the subject. "Notice the rain has stopped," Janet eventually said. Why don't we take a boat ride around the lake and have some fun?" Janet tickled Steven's side.

"That's the coolest idea you've had since I arrived, Sister. Let's go!" Steven was up and heading to put some clothes on. He was at the door and waiting before Janet had time to prepare herself.

"Wait! I still need to get the boat key. I need my house keys. I need my cell phone." Thinking of her phone reminded her of calling her parents. "That reminds me, Steven, do Mom and Dad know you are here?" Janet asked with hopes of being able to share the news. "I haven't called them today. Mom is going to be so mad at me. I need to call her before we go out."

"I don't want Mom and Dad to know I'm here just yet," Steven requested of Janet. "I have a lot to say to people, and I'm not ready to deal with them. I'm trying to spend time with you right now. Let's just keep this as our time, hmmm?"

Janet wasn't happy about keeping that from her parents. She also felt that Steven being there was big news and they'd want to speak to him. Also, she wanted to respect Steven's wishes. He deserved a little time, and she did not need to be a gossip. "Okay," she agreed. "But I need to call them anyway."

"Hi, Mom! It's Janet," Janet could be heard saying by Steven. "Sorry to get your answering machine and to have missed you. I've been so busy cleaning up the apartment. You'd think two people did the work up there because so much has been accomplished. I'll be painting up there soon. The rain just stopped. I was going to take the boat out for a short ride. The storm last night was terrible, and I want to make sure the boat survived it. And, Mom, I have bad news. Irwin is dead. Yes, you heard me right. He fell down his basement steps. Gertty and I were there to find him, but I helped Gertty through it. You'd have been proud of me. I'm okay and being looked after just fine by everyone. I'm looking after everyone too." Janet winked at Steven. "I'll talk to you later. Kiss Dad for me. I love you guys. Bye!" Steven was comforted that Janet handled the call very well. Janet seemed to him to even be handling the death of Irwin very well. He'd have predicted she'd still be very shaken by the experience. Instead, she talked about his death as if it didn't bother her in the least. His baby sister had grown up a lot, it appeared to him.

Their boat ride had taken awhile before they returned home. Janet had time on the boat to ask Steven where he had been the last few days, and he told her of his trip from California to Illinois. He described all the towns he had seen along the way, hotels he stayed in, and diners he dined in. He never did state when he had actually arrived in Illinois. Just as Steven got to answering that question, the boat had pulled into their dock, and he jumped off to tie it up without discussion. The question had been evaded.

Venison was in the oven, slow roasting and already filling the house with the aroma of herbs and an array of kitchen fragrances that would linger for hours until they would actually eat. In fact, it would eventually linger even longer after they'd finish eating. Steven sat quietly in the four-seasons room playing a solo game of cards while watching the oncoming sunset, which peeked between dissipating rain clouds. The house smelled wonderful. The view was marvelous. He felt well and comforted given his medical conditions. It upset him that he had felt he had to flee the places he had known in Illinois just to get away. Being back here, there was a touch of jealousy that Janet was able to live the life he could have been living near his family. That is, if they had loved him the way they loved her. He believed they did not. Before long, all of his freedom could be taken away altogether if he wasn't careful in the future.

Janet entered the room and politely asked permission to be excused. She had not heard from nor seen Armani all day and wanted to speak with him. It was something she had wanted to do while Steven went into town, but time had gotten away from her. Although she thought it best not to tell Steven that was where she was heading. Steven agreed to keep an eye on the cooking dinner and had not protested the request Janet made. He probably didn't protest in most part because he did not know where she was going. "I'll see you in about thirty minutes. Home in plenty of time for dinner and a board game tonight. Be prepared for me to beat your ass at any game you choose. Just like always!" Janet left.

Armani had watched Janet come up his pathway. He met with her halfway to the street. He kissed her passionately and said, "There's my girl."

"Am I your girl?" Janet asked. "You and I haven't had much time to talk about what has transpired between us. I hear some good and some bad about you, and I just want you to know I am a very good girl. What's the deal?" Janet hoped she had not pressured Armani too soon into vocalizing his feelings for her.

"I was just heading into the garage. I've got things to do in there. Come with me," Armani invited her. "I see you have company: Steven. I've stayed away not wanting to impose upon your time with him. Is he visiting for long?"

"Not too long. He said he has business. Business with you too, apparently."

Janet hoped notifying Armani might speed up the timing of the eventual discussion he and Steven would eventually have. Armani stopped what he was doing and looked at Janet blankly and quietly. Blinking and breaking his stare at Janet, Armani went back to sorting through the keys on his key ring to find the one that would unlock his garage.

"Did he say what he wants to talk to me about?" Armani asked Janet.

"No," she admitted. "Since he will not tell me, I thought you might?" Janet boldly asked. "Not that it's any of my business."

"I assure you that I don't know. I haven't talked to him in such a long time." Armani thought he had sidestepped the question.

"Maybe that's it? Maybe he just hasn't seen you in a long time and wants to catch up? You two were friends at one time. I guess nobody cares to tell me why you still aren't? As I said before, maybe that is also none of my business? If you get to know me well enough, you'll find that people I care about are my business. It's a trait I learned from my mother," Janet firmly stated.

"Any reason I should be friends with him? I saw him here some summers. We didn't have much in common. Even less in common as we got older. He went on with his life, and I went on with mine. We have an understanding. So? There you have it." Armani felt no need to say more.

"Armani…he said I should beware of you. It is something some people say about you. Why do they warn me to avoid you?" Janet hoped for a reasonable answer.

Armani took Janet's shoulders in his hands and again looked directly into her eyes. "I'm not here to please other people. I don't even care what they think of me. I don't allow people to control me. Maybe they don't like that? I only care what you think of me right now. If they said something to disturb you, you tell me, and I'll address it with Steven or whoever else you think has an issue with me. If I don't know what you or they are talking about, I can't give you an answer. Maybe it's actually something good Steven has to talk to me about? I will not know until he decides to speak up. Understand me?" Armani wanted a confirmation.

"You are right," Janet admitted. "I don't know. Somehow, I always think it's what I don't know that is someday going to haunt me," Janet worried. "I become concerned. I'm always thinking the worst, and I am sorry for asking so many questions. Before I stop questioning you, Armani, I just have one more question," Janet wanted to ask. "Strange things are happening around the house, and I just need to ask you some things." Janet stopped to compose her thoughts.

"What's on your mind?' Armani wanted to know. "What is it?"

"Things moving around," Janet complained. "Steven is there, but he claims it's not him moving things. If it's not me and it's not him...well, I know I gave you a key. Even if the door was unlocked and you just came in, I need to know what's going on so I don't think I'm cracking up?" Janet looked down.

Armani grabbed her chin and lifted it up. Looking her straight in the eyes again, he said, "Janet, I assure you I don't know what you are saying. You keep those doors locked. I cut that lawn for the first time when I was nine years old, and I've looked after that house ever since. I've chased away other kids. I've chased away potential robbers. You get what I'm saying? You keep your doors and windows locked or mind closely when they aren't. It's not unheard of for unwanted people to come around."

"I get it," Janet replied with a comforted smile.

"I'm glad you get it because I don't. I have no idea what you are talking about. Now I could have spent this time tasting your sweet lips. Instead, I had to listen to a chattering woman speaking of matters I don't understand. You women are all alike. Do you all go to some class to learn to confuse men?" Armani lightened the subject.

"I think we are born with a natural ability to do so. What I was not born with, my mother taught me. You know how neurotic she is. And my dad is just crazy. I'm a by-product of both. They were good teachers." Janet smiled coyly.

"As for that sweet taste of your lips…" Armani touched her lips gently. "The smell of your hair…" Armani took some strands of her silken, flowing hair and sniffed them deeply. "And your baby-soft skin, which has the most incredible aroma…" He drew closer in and nuzzled her neck before gently planting tender kisses upon it behind her ear. "What is that smell that drives me so wild? I just want to eat you up."

"It's just my natural feminine mystique," Janet jokingly admitted. "I exude it!" Janet whispered as they now planted their lips upon each other and kissed deeply. Passionately, their lips embraced until they stopped for air. "That and my own line of body products chiefly consisting of vanilla cream and peach oils," Janet revealed.

"Smells out of this world," he said after inhaling deeply. "Heavenly. Just like you." Armani complimented Janet as she blushed and glanced away in shyness. He continued to gently plant kisses on her here and there about her face.

"And speaking of smelling out of this world, Darling... I have venison cooking at home," Janet said, pushing him away when she felt his time was up. "Steven brought it. I wanted to invite you for dinner, but it seems he wants to speak to you about whatever it is in his own time before I ever do anything like that. He's that way with a lot of people these days. Probably best I have him speak to you before I ever put you two in the same room together. I'm sorry. It would have been lovely to have you over." Janet truly felt sorry and stated she had to get back home soon.

"I'll lay low until Steven comes around," Armani said, not wanting to make any disturbances. "Enjoy your time with Steven. It's been awhile since you've heard from him, and now he shows up from out of the blue? Strike you as being odd?" Armani seemed concerned.

"Yes," she agreed. "Then again, some people think he's always been a bit odd," Janet stated the obvious, knowing Armani knew certain things about Steven. Yet Armani never once cut Steven down in front of Janet. Armani seemed to be more respectable toward Steven than Steven was toward Armani.

It was apparent that Steven was the one with unresolved issues.

"What about his perversions and things he had done? How do you feel about all that?" The question hit Janet hard.

"He said he wants to talk to me about that. He says there are things I don't know. I guess there is a lot I don't know," Janet openly admitted. "He hasn't had the chance to explain everything about his life yet. I'm giving him a little space, being that he only just got here. There is just a lot going on with everyone in the family, and not everyone is quick to open up." Janet looked saddened.

Armani felt for her. "I heard about Irwin. I knew him well. You doing okay?"

"Am I doing okay?" Janet exclaimed. Now Janet felt badly that she had not even mentioned Irwin to Armani. All Janet thought about had been her concerns, and here Armani had been friends with Irwin for so long. So close they were over the years that Irwin had been like a father to Armani and Gertty like a mother to him. Since he lost his own parents, they had been there for him. "I'm so sorry, Armani. I feel I have been so self-absorbed. How are you doing? Forgive me for not asking sooner."

"I'm strong enough to deal with it," he confessed, wanting to appear neither too sensitive nor insensitive. "Guess you already know he's not having a funeral. He had no family except an ailing sister, I've always been told. I hear he may have left the house to me, and I need to go downtown tomorrow to handle some details. The sheriff still thinks there may be foul play involved and thinks maybe his fall down the stairs wasn't a complete accident. Since I stand to inherit, our dear sheriff friend may be making some trouble for me. Guess he has something personal against me too. Your brother and also the sheriff? Who knew so many people could have issues with little ol' me?" Armani still had his humor even at a time like this. "Jealousy," Armani continued…"I think Dean is just jealous of the past. As for any jealousy, does Steven know about you and me? That topic should flare up some jealous and protective natures." Armani was certain he already knew the answer.

"Yes." Janet didn't deny it. "Steven knows this and that. He knows what I wanted to tell him. I don't fill him in on intimate details of my existence. He knows that some unmentionable things have transpired between you and me in the last few days. It has only been a short matter of time, and I have been busy. It's not been the foremost topic of discussion between him and me. He doesn't know everything." She opened up, and Armani didn't seem to respond. He seemed to be thinking.

Armani grabbed Janet again and kissed her powerfully and started to rub her breasts. Janet pulled back gently and stated she had to get back to her dinner with Steven. Really, she only had minutes left before she really should get home and wanted to check on Gertty but felt no need to announce plans of her every movement. Although she hated to leave

Armani. His kisses and touches burned with eroti-
cism, and he had made her feverishly hot. She could
hardly wait until he fucked her next and wondered
where they would do it.

Gertty took a while to answer the door. "How
are you?" Janet expressed her concern.

Gertty looked depressed. Attempting to hide
her depression, she smiled unsteadily and nodded
while softly speaking, "I'm just okay."

"Just thinking… Have you had dinner yet?
Steven and I were going to have venison, and I'm
sure he'd not mind if you joined us." Janet was all too
pleased to extend the invitation.

Gertty seemed to perk up just a bit and then
softly, but in a bit louder voice, said, "How do you
cook it?"

Janet claimed she cooked it just as her parents
had taught her. These thick steaks were piled like
a roast and being slow-roasted in fresh herbs until
fork tender like a juicy prime rib roast. Janet's father
was a hunter, and her mother was always cooking
what he brought home. Janet learned how to cook
many unusual dishes most people have never tried.
Although she did not approve of hunting and only
made an exception for this deer this time because it
had been hit by a car.

Gertty accepted. "You got any of that gin left?"

"I'm sure I do. I also have a fabulous dessert
Steven picked up from the bakery in town."

The old lady was suddenly all smiles and very talkative. She talked Janet's ear off all the way next door. Janet wondered if she had done a good thing by inviting her. Mostly, Janet was concerned because this woman could talk through the night, and she wasn't certain Steven would be up for it. However, Janet would not enjoy her evening if Gertty were home alone depressed over Irwin. Steven should be able to understand that should the need arise to justify the unexpected invite.

When Janet entered the house with Gertty in tow, Steven seemed indifferent. He didn't mind her being there at all. He, too, had not really had much to do with Gertty over the years and really didn't know what to make of her at first. Gertty was very chatty; not only did she do a complete turnaround in emotional actions from when Janet went to Gertty's today but Gertty was also now acting as though she was the life of a huge gala. She seemed to know enough about any topic to keep a good conversation flowing and was a smart cookie.

Steven set the table while Janet gathered the cooked food into what dishes she could find, which Peggy had left behind. Picking out china patterns and shopping for new things for the home was an event Janet was building up her excitement for. At the moment, any hand-me-down china Janet could find would have to make do.

Gertty questioned where the bar was and then proceeded to it to pour each of them a drink. Carrying the drinks into the kitchen, Gertty also managed to bring the entire bottle of gin tucked under her arm. Although by Gertty's standards, there was not much remaining in it.

The meal was served, and Janet requested they say grace. They all agreed, and Janet led in prayer. It wasn't a regular regiment for Janet, but she had been thinking of how much they all had to be thankful for. The three concluded with an "Amen" before digging into the delicious plated meal. Everything looked exquisite sans the mismatched selection of serving dishes. But the food taste was unsurpassed. They ate rather quietly, and Janet thought this was a good way to quiet Gertty's food-filled mouth down for a spell. Just stuff her face with food, and she stays quiet! Janet ate eloquently, while Gertty and Steven wolfed food down with hearty appetites. Gertty complimented her hosts on having prepared such a delectable feast. Steven contributed to conversation by the telling of how he came upon obtaining the venison.

When the meal was done, Janet cleared the table and washed dishes while Gertty nursed the gin. Steven and Gertty remained seated at the kitchen table. Janet could not hear much of what was being said over the running dishwater and clanging dishes even though she tried her darnedest to listen. All she could catch were every few words. Maybe she comprehended the conversation topics. Maybe not. She thought she had.

In general, the conversation was rather insignificant between Steven and Gertty. He did not have much to say to her but didn't mind her speaking.

He found her to be a bit nosy and pushy when she inquired about his life. Steven was doing well at avoiding answering most questions 100 percent truthfully. He mostly opted to allow her to speak about herself, and that he found to be tolerable.

In little time, Janet had joined them and requested they speak in the living room where the seating would be much more comfortable. Conversation lasted late into the night and ended up on the topic of Armani. Instead of ignoring the topic, Janet informed Gertty that Steven was not fond of Armani and he may not be a comfortable topic to be discussing. Gertty spoke up and began to slur her words. "You folks be nice to Armani. He took care of me when nobody would. He is like a son to me. I may not always be on his side, but I do what I can for him. I take good care of him, and he takes care of me. That does not mean we don't fight like family when situations arise. They arise. They do arrrrriiiiisssse." Gertty's words became slurred and incomprehensible from all the gin.

Just as Gertty finished speaking, she leaned over and vomited on the carpeted floor alongside the sofa. Steven thought the drunkard was a hoot to watch. Janet was concerned for Gertty. Janet was also concerned that she would have to clean the carpet. This may be a good time to just rip the living room wall-to-wall carpet out and start renovating that room. Not at this moment, but tomorrow. Maybe? Janet smiled at Steven, and neither were offended by Gertty's actions.

Janet hastily led Gertty to the guest bed after cleaning her up and permitted her to sleep off her drunkenness until morning. Outside the bedroom door, Steven began playfully joking with Janet over the entire evening. Janet contemplated the best way to clean the alcohol-based vomit from the carpet and joked along with Steven.

"Nice party, Sis. Nice neighbor. What did you do? Poison her with your cooking?" Steven was laughing and enjoying himself.

"Laugh all you want, Steven, but tomorrow you are going to rip out all this carpeting for me. And you know that was a wonderful meal. If I were going to poison anyone, I certainly would not go through all the trouble of cooking a meal for them. Thank you!" Janet was being honest and funny at the same time.

"It was a wonderful meal, and I didn't mind the company. She's different. I'm glad you and Gertty have each other to look after around here. That woman had a hard life. I feel bad for her," Steven commented with sympathy.

"Steven, tomorrow, I'd like for you to speak with Armani about whatever it is that has been on your mind. Armani and I have something going on, and it's rough on us with you being here having some unmentionable, unresolved issue. I love you, and I need to know things are okay. Otherwise, it is very unsettling to me," Janet suggested with a demand in her voice. "Then we also need to tell Mom and Dad you are here. I have a feeling Mom is going to be talking to Gertty anyway to ask her if she is okay with Irwin's passing. Gertty is bound to tell her she had dinner with you here. I can only keep a secret for so long before our dear parents find out and become upset that we haven't said anything. Am I right?"

Janet was right about some things, and under this circumstance, Steven knew what he should do. He was not all too happy. He had already anticipated that Janet had talked with Armani to some extent when she had left the house. Janet had been outside too long to have only talked with Gertty and then have ended up inviting her over afterward. He had also watched her head over his direction when she had left. Steven also realized that Janet would have known Gertty's having seen him would get back to his parents all too soon. Steven was not going to allow Janet's actions to nudge him along. Knowing what he should do did not mean that was what he was going to do. For now, he'd be agreeable with Janet for the sake of quieting her.

Chapter 12

Morning came quickly, and everyone was up at once. Janet helped Gertty home, and Gertty was very apologetic. She presented Janet with her homemade cupcakes as a kind gesture for taking care of her. Janet didn't question Gertty's gesture, but it made no sense. Gertty had already promised them to Janet when she had been letting them cool before they went to Irwin's, and Gertty could have brought them over with her last night. Steven did his own thing that morning. By the time Janet came back home from next door, Steven wasn't there, and his rental car was gone too.

Janet began painting the apartment above the garage but knew she did not have great painting skills. She decided to roller-paint the ceiling and walls and have Steven or Armani do the tedious edging at a later time. Once she'd observe someone more experienced in painting and experimented a bit herself, she would pick up the skill tips to be able to work on the main house with less help later. The apartment was small, and Janet rolled quickly, considering her lack of professional expertise. A lot got accomplished by early afternoon, and she had accomplished all she could. At least all the painting she wanted to accomplish.

Steven was still not home, and Janet could not decide if she should call him or give him his space. There was no reason to call him. If she did call, it would be only because she was being nosy and keeping tabs on him. Wanting to give him space, she went about her business and tended to basic chores. There was an endless list of chores always waiting for her spelled out on one of her many organizational lists.

By early evening, Janet's energy level was winding down. The day went quickly for her, and she was not anxious to start in on any other tasks. Her mental ambition was there to have done so, but her physical body was plain exhausted. Muscles she had not normally used ached from a good day's work.

No sooner had Janet gone down into the basement to get some more meat out of the freezer to defrost for a later night when the doorbell rang, followed by a knocking sound. Janet begrudgingly climbed back up the stairs and made it to the door. She had hoped it was Steven, but it was the sheriff.

"Hello, Jan," Dean said with a polite greeting. "I hope you don't mind me stopping by unannounced. I was going to call you later. In the meantime, I ended up on a call in the area and figured I'd take a chance I'd catch you here." The sheriff seemed serious.

"You seem rather serious and tense, Sheriff. Anything wrong?" Janet expressed concern.

"No. Nothing like that. It's rather a personal call. Don't mind me. I'm just sort of shy when it comes to these things at times. I was wondering if you'd go on a date with me sometime? Maybe a dinner?" The sheriff was being shy and could not even look Janet in the eye. His cheeks blushed with rosiness.

"Listen, Dean, I like you. I like you a lot. The truth is that I hardly know you, and I've kind of got a thing started with someone else right now. I don't know where that is heading, but I don't mind taking time to get you know you though. No hard feelings and nothing to be embarrassed about. I thank you for asking. I'll tell you what: I have almost a full venison in the basement freezer and was about to start defrosting some. I've got my brother visiting for just a short, undetermined time. Why don't I phone you in a day or two, and we can set up a friendly dinner for after he leaves my house? What's your night off?" That seemed like a satisfactory way for Janet to handle Dean.

"I know your brother is here," said Dean. "Obviously, we saw each other here the other night. He'll be in town for a while though… Being he's a suspect in the Kinski case and all. I never really get time off. My work is never done. I just make time off as I need it. Whenever is good for you? I'd be pleased to try your cooking. I never had venison but look forward to trying anything you serve me."

Janet almost stopped listening after the first couple sentences. "What? My brother is a suspect in the murder of that woman in town?"

"Yes," said Dean. "I thought you knew. Didn't he tell you?" Dean was as surprised as Janet was, and

Dean had hoped Janet might disclose something useful to the case over dinner together—sooner than later.

Janet couldn't figure it out. "No. I didn't know. How? He did not even get to town until after the disappearance, and I wouldn't think he even knew her."

Dean explained…"That's not accurate. Your brother was here before the murder. He was seen with the Kinski lady the night of the disappearance, and she is still missing and presumed dead." Dean felt horrible revealing the details Janet didn't know.

Janet was still surprised and replied, "I don't know what to say. Steven didn't mention it. I don't think he ever told me when he got into town. I just naturally assumed he came straight here. Wait a moment and let me think… When Steven arrived, he wanted to go to bed early because he said it had been a long drive from California. I know he told me that." Janet was scared. "Maybe Steven didn't want people knowing he was in town sooner?"

Sheriff Dean was pleased with what Janet revealed. It could be of some importance to the case. Why hadn't Steven told his sister anything? The information Dean learned was exactly the type of information Dean hoped to learn over a dinner date with Jan.

Janet asked one last thing of Dean… "I was just curious if you learned anything about Irwin's death? I've been thinking about him."

Dean answered her question… "No. If you think of anything at all, please call me. You might think of something that could turn out to be important to any investigation even if you don't think it is."

Janet excused herself and closed the door. Her first action was to call Steven. To her surprise, the phone was already on the information to dial Steven. Why? She had never called Steven. Had she dialed when planning to call him earlier? She was sure she hadn't. It made no sense to her, and this hadn't been the first time her phone had been preset to make a call. It was just like so many other peculiar things that had happened to her at the lake recently. Upon calling, she got his voice mail just as she typically did.

Leaving a message, Janet said, "Steven honey, are you in trouble? Sheriff Dean was just here and told me you were in town before Kim Kinski disappeared and that you had been seen with her. You are a suspect in her disappearance, and I haven't seen you all day. I didn't know any of this. Have you seen Armani? Does this have anything to do with him and what you weren't telling me yet? I'm worried and very concerned about you. Please get back to me sooner than later. I love you."

Janet poured herself a drink and tried to relax. She was tense. Maybe Armani would know something? Maybe Steven had talked to him? Janet picked up her phone to dial Armani and got his voice mail too. "Armani, please speak to me soon. I was wondering if you spoke with my brother today? I also wanted you to do some edge-work painting above the garage in the apartment. Thank you!"

Now there was nothing to do except wait to hear from someone—anyone. Even phoning her parents still needed to be on hold until Steven called back. It was a perfect time to just relax with her cocktail and look at the lake from her four-seasons room. The lake always had such a calming effect. It was mesmerizing. Janet sat until into the early evening, never moving from the room. She thought all she could and either felt unsatisfied that she could not reason things out or contented that she organized other thoughts she'd not previously had the time to.

Chapter 13

Morning sun arrived and placed warmth upon Janet's flesh. It was going to be a sunny, hot, and humid day. It was to be the kind of weather Janet didn't like much unless she was enjoying activities in the lake water to cool her down. At this stage of her life, she avoided going into the murky waters.

Steven had not been there all night nor had he phoned. Armani had not returned her call either. Picking up her phone, the time on the screen stated *7:01*. She felt that was late enough in the morning to call the guys again to see what they had to say for themselves. Janet was not their keeper but felt they could have extended common courtesy by returning her calls. Either of them were people she would have not minded had they called her anytime day or night.

Instead of experiencing any relief from concerns where these two men were concerned, she felt only more bewildered they had not bothered to return her calls. Now she was even more bewildered that they still were not answering. On the other hand, their business was really not her business. It would only be her business if she made it her business. From this moment on, she was not going to stress herself out

146

over them. She'd made up her mind, and that was never an easy task for her. But when Janet made up her mind, that was it. Her mind was made firmly up. "Screw them!"

Frustrated, Janet made another call. She phoned her mom and dad. Peggy answered, and Janet told her Steven had been by. He had come and went without telling her he was leaving, which was not untypical of him. Janet and Peggy knew Steven all too well in that way as he had a habit of doing that. As always in the past, Janet did not know if he was ever coming back. She never knew when she'd next speak to him. Certainly, he would have told her he was leaving for good this time. He'd have told her had he been leaving town. Maybe he was in the hospital with his illnesses, or something worse had happened to him? "Unfortunately," Janet concluded with her mother, "Steven has not answered my calls I made to him. It makes me worry, and I'm not going to worry over him." Janet elaborated to her mother that she did not know what Steven's plans were in the least. While Janet suspected there may be trouble with the Kinski case, she did not want to alarm Peggy by being the one to speak of it. Janet believed that was Steven's business to discuss with their mom and dad soon, or else she would at a later time should it become necessary for her to be the one to do so.

By the time Janet got freshened up to start the day productively, it was after 8:00 a.m., and she was able to make a couple of business calls. Afterward, she made some toast for breakfast. Opening the refrigerator to take out butter, Janet poked at the two defrosting packages of deer meat she had taken out of the downstairs freezer. The packages felt soft to the touch, and that pleased her. What Janet noticed about the last fresh venison she had partially defrosted in the microwave was that the microwave may have altered the flavor and texture somewhat. Nobody else seemed to have minded, but she could tell.

Janet then decided to take a trip into town. In fact, one of the professional calls she had made was to the psychiatrist who had once prescribed her anxiety medication long ago. Janet was concerned she may want more to help her ease into her new lifestyle, and Doctor Artemis Paul was one who could help her do it.

After doing some shopping, Janet felt somewhat better already and believed that shopping could be great therapy for her. It had taken her mind off the house and people for a while. She loved the small shops that lined Main Street and enjoyed speaking with the proprietors and clerks who worked in them. It was a delight to see them.

Now that she lived there full time and was able to entertain, she was sure friendships would grow with them. She wasn't quite sure if she wanted to start entertaining yet with the house in need of so much work. Was it better for people to see the now and after or wait until she was settled in and the place was a sure showplace? She'd think about later.

Some people she knew there were envious of her because they knew she had a boat on the water. That was a very impressive status-symbol toy in Antioch. A nice party boat on the water equaled popularity. Janet wanted to be popular in her new life. She was well-liked but always had presented herself as being a bit of a wallflower. She wanted a change in popularity.

Now most acquaintances Janet once had from Prospect Heights had moved away since they all went separate ways in life. Education, relationships, careers, and family had distanced them from her during their metamorphous into adulthood. She rarely spoke to any of those people except for a couple close friends who still resided in Prospect Heights and had not moved on in life. She would need to make new friends locally if she wanted to be social. Knowing that the house remodel and making friends would all take time, Janet was eager to be completely settled in and could only imagine how grand her life would be.

She even stopped by the local pet shop and contemplated buying a pet to be her new friend. They didn't have anything that appealed to her at this time. She really wanted a puppy and a kitten who could grow up together and keep each other company when she could not be with them. She'd be especially fond of any pet that would grow up to love boating and being on the water as much as she did.

Her meeting with Doctor Paul went very well. Janet explained the stress she was under, and Doctor Paul wrote her a prescription without hesitation. "It was normal to be experiencing stress after a major move in a person's life. Moving is one of the leading stress factors among people," the doctor explained. He said little else. Janet did most of the talking and wasn't even sure of what all she had said when her time was up. That made Janet realize that maybe she had been doing things at home and not even realizing it. Her mind was stressed and so preoccupied, and it would be that way for quite a while to come if she allowed it to be. The pills would hopefully help.

After Janet left Doctor Paul's, she drove downtown and stopped into the Antioch Police Station to see Dean. He was there and was surprised she had stopped in. Janet invited him to dinner tonight and hoped that maybe he'd shed some light on her brother's situation and Armani. Considering she did not know where the guys were, perhaps Dean even had another way to connect with them for her? She hoped and was glad that Dean accepted on the spot.

Having completed her errands downtown, Janet returned home with a slice of pizza she had brought home with her. She sat down and unpacked everything she shopped for as she briefly thought again about Armani and Steven and how rude it was they had not returned her calls. But she also believed that just showed how irresponsible and juvenile they both were. It seemed to her that all the single men she had known were very independent and thoughtless. That was probably why she didn't have a husband or steady beau yet. They all seemed to lack attentiveness and be too immature when it came to being responsible and reliable. Knowing Janet was so young and was inexperienced with relationships showed her own lack of ability to understand that all men were not like this.

Janet wondered if Sheriff Dean was immature. He had such responsibility and was holding such a regal position within the community. *The things a sheriff must deal with every day certainly would require some integrity to deal with it*, she thought. Dean was one man who must certainly have a lot on his plate. Does that make him responsible, or was he so tied up in his own life he had no time to think of others on personal levels? Another one of Janet's immature ideas. If Janet thought of Dean, could she think of him in a romantic way?

What about Armani? Does not calling her within so many hours after requesting a call warrant scrutinizing, and did she owe him a monogamous relationship? She had never dated multiple guys at once, and the relationship she allowed to be created with Armani was very different from any she had before. Different because she had known him for so many years. Different because he took her virginity and made her think of his cock often. Could another man make her tingle the way Armani did? It was not as though she had just met him and knew nothing about him. She had, after all, fantasized about him since she was a little girl and had longed for his attention. All of this must mean something special. For the time being, everything is okay, she figured.

Dean was just going to be a friend, and she needed to learn over time how Armani treated women and not focus on what other people thought of him.

Maybe Armani's poor treatment of women was why Marissa had left as Steven had said. How would Steven know what Marissa was thinking and feeling? Had Steven ever even met Marissa? Janet would find the answers to questions she sought someday on her own.

Janet went about her day and began to cook a feast for Dean. She even planned to cook enough for Steven, hoping he'd turn up and join them. With any luck, they could all sit down to a civilized evening, and she could help clear any suspicions Dean was having about her brother.

Wouldn't that be fantastic if she could be a part of bringing peace to those she knows? That led her to reach for the larger of the two packages of raw meat she had been defrosting. If not Steven, who would help them eat all the food? She could always bring a plate over to Gertty; Gertty would be appreciative.

To Janet's surprise, the top of the refrigerator shelf containing the meat packages was coated with a thin membrane of blood even though the meat shouldn't have yet been fully defrosted. The refrigerator still felt very cold to the touch inside, so it couldn't be too warm in there. "Strangest thing," Janet said aloud. As the venison package defrosted more in the sink, Janet gave the refrigerator shelf a good disinfecting.

Blood never disgusted Janet much. She had, since youth, worked side by side with Peggy preparing fish and game her brother and father brought home to the kitchen. However, this blood seemed different. It was thicker and a richer red color despite taking into consideration the recent age of the meat. Wild game always had many differences from that of grocery-store meats. It wasn't at all like the hemoglobin red-juice injected stuff that stores sold and kept the meat from losing its color. This meat had real blood. Yes, fresh game meat was certainly different, and it had been a few years since seeing or tasting it. Even the meat sold in the suburbs seemed to be very different from the meat sold in the countryside stores.

Yet this particular package seemed very different from anything else she'd ever known. With this package, everything looked, smelled, and leaked from the paper package differently. It was primal and very appealing to her senses. A hint of aroma from the defrosting flesh delighted her in a savage way. In a matter of time, Janet had marinated the meat in seasoning for later cooking and had cleaned the kitchen thoroughly. Bacteria and germs were always of concern, and a clean kitchen was the cornerstone of good cooking, Peggy had instilled in her.

When Dean arrived, Janet was elated with how much different he looked out of uniform. Not necessarily better, but not so rough, tough, and industrious-looking. He could have almost passed for a mature professional model. He was clean-shaven and had on a designer tie over his dress shirt. It put her garb to shame. She had on her usual short shorts and an out-of-date 1980s-style tube top covered over by a short-sleeve blouse. Definitely another trait showing

Janet had some maturing to do when it came to dating more mature men and relationships. The clothes she had probably had been stored in a dresser drawer here at the house since many years ago. They surely were not in style today, and she had not even bothered to apply any fresh makeup, which was never a major concern of hers while at the lake house. However, Dean noticed.

This house had always been a place where she could let her hair down and be a bit of a tomboy. Not that Janet considered herself in any way to be a tomboy. She was just adventurous and a good sportsman. Men always seemed to like that about her. She could be the woman they could lust after and the friend they could hang out with and do rougher guy stuff. She knew the ropes of being a woman and also the ropes of being one of the guys. Normally, guys around town would not consider a girl from out of town for more than a one-night stand. Janet was not a one-night stand sort of woman. With all being considered, Janet was now around all the time, and Dean was not one to let an opportunity pass. He would do what he could to impress her.

Janet led Dean to the bar in the living room and requested he pour drinks while she went to freshen up. In only a few minutes, Janet returned looking stunning. It did not take much to turn her from a plain Jane to an absolute knockout. She'd never seen herself as being one, and it was not her intent to arouse Dean. He was to be just a friend. However, Janet noticed how she kept reminding herself of that

154

and wondered why she felt the need to do so. In such a small town, it really didn't take much to drive a single man wild.

Dean stood from his seated position on the couch out of gentlemanly respect as she entered the room. "Wow, you look terrific! I'm sure you know that already!"

"That's a nice compliment from a friend," Janet said, with emphasis on the *friend* part. "You look special tonight, and I didn't expect that. A tie? It is just a friendly dinner between two friends. Just sit back down. Make yourself comfortable. I'm sorry if it smells a bit like booze in here. Gertty introduced gin to the carpet, and I'll be ripping it up soon."

"In the back of my car with my uniform is also swim trunks if you are interested in a midnight swim later?" Dean provided alternative options to his evening attire.

"It's mostly all fine," Janet responded. "I don't swim at night though and not ever with a swimsuit on," Janet tried to modestly jest. "Seriously, I've become kind of weird about actually getting into the lake water, Dean. You know... all the strange stuff that has happened in there. Entering the water is like entering another world. I've seen some huge marine life in the water over the last few years. I swear those catfish will start swallowing people whole someday. Not just that. I cut my leg on a broken bottle under seaweed and sediment a few years ago, and I worry about what is down there. It's probably now littered with hypodermic needles from those crazed druggies who hang out around the lake. I surprise myself that I even eat the fish from there these days. Fish need to come from someplace though, I assume." Janet seemed to be overdramatizing things a bit, but Dean seemed to be fine with her chattiness.

"Maybe a casual boat ride would be more appropriate? If you think you'd be more comfortable in your swim trunks, go ahead and put them on. Style has always been casual around here. I think you may very well be the first man who ever sported a tie in this house. This is a swimsuit environment. I liked that you dressed up, Dean, and took the effort to do that."

Dean was so taken with how breathtaking Janet looked in the dimming sunlight filtering into the room through luminescent blinds that his mind was elsewhere. Janet considered snapping her fingers to snap him out of it but decided she would test him with a question to see if he was paying attention. "Dean? So what are you drinking?" Janet inquired.

"Soda. Diet soda," Dean said and smiled.

"Yet I have a cocktail in my hand. Are you trying to get me drunk?" Janet shook her head disapprovingly as she posed her question.

"I-I-I don't drink much since I'm always on duty and need to keep my wits about me at all times. I figured you wanted a cocktail since you led me to the bar when I got here. The vodka was in the forefront. I assumed you drink vodka since it was out and the most accessible."

Dean noticed how silky her hair looked, and he longed to run his fingers through it. Strands danced like a silken spiderweb in a breeze as her head turned. It looked so soft and flowing. Dean mustered up the words to answer her and stumbled over them.

"Always on duty?" she said, repeating his words. "I know you said that to me once before. I hope you don't just run out of here on me tonight." Janet understood what he meant though. Emergencies come up. "I understand police emergencies occur," she assured him. "As for the other subject… I just stocked the bar the other day, and it seems Gertty swam home in the bottles of gin I had here, and Steven apparently has taken all my bourbon. One of them left the vodka there.

"I do hope you have a nice, little glass of wine with me later. It's sort of a requirement to pair with the meat at dinner. It brings out the flavors and seasonings. In general, I prefer wine if I have a choice. My body is not used to hard liquor too often. I'm barely old enough to drink, you know! I'm only twenty-one, and I have not been into going to bars. My mother, father, and I certainly did not drink together at home. This social drinking is all new to me. I'm not sure how I feel about it. Watching Gertty drink is enough to turn anyone off to it." Janet smiled.

Gertty's lust for alcohol was a secret to no one. Dean agreed to indulge just a bit tonight with dinner.

Dean wasn't always so on guard. But things were off kilter lately around town, and business preoccupied his time because he let it. The police department wasn't the only place riding his ass about safety within the community. The mayor and city council were lecturing him regularly, and he feared for his job. Even tonight, as far as his coworkers were concerned, he was visiting with Janet as part of his job to learn about Steven and had requested he not be disturbed unless there was a serious emergency.

"On the subject of Steven," Janet had mentioned him a moment earlier, "is he really in a lot of trouble? I've known my brother my entire life, and I'm certain he is not capable of murder. He may have his faults, but being a murderer is definitely not one of them."

Dean then stated, "Nobody thinks their brother is a serial killer. Then again, you do know Steven better than I do, and it's my job to be suspicious of people. I don't judge, but it is simply my responsibility to observe and report data. I'm not a judge and jury. I'm just a messenger of sorts. There are staff trying to solve cases who need my help—detectives, other individuals—and I'm just as much here to help your brother. If you want to help Steven, he and I both need your help."

Dean hoped to be the silent one and let Janet do the talking this evening but knew he'd need to relax her if she was to trust in him, so Dean had ulterior motives still. Janet needed to feel comfortable with openly speaking to Dean. Maybe she'd say something that would be of benefit. "I need information on your brother. For example, you did say Steven drinks? We know that from the reports the Come On Inn bar gave us. Has he ever had a substance abuse problem that you know of?"

"Yes. He has been in rehab off and on during his life," Janet replied. "I've witnessed him drinking while he has been here, and that's not a good thing for him to be doing. Just a cocktail or two though," Janet said, confirming that she knew of.

"Generally speaking, my parents never included me in on his family problems when I was growing up. I was the baby, and they overly protected me from conversations they were having over anyone's bad behavior. My mom, Peggy, was very concerned about what other people thought of the family. She did not share any scandalous information with anyone. She's a very righteous woman. The fact that Steven was and is still gay is something my parents never exactly approved of either. They love him, but not his lifestyle choices. I knew Steven was drinking at times, but I never judged him for doing so. We were close, and I would have known if he was overly using to the point of abuse. It was apparent to me that he simply partied with friends when he could. Being that he felt like an outcast, I'm sure it made him feel like one of the guys. Don't tell me you never tried alcohol when you were underage? When my parents found out, that started a cycle of rehab centers for Steven. Since Steven moved to CA, I really couldn't say what he does.

"The family assumed that he keeps to himself because his lifestyle doesn't fit in with the rest of the family. It seemed he had found a place in this world where he felt comfortable and could be himself. There definitely was not much gay lifestyle around Prospect Heights or Antioch for him to grow up around and relate to. I couldn't very well blame him for indulging himself in some recreational partying to pass time. My parents did. I think part of sending him to rehab was with their hopes they'd somehow change him in a way they'd be more approving of. It appeared he stopped using completely after having been to a quality rehab center upon his arrival in California. That's what I had been told.

"Now he said that he has an occasional drink to kill the pain from a medical issue he has. He is going to do as he does. Tell me, why would a gay man be interested in a woman like Kim Kinski? I have gay friends, and I'm not blaming her if she had any. I simply am not aware Steven knew Kim. I only learned of her myself from reading the newspaper when I moved in. Had she always lived around here?" Janet was considering the amount of time Steven may have known Kim.

"No," replied Dean. "She wasn't from here. A bartender reported that Steven had been talking to her as though he had been meeting her for the first time. We have no idea what transpired after that the night of her disappearance.

"Of course, gay people can be disturbed just like anyone else. In fact, quite often, they can have a dislike for the opposite sex. It can be such a dislike that they may act out. Maybe Kim challenged his manhood in some way that made him snap? Steven hunts, so maybe it was all about the hunt? Don't get me wrong. I don't want to think your brother had any part in her disappearance. I just need to know if he did do it. The fact you said to me that he took off from your home and you haven't heard from him is even more concerning to me. I've already got every officer in the states of Illinois and Wisconsin secretly on the lookout for him. I've been wanting to speak to him again. He was the last person who reportedly had seen Kim alive that we know of. If he isn't the danger, he could be in danger himself. It's best you not worry until I know more. I should say, until we know anything at all.

"I really don't know anything, Janet. Steven came to town after a period of absence, and now he has disappeared into thin air as far as we are concerned at the moment. He was warned not to leave town without notifying authorities. He returned his rental vehicle, and I don't know how he is commuting now. If the powers that be hear he left when he was told not to… I know he'll have even more trouble on his hands if he did. You never had much contact with him in recent years, you said, and it's not likely to think he's going to come running to you for help now. He might even be scared. I just hope he didn't come here as if to say a goodbye before he does something drastic. If there is a problem, the more I am here, the less likely he is to come around. Don't worry. It's my priority to get to the bottom this. I don't want to see you worry your pretty face, my friend. You'll wrinkle it!" He laughed aloud to ease Janet.

"Did Steven tell you why he left California to come back to Illinois?" Dean wondered.

Janet didn't know what to say. Wanting to say something, she racked her brain. "Steven really isn't my business. He's always been kind of private and to himself. He called on family only when he wanted, and we have not seen him in recent years. But he really never returned our calls. If he did, it would take weeks to hear back from him. In fact, I tried calling him last night and today and can't get him to call me back. I'd worry, but he's always been like that. If I can help, I will. All I can tell you is that he told me he was here on personal business and could not or would not share with me what that business is.

"Let's change the subject for awhile, shall we? For this evening, maybe we should take a boat ride in the setting sun before it gets too late? Dinner will hold just fine."

Dean was enthusiastic about the plan. He loved boating but did not own a nice boat. His only boat was a small fishing boat with oars and a tiny sputtering outboard motor, and it had not even been in the water this summer. Other people with nicer boats never invited him out on the water much. It was only the more upper class around Antioch who could afford waterfront homes and boats than the working class, which Dean was. His public-servant salary couldn't afford a great lifestyle but was comfortable for a single guy.

Dean went to his car to grab a more suitable change of clothes for boating, and the two ventured off when they were ready. Boating did them both a world of good. Janet forgot her troubles and simply enjoyed herself to the fullest. The world around the lake appeared so different from actually being on the lake. For the center of the water, Dean could spin in a circle and see all of the lake's distant perimeter except for what a tiny sandbar of a rocky island covered in trees blocked in view.

"It has been so long since I have been out on this lake, Janet. I forgot about the sandbar island. Can we go over that way so I can take a look?" Dean thought the trees there might be concealing something he'd be interested in.

"I won't go too close. A motorboat is not the way to get there, given there is too much seaweed and any sharp rocks, too, that could damage the boat. It's not a place for a novice boater to venture. I've only been there fishing a couple times when guys rowed us out there in a rowboat. My dad had taken me once. Fishing was good there because the fish love to hide in the reeds and rocks. See all the cattails and water plants? Fish love it there. The whole island, if you can call it one, seems to rise above and sink below the water surface depending upon how much rainfall we get in a given season. Really, nothing worth seeing over there. There are a few other sections of reeds and cattails around the perimeter of Lake Marie, which are likely to be more scenic." Janet was aware Dean was scoping it out but hoped to turn his interest away from it.

No matter if it was professional business he had on his mind or if it was just part of his personal curious nature. Janet hoped he'd be a bit more interested in their friendship tonight instead of business. The evening mood and atmosphere on the water was so nice. The rains had left everything clean and clear. Besides, less disturbed areas, such as that island, were teeming with insects this time of year, and it was best to stay clear of them. "Let's keep the boat moving and head back before the mosquitoes start biting," Janet suggested. "I don't want us to be sitting ducks for West Nile virus."

Dean joked and said, "I don't blame the insects. I'd bite ya!" Then he made a chomping motion with his jaw.

Janet wasn't sure how to deal with Dean at this point. He seemed to be so complicated. On one hand, staying just friends, but then he flirts and looks so nice. It was going to be a difficult task. Keeping him interested enough in her to be friends without overstepping a friendship boundary would be difficult for her too. Taking his mind off work enough to have fun without giving the wrong impression would be even more difficult as well.

If Steven needed help, why were they flitting around without care? Janet wasn't trying to be fickle. But how could she keep their friendship relationship balanced while helping her brother? Then again, her brother's business wasn't her business. It was so confusing, and Dean was now looking very sexy to her. He had so much hair on his legs, arms, and chest.

Janet had never run her fingers over a furry man before. She wanted to. If she asked if she could, would that be overstepping the boundaries of a friendship? Armani didn't have the body hair that Dean had, and it was a difference Janet had noticed.

The boat docked back at the pier at the home where Janet resided. Dean leaped off and tied it up. Then he reached over and extended his hand to Janet to assist her out of the boat. Nobody had ever done that before for her in her adult life, and it impressed her. Now she was seeing another side of Dean, which showed how the man in him differed from the other guys who behaved more like boys lacking social etiquette, including Armani. Dean had a class, maturity, and individual charm about him. His job position made her feel secure. That made her think of her father and how her own father made her feel secure when she was a little girl. Now she was not a little girl, and being around Dean was a newer adult experience for her. He was keen in his wit, smart, and charming. She'd never known a guy anything like that except for her own father when she was young. As Janet aged, she even stopped thinking of her father as being like that, and he changed, growing old. She had learned from her father and had come to display her own wit, smarts, and charm, which she portrayed in her own personality. Here was a man she was coming to know who was using her own game of wit, smarts, and charm on her. Something else she would need to keep in balance around Dean. She did not think he would appreciate the little-girl persona that she sometimes still kept hidden inside her. Spending time with Dean showed Janet that she could be a woman. While Armani protected her, she was already noticing a difference in Dean compared to Armani, even though she had sex with Armani, that the relationships she has with both guys had differences—both appealing to Janet but in different ways.

Moving to this lake was what she wanted in a growth change, and she knew Dean would be the teacher who would be helping her make those changes. No more boys in her life. It's time for her to be and act like an adult while carrying herself as a woman and expect a real man to accept her as a woman. Time for her to become a lady. Lord knew this country town could use some class, style, and refinement these days. That was what Janet wanted to change into. *Refinement* was the word.

Once in the house, Dean went to the bedroom where his belongings had been left when he changed. Janet went immediately to check on dinner. Dinner was fully cooked and ready to be plated.

"Janet! Janet!" Dean yelled loudly from the back of the house in a panic.

"What is it, Dean?" Janet called back to him.

"Janet, my clothes are gone. They were here on the bed. Worse, I know I had left my keys in the pants pocket. I didn't want to bother you to come back for them after we were on the boat, and I realized I had not brought them with me. I assumed they'd be safe here in the house. The house was all locked up, wasn't it?"

"The house was completely locked up, Dean. I swear it. I'll double-check all the locks and latches if you want to be sure, but I am positive of it."

"Who would do this? Do you think Steven could have come back and taken my things?" Dean was in a panic. "My car! I've got to go see about my car." Janet and Dean ran out the door and to the roadside of the garage. There sat Dean's car with the trunk open. His keys remained in the trunk lock, and the vehicle had been searched through. "Gone! My work uniform from the trunk is gone! This is terrible! You have no idea how bad this is going to be when I tell the station I have lost one of my uniforms. Even much worse when I tell them it was intentionally stolen." Dean was stressed but was composed. Janet's heart went out to him.

"It had to be Steven or Armani. They are the only two with keys to my house. I can't imagine Armani would just enter. Then again, I can't imagine Steven would come in and take your things either. I've known these men all my life, and they are just not like that, I tell you."

"I've got to go over and see Armani and then call my station." Dean was not pleased at the thought of doing either of those things. "I'm hoping this is just a prank, but I would not put this past any of these guys."

Janet followed Dean to Armani's house, and nobody answered. "Seems he is often not home," Janet said and looked at Dean as if it was meant to mean something of importance. "Let's go see Gertty, Dean. Maybe she saw someone out her window."

"Unlikely because none of her main windows face this direction, and she'd be too far away. But one never knows."

Gertty answered the door but knew nothing. "I haven't seen anyone or anything. I haven't been looking. I'll start watching if you'd like? Were your doors and windows latched?"

"Yes." Janet knew what Gertty would say if they had not been. "I know better. They were locked, and someone came in and took his things. The keys were in his pants on a bed where he changed to take a boat ride. Someone then used the keys to get into his locked vehicle and took his sheriff's uniform from out of the trunk. It just had to be Armani or Steven. They are the only two people I gave keys to."

Dean walked ahead while Janet remained behind to speak to Gertty for an extra few moments. Calling his station, Dean got his best work buddy, John. Janet concluded her conversation with Gertty and attempted to reach Steven and Armani with her phone. She had no luck getting either of them to pick up.

"That was my station I was on the phone with. My partner, Sylvester, was available to speak to me. I explained what happened. He'll try to soften the blow with our superior by telling them my car was broken into. I would not even have mentioned it to anyone if I did not think this was important. I don't know who has the uniform, and I'm too honest to keep this a secret and act ignorant if it ever showed up without me having said anything. Sylvester is going to bring me out a spare uniform from my locker. I keep spare sets of important things in my locker for safekeeping and emergencies. No place I know is safer. It will take Sylvester a while to get here. He's got things to do first. I just thought it would be best if he turned in a theft report instead of me. Perhaps he'll see something I've overlooked." Dean was still upset but a bit more relieved, yet composed but perplexed.

"I'm sorry this happened, Dean," Janet said in an attempt to console. "I guess I should tell you that I have been having a feeling I am not alone in the house. Things have been moving about. Strange occurrences similar to this have happened. None as severely disturbing and important as this, but they seem to be getting worse as time goes on.

"A light bulb had been unscrewed, and when I asked Steven about it, he denied having done it. I had asked Steven to take a spare key into town, and it was not where I had told him to get it from. A plant had been moved from my kitchen into the bedroom your pants were in. Steven claimed he had not moved it. Steven played pranks on me when we were kids, and I just assumed it had been him. I also thought it could just be me losing my mind if it hadn't been him. I've been so busy around here and thought maybe my memory was playing tricks on me. Maybe I never put the key under the planter, and maybe I carried the planter off to the bedroom and set it down but didn't recall. Anything is possible.

"Whatever the case, there is still a key missing, and I have not been able to figure out where it is. I can't help but wonder if someone has it and has been coming around when I am unaware or not home. If that is the case, how they got into my home with new locks to get a key is a mystery. If they could get into my house without a key to have found my hiding place under the plant and taken a key, why would they need that key in the first place? Why move the planter? It's all been a mystery I haven't been able to solve. Now that this has happened, I am glad to at least know it isn't me going insane.

"It's my own fault for forgetting my keys, Janet. I should have come back for them. How irresponsible of me. I'm not the irresponsible type, and this matter disturbs me greatly." Dean didn't want Janet to think she was to blame. "I'm just concerned that someone is out there putting my uniform to a bad use. Otherwise, why would they have taken it? Now that you have told me about your missing key, I'm even more concerned. These are the types of situations I've been wanting you to speak to me about. What may seem insignificant to you is possibly not insignificant at all. Trespassing and theft are crimes."

"I'm guessing you will want to leave when Sylvester arrives? I'm sorry if this ruined our evening. Should I put dinner away?" Janet didn't know what else to say. "I can't think of anything else to tell you. If there was ever anything to tell you, that is all of it."

"We have a little time before Sylvester gets here. I don't know how I feel. There is so much I should be doing even though I'd rather be here with you. I hate to waste your good cooking." Dean brought up a disturbing thought. "If we ate, do you think your food could have been tampered with? Nobody would be trying to hurt you for any reason, would they?" Dean was considering extreme circumstances from all angles.

"No! Dean, Steven and Armani have looked out for me my whole life." Janet went into a long winded explanation. "If not them playing pranks on me, what reason would anyone ever have to harm me? That's absurd. I'm pretty helpless here, and there would be many ways for a person to do me in if they wanted. Plenty of opportunity too." Janet was trying not to be offended, and Dean knew it. "It's not that I am keeping anything from you, Dean. So much is all new to me since I moved up here, and I'm not a very worldly person.

"So much never makes sense, and I let it roll right off me," Janet stated. "I ask people questions like some of the ones I asked you, and nobody wants to be direct with me. I don't understand anything anyone is doing. It normally would not bother me because I'm just not the analytical sort of person to dwell on this kind of stuff, I guess. I think it's strange, and I brush it off because I would go insane if I tried to analyze every person I know the way you do. The things people do and the things in life that I can't explain are numerous. I can't explain Steven, I can't explain Armani, and I can't explain Kim Kinski. I can't explain what goes on around this house. As much as I want to know you,

I'm still learning about you. I'm still learning about all this stuff."

Janet continued her chattiness and unbecoming childlike immaturity that clearly was coming through and, in the same breath, stated, "You helping me to discover all the answers is going to apparently be a huge part of our relationship, and I appreciate your help. I don't blame you for suspecting Steven and Armani of things, but you also need to support me when I don't suspect them of bad deeds. Nobody is out to kill me, and my cooking doesn't poison people. Don't try to make me paranoid! There must be a simple explanation, and I'm sure it is meant to be a prank. If robbery was the motive, the burglar could have taken any number of my things. And we've now checked the house, which was all secure, just like I told you."

"However, something was taken, my uniform. And them breaking into the house and stealing my uniform and breaking into a government car is a felony at this point. And your missing key?" Dean reminded her.

"I put it someplace I don't remember. It's not uncommon for me to do stupid things and not recall every detail. I've had a lot on my mind lately. I'm sure it's not anything to worry about." Janet started calming down.

"I'm so sorry, Janet. I'm just thinking, and I don't know what to think. These are uncommon and bizarre circumstances. I do worry about you. I worry more about people who would try to hurt me." Dean looked slightly concerned. "Doing my job doesn't always set well with everyone. Not everyone is a friend. While I need to be aware of my surroundings at all times, I can only assume that what has been happening around this house has more to do with you. Let's try to relax and not let your dinner go to waste tonight. What do you say? We have a little time before Sylvester gets here, so why don't you serve dinner up?" Dean was feeling guilty for having offended Janet and leading her to paranoia. He knew she was innocent of anything. That did not mean she was not going to be caught up in terrible situations beyond her control if she was not careful. Dean did not want her getting hurt in the least.

They dined quickly. Conversation was mute for the most part, just as it had been with Gertty when she had dined there, and mouths were full. Janet knew Dean's mind was on business, and she did not know how to get it off that subject at this point. Since she did not like to talk with her mouth full of food, it wasn't fazing her that conversation was somewhat hushed. Some small talk seemed forced when they did attempt to exchange words. The exception was conversation regarding the food. Dean was very pleased with his meal. It was better than he'd ever had at the finest of restaurants he'd ever been to, at least what he could compare it to.

Janet agreed but could not help but think the meat tasted like pork and very different from the last time she'd prepared it. The gamey taste was lacking, and the meat was lighter in color. Maybe it was because she had not defrosted it in the microwave this time and had left it longer to set while they dealt with the uniform situation. Perhaps more of the blood had drained out.

Just as they finished their last bite, Sylvester knocked at the door. It was not the end to the evening Dean had planned with Sylvester standing there. This had not even been the evening Dean had hoped for. Janet understood the circumstances, and she apologized as best she could. To make peace with Dean, she said, "Let's try dinner together soon without any of the drama. Shall we?"

"Sure thing, Janet. I am going to place Sylvester in an unmarked police surveillance car in the area tonight. Not that it will do any good. Armani is expected to be in the area since he lives here. Steven or anyone else apparently has already come and gone. I can't place the car too close to your house where anyone would notice and become suspicious. Not much traffic around these parts for a car to blend in with obviously." Dean made sense.

As soon as Dean departed, Janet wondered if the missing household key was something to be worried about. She could always change the lock on the door that key fit. All the locks had different keys, and that one having been potentially compromised had been the only one in question. Even if she wanted to, it was too late tonight to go to the local hardware store.

Janet did all she could around the house and went to bed early. Unable to sleep, Janet got out of bed at random times. She walked around the house and looked out the windows. She checked all the windows and doors. They were locked securely, but she could not help checking them over and over to be sure.

Shortly after midnight, she noticed lights on at Armani's house. Janet felt the urge to run over instantly and acted upon that impulse.

Armani opened his door for her. "It's very late. What are you doing here at this hour?" Armani didn't mind that Janet came by, but he wasn't in any mood to entertain for any length of time as he'd had a long day.

"Maybe I was taking a walk and saw your lights on? Maybe all hell broke loose tonight and you haven't returned my calls? You decide. Which answer works best for you?" Janet waited for him to respond.

"If you have been calling, I'm sorry. My phone disappeared, and I don't really pay much attention to it anyway. It's usually just neighbors calling me with work, and they wait for me to return calls. They know how busy I get at times, and I don't get many calls otherwise except for annoying telemarketers.

"I was away from the house and didn't have time to look high and low for my phone before I left. Sorry. I didn't know I was being kept tabs on. I know things have progressed between you and me, but I haven't married you yet. No lead weight on this wedding finger. Besides, I'm not the henpecked type. What the hell has gone on? I sure don't know what police are doing around here. I passed one in an unmarked car coming in. It's easy for me to pick them out since I know their cars after all the years of living here. I have been around longer than they and their cars have been."

Janet said it was to be a secret. "Maybe they don't disguise themselves well enough, do they?"

"No. They stick out like a hitchhiker's thumb. Can you explain their presence?" Armani was sure she could.

"Where did you see them?" Janet asked before answering. "I haven't noticed any cops out here, and no cars either." Janet was surprised Armani had spotted them.

"You are really concerning me here, Jan honey. What about the cops, and what's going on around here?" Again, Armani was sure Janet knew something.

"A lot has gone on around here today. The police know someone came into my house uninvited, and I was not aware. While Dean and I were out for a boat ride, they took his stuff while we were gone. I've only given my key to you and Steven and had to tell them as much. They knew you'd be here because you live here but wanted to post a car in case Steven came back. They want to talk to him about something, but Steven has left without telling me. I wanted to know if he ever talked with you." A feeling of unease came over her. Janet felt a need to say, "They're probably watching us now. I've not noticed them."

"I don't like justifying myself to people," Armani said with a firmness in his tone. "I can justify where I have been should the police ask. I was nowhere near your home. I'm uncomfortable with you and your male consort thinking I might have been. Maybe I better give you your key back and we'd best talk about us another time. It's late. You can bet that I'll call Sheriff Dean and settle this matter. I have not talked with your brother, and I've not been home." Armani made Janet feel horrible.

"I didn't say you were in my house, Armani," Janet clarified. "They wanted to know who had keys, and I told them. I've been worried I haven't been able to reach you nor Steven while stuff like this is going on. I've missed you. Do you think you haven't fondly been on my mind?"

"I'm sure Dean has been occupying your mind just fine. Well, I'll talk to him and you another time when it's not so late. I still have to find my phone if I can, and I'd like to get some sleep. I have a job to do in the morning." Armani closed the door in a manner indicating he was not happy with her.

Janet felt even more horrible now. More than anything, she wanted someone to talk to. Maybe she should go see her psychiatrist in the morning if he has an appointment opening? Maybe Gertty would have some advice in the morning? Janet knew this was to be a long and sleepless night ahead. She had meant to be crude to Armani for not returning her call but now felt terrible for having done so. His words outmatched her words in a debated discussion, and he had a right to be upset. It had never been her intention to be leaving his house on such a bad note. She felt only guilt.

Tossing and turning the rest of the night, Janet utilized the hours resting in bed without one wink of sleep. Every animal that crept and every leaf that rustled had Janet jumping up to look around. She didn't even know what she was looking for. Perhaps she was just hoping Steven would return or the patrol vehicle would pull up with news? Maybe Dean might even come by? If anything, that would make her feel most comfortable. She'd not have even minded if Dean were here now watching over her as she slept. That was a peculiar thought. Why would she be thinking of Dean being there and not Armani? She deduced it was because Dean provided her with a feeling of comfort where Armani didn't.

At four in the morning, Janet's phone rang. It was Dean. "Are you okay there, Janet?"

"Yes, Dean. Sleepless and a bit wound up, but just fine." Janet was comforted to hear Dean's voice. "I'm glad you are calling, but why a call at such an hour?"

"There is a problem, Janet. Sylvester had been found dead outside the car. We don't know what happened to him. There is no sign that his death wasn't natural, but it's peculiar. He was apparently relieving himself in a bush and dropped where he stood. I know this man, and he was a good family man. I want answers. Unfortunately, I am not the one assigned to his investigation. Detectives are on that. It's over my head. It could take time for them to get any answers. Detectives are still looking at Irwin's death as well. I'll know something when they are ready to tell me.

Unfortunately, at the moment, I have nobody else to put in your area. We are a small department, and budget cuts have this crew cut to the bone. Too many mundane misdemeanors and too much paperwork keeping us all busy at the station. Without a verifiable reason, I can't place another car there, Janet. I desperately need some sleep myself. I've been up too long." Dean sounded groggy.

"Come on over," Janet offered. "Sleep here. I'm jumpy, and I'd feel so much better if you were around." Janet was both hopeful and shocked her lips would extend such an invite.

Dean admitted that under normal circumstances, any time Janet wanted him to spend the night, he'd be mighty pleased to do so. A time like that was intended to be reserved for a sexual interlude. Not now. He was concerned it would keep Steven away if he was there. It would also keep anyone else away. He also knew he could not rest with Janet being so close. It was evident that deep inside him was a kindling fire burning, and he was yearning to seduce her. While confident that time would come, he'd need to wait until situations were more under control. Dean declined. "I need to go home and get a wonderful rest in my own bed to be at my best. You keep your phone near and call me if you need anything." Dean was reassuring, and Janet needed to be comforted by him with that sentiment alone.

Janet never went back to bed. Instead, she began picking at and peeling off the old country wallpaper border in her kitchen. She had hated it ever since

Peggy had hung it up and now was glad it was coming down permanently. Labor didn't keep her mind occupied so much but did wonders for her physical anxiety. It kept her from pacing the floors and double-checking locks.

Watching the time, she was wondering what time would be appropriate to call Dean back or visit Gertty. At seven, Janet decided she'd visit Gertty. It was known from past conversations that Gertty was usually, as per her own quote, "up with the chickens." Gertty was indeed awake and happy to see her. "I wake up by six every morning," she told Janet. "If I don't know it's six, my bladder sure does. It's more reliable than any old clock." Gertty seemed like a ray of sunshine when it came to taking away Janet's darkest concerns and fears.

Over a glass of fresh squeezed orange juice and a cupcake, Janet unloaded her worries. "I'm so beside myself. I don't know what to do. There's Steven who seems to be in trouble over that missing Kinski girl. There's Armani too. We got really close as soon as I got here, and now I think I should not have. Armani and Steven had keys to my new locks, and Dean knows that. Armani became a suspect of Dean's missing uniform because he has a key. He was going to confront Dean and clear himself of that. Now Armani is mad at me for spending time with Dean in the first place and for having presented him as a suspect. Dean is so sweet, so different, so mature. All the guys look out for me, but Dean makes me feel secure. You know what I mean?"

Gertty finished swallowing her orange juice before she spoke with a sour look upon her face from the pulpy citric acid. "What I know is that I see your face light up when you speak of Dean. You're warming up to him. Armani has been independent for a long, long time. You watch yourself around him. I can't speak for Armani, but I doubt he wants you getting him hog-tied under your thumb the minute you came to town. A pretty girl like you has certain powers over men. You won't change that particular man, not a man like Armani. Your brother is another story. I don't know much about him. A missing uniform? What reason would Steven have to come to town and then take Dean's uniform from your house? Why would Armani go into your home and take it? Meanwhile, I slept with my handgun by my side last night. Don't like what's been going on much around here. At least I sleep well knowing I have protection near. While you want to find a man to protect you, I prefer a gun. I have more control over my gun than any woman will ever have over a man. Take it from me... Old Gertty here has wisdom and firsthand experience."

"I wish I knew what to do, Gertty. I wish I understood any of this as well as you seem to do. I hoped talking to you might help me sort things out in my mind. While it's nice to see you and talk, I don't think I'm any further ahead with my thoughts at the moment. I'm not a gun-type person. Dad and my brother fired them a lot for hunting. The noise just makes me so jumpy. They scare me to death. I'd not trust myself being around one.

"Say, I started to take down that wallpaper boarder in the kitchen to ease my nerves. I was thinking I might go to town and get some things for in there. I'm hoping that will take my mind off men for a while. Do you need anything while I'm in town?"

"No, darlin'. I'm just fine here, Janet. Maybe. On second thought, if you'd not mind, could you bring me back a couple bottles of cheap gin? From the grocer, but not the liquor store. Who can afford their prices?" Gertty didn't drive often with her physical conditions and was glad Janet offered. It would save on a delivery charge and tip.

"Sure, Gertty." Janet excused herself and showed herself out.

Never had there seemed to be such a beautiful day, Janet felt, and a trip to town was just what she felt she needed. Looking at bright colors of paint for her kitchen at the paint store in town would also brighten her day to a greater extent. As quickly as that, Janet's concerns were lessened, and her mood turned around. Lack of sleep had not put a damper in the bounce in her step. Not in the least.

Dean eventually called, and she was happy he cared enough to check up on her. His call brought extra joy to her life. Although her talking with Gertty and the beautiful day outside had already cleared her mind. Dean had nothing to report to her, and she no longer felt a need to be speaking with him. Not for comfort's sake anyway. A desire to speak with him, yes. It was appreciated to receive a social phone call without him being the first to bring up business. She knew she had to. It was unavoidable that she offer her sincerest condolences regarding Sylvester. Like Irwin, the life of a friend lost so unexpectedly in just a few days. Both in her own neighborhood and just doors away from each other.

Hours later, the sun was bright overhead, and Janet returned to Gertty's house with the gin. The smile was grand on Janet's face as she whistled a happy tune. Gertty saw her coming up the path and greeted her outside knowing Janet was bringing the liquor she longed for.

"Are you working on your own garden today, Gertty?" Janet inquired. "I thought Armani did all that work for you?"

Gertty quickly replied, "He mows the lawn and does my initial planting for the season. He doesn't do weeding and all the little stuff. I can't afford that. I do the other work myself when my hips are able. It gives me some exercise. That's why I need the gin to kill the pain and make my hips function. Couldn't live without it!"

Janet smiled, knowing Gertty was telling the truth. "Go easy on that stuff, Gertty. A little goes a long way with the cheap stuff. You could probably run an engine on that octane. Look in the bag. I splurged and got you the good stuff. My treat! If you want, stop by later for some leftovers from dinner last night. Dean had to leave early because of his missing uniform, and he didn't stick around for second helpings. There is plenty enough left over for us. Also, I kind of hoped Steven would have come back. I cooked extra for him in case he was hungry. He never showed up. There is plenty enough for both of us if you want me to warm it up. Otherwise, I'd be just fine with you taking it to go. Whichever you prefer is okay with me, but we can talk about it later.

"That reminds me… I even took out an extra package of uncooked venison. I'm just not going to eat all that meat myself. You can have it, and I can give you some apple pie to take home too. Fresh from the bakery that I just picked up in town. They were so fresh that they were still steaming from the oven when they boxed it for me. I just couldn't resist! Some people have a sweet tooth, and my whole mouth is filled with them, Gertty."

"There are so many cupcakes I made. If you had a sweet tooth, you should have come to see me. Don't tell me you already ate all the cupcakes I gave to you, Jan?" Gertty had a look of questionable surprise.

"Not at all, Gertty." Janet did not want to appear to be a pig about it. "I have had more than one, I admit. I froze a couple for another time when I know I'll have a craving. They'll be gone before I know it. Pie and cake are two totally different things and separate food groups, I think. Aren't the four food groups cakes, pies, cookies, and ice cream? Before you ask, I have ice cream too. No. I get what I can get when I can get it and pack it away. I am a hoarder of food. One day, I will say to myself that I want one of Gertty's cupcakes, and I'll know I have one in the freezer. You'll come to know I'm an impulsive shopper. Just can't pass up food, and it won't let me pass it by. It's a mutual understanding, you see. I confess. I got some cookies at the bakery too. I'll share if you stop by later. You keep on baking for me, and I'll keep on shopping at the bakery for you. Come winter, perhaps you can teach me to bake?"

"What it's like to be young and burn off calories like they be nothing, Janet? Most any older woman would long to have your figure." The compliment came followed with a warning. "A metabolism and figure like that doesn't stay around forever. Enjoy it while you can!" Gertty then offered, "I'd love to show you some of my baking tricks when the weather cools off. It would be nice to have someone to pass my knowledge down to. It's not hard. Just follow the instructions on recipes. I have some old family classics I'd love to pass down to you."

"You sound just like my mother, Gertty." Janet really thought so.

Chapter 14

Paint cans and things Janet brought from town exhausted her carrying them inside. No sooner had she plopped down in a chair, and Dean called again. For the second time today! Looking at her phone to see who was calling before deciding to answer, she did not want to pass on his call. Labored in breath, she answered the call. "Again? To what do I owe this honor?" Her face lit up.

"Jan, there has been trouble again. Today, Dan, at Baskin's, found Eli in one of his boats. Eli had been murdered and was hidden under a tarp. Strangest thing, and I probably shouldn't be sharing this, but I just can't help but feel all the death around the lake is somehow tied together. Police were called out once before to take a report for blood on Eli's boat.

"We investigated that incident, and it turned out to be animal blood. Now we've been told by other people that this had happened to Eli's boat on other occasions. Eli did not want to report it after the first time because he thought it might, in some way, be bad for business. The blood apparently always has been found in patterns as though it had been painted on. The blood on the boat was always painted in the same fashion, according to the people we talked with. Some kind of symbols, we think. I just don't have the expertise on my staff to be dealing with this kind of stuff. We are a small town and deal with traffic tickets and barking dogs. Anyway, the symbols are reminiscent of those found on a couple of girls found dead two doors down from your house years ago. Nobody ever could figure out what they were. I know you aren't squeamish about blood, as you mentioned the other night. I was wondering if I could show you the pictures later and see what you think. I would appreciate it. Having been around the lake as long as you have been, maybe you can think of something I can't.

"Murder and missing people require more advanced detective work than the state sends us in this Podunk town.

"I don't think these symbols are globally universal. I think they have something to do with someone or something locally because outside experts have not been able to figure them out. You can't deny some strange stuff has been going on."

Janet eagerly agreed to help. She desperately wanted to be of any help she could. Maybe it was to help Dean? Maybe it was to clear Steven if these incidents were in any way connected, including the day she spoke to Eli and he mentioned the cult gatherings and rituals? Maybe Eli was trying to warn Janet? Maybe it was because she wanted all this put in the past and to move on with a peaceful future at the lake? Maybe she was looking for drama and excitement in what had otherwise been a very non-exciting life? There was a tiny part of her that worried that she may be becoming too wrapped up in things that did not concern her. That wasn't enough to prevent her from being of assistance. Deep down, she knew if it concerned people around her and her community, it concerned her too. One by one, they were being picked off for some reason.

Dean later brought over the pictures, and Janet thought she might have some knowledge of the symbols Dean was trying to interpret. Jan was happy to tell a story that she thought might be of help to him. "Years ago, I told you before, I went to the sandbar island in the middle of the lake. It wasn't always so hard to get to by boat and walk around. The water has risen over the years, and much of the land there has eroded with time. Even since I was a child here at the lake. Stumps of old trees, rocks and boulders, and varieties of seaweed-type plants have now made access there much more difficult. Not impossible, but difficult for many types of boats.

"Low water levels mean more of the area is exposed. High water levels mean more obstruction and more sinks under the water surface. Obviously, the more the island and area around it is exposed above the water surface, the more island there is to explore, and parts become easier to walk around. It's always dangerous. The ground isn't firm around the wet edges and even in the center parts. What I'm getting at is, I seem to recall some of these symbols carved into very old trees there. I would not know if the trees are still there or if their barks are bare by now.

"My father was with me one time I had seen them, and I asked my father what they were. He told me that those trees are so very old. Many were there before white man ever settled this area. American Indians once lived on these lands, and the lakes were an important way of life for gathering water, washing, getting around, or for whatever they needed. White man basically came in and took the land away from the Indians. The Indians fought but lost and moved on. Back in the day, that swampy, rocky sandbar was more of an actual island. Indians who died in battle with the white man and other tribes were supposedly buried there—warriors. Those bones would have been underwater many times over and probably washed away by now, I'd think.

"To answer your question, these symbols look just like these you are showing me and, according to my father, are some sort of warning to any adversaries. Not the type of the usual "Keep out" warning you'd expect. They were more like a curse placed on those who trespassed on their sacred land. That's if these are the same symbols. Legends. I've been there and never had anything bad happen to me. Another story I have heard is that Indian ghosts gather there for ceremonies. One can supposedly hear them late on quiet summer nights. Just legends."

"I've never heard anything." Dean laughed. "That laugh just did me a bit of good, Janet. You're saying I am dealing with an Indian curse that is murdering people and perhaps ghosts?"

"I didn't say that, Dean," Janet said, smiling. "My father and brother loved to scare me with stories like that when I was little. I am telling you that I am sure I have seen symbols like these. The rest may have been my father's tale meant to interest me or keep me from ever going back to the dangerous island. If these are Indian symbols, they must have some meaning to Indians. You may know the folks around here love their spook stories.

"It was a different time, Dean. I mean, back when I was a kid. This is the countryside, and we kept ourselves preoccupied with Dad telling us stories while out fishing. Some were true, and some were not. That reminds me… I think my mom and dad would love to get a call from me shortly. They have no idea what is going on, and it will worry them so when they find out. Best I be the one to tell them about Eli. I can call them, and I could ask my dad if he believed that story he told me was a true story or just one he had made up. Even if we think it's fictional, Indians have differing beliefs of their own. I don't mock them. Who's to say?"

"It might help if you asked your dad, Janet. If it really is a local legend, it could imply that the killer has ties to these parts. I don't think tourists would know this stuff. You're sure the symbols look the same? How can you tell?" Dean was willing to follow any lead he could find.

Janet recalled them vividly. "Because my brother has an old photograph of those trees with the symbols and I'd seen the picture now and then over the years."

Dean looked at Janet, and they both realized what the meaning could be behind what Janet had just said. "Steven knows about those symbols too?"

Janet made up a reason not to call her mom and dad right then. She wanted to discuss what had been happening in her private life, and it required a bit of time to compose her thoughts before calling. Her family had known the Charter family, and news of Eli's death was not going to be taken without saddened feelings. So soon after the death of Irwin, it would likely be even more emotional. Any word of murder would have her parents calling her every hour to make sure she was fine or her mother showing up for an extended stay. Janet did not want either of those things happening.

"You be very careful, Janet. I need to go for now, and I'll be waiting to hear from you." Without thinking, Dean leaned in and kissed her cheek goodbye. He was honored that she had not protested his action. She did not think even think anything of it. It was just a friendly gesture as far as she was concerned.

Janet returned to her housework and started removing the wallpaper border in her kitchen. It had not been the easiest task one could attempt, and the remaining section was coming off in tiny bits. She wanted to acknowledge to herself that she was at least accomplishing something. However, it was the perfect time for her to call her parents and ask her dad if he had any suggestions. She got down off her ladder and dialed the phone. The answering machine picked up. She left no message.

The moment Janet disconnected the call, a lawnmower engine started in her yard. It was Armani mowing the lawn as he had done for many years. Janet went to him thinking he may not be too anxious to approach her after she'd last seen him.

Armani didn't even shut down the motor as she approached. He wanted to avoid looking at her and kept his mind on the lawn. He knew it would be inappropriate not to speak to her but was in no mood for extensive conversation.

"You know, Armani, I have been at home. Not that I expected you to come around after the other night. At least not anytime soon." Janet felt remorse. "You have no idea how terrible I felt after having left your door in the middle of the night. It was all so wrong of me." Janet took full blame.

With an annoyed look on his face, Armani stated, "You did nothing wrong. I just don't like being questioned. You don't own me and seem preoccupied with Dean. Your parents had paid me to mow the lawn one more time, and I wanted to fulfill my obligation. Of course, it's your home now. And right now, I have this lawn to mow and a lot of work to do elsewhere unless you don't want me to mow here? We can talk another time." Armani was otherwise preoccupied. It was hot. He was sweating profusely, laboring in the humid heat. Moisture droplets covered his tanned skin. He was anxious to get his work done and had patience for little else.

Janet reached over and switched off the lawn-mower power. "I'm not looking to control you, and I'm not even sure that us dating or otherwise being involved is a great idea. I do value you as a human being and the friendship we have. I don't want to lose that. Let's just emotionally step back from things for a while. You can finish your job now if you please, Armani."

"I knew that's how you'd feel when Dean started showing his face around here. Gertty told me he was here for dinner the other night. I had known he was around but thought it was all business until Gertty discussed his dinner at your place. Then I saw him kiss you earlier. He's here too much for my comfort. Boat rides, dinners, kisses, and maybe other things you haven't told me. I know what's not going on between you and me, and I know that Dean is at the heart of it. Maybe you should grow up a bit and figure out what you want before you start going after things. My feelings are not to be toyed with."

Armani started the lawnmower with a forceful pulling of the starter cord and continued about his work. Janet wanted to say something. Anything was better than nothing, but she just couldn't.

Janet didn't know what Gertty may have said to Armani, and she knew, in some way, he was right. Dean meant something to her, and Armani would always be the jealous type. The last thing Janet wanted to do was hurt anyone's feelings. Gertty's advice was right, Armani was right, and Dean was right. Janet clearly was not as mature as she thought she was. However, she was right herself. This was all too much drama too quickly, which came along with her life changes. Armani was never a problem issue before, and Dean had just entered into her life. To add to it, Janet was starting to feel ill in her stomach. Too much stress, Janet concluded.

After the confrontation with Armani, Janet no longer was interested in the wallpaper in her kitchen. Janet tried to otherwise occupy herself. She wanted to relax and suntan on the pier, but certainly not with Armani working outside. Wearing a bikini on the pier with him nearby would just appear to be a blatant, flirtatious, flaunting of herself in front of him and ultimately look cheap even if it was a natural thing to do by the lake. Being outside at all would appear obvious, and he would certainly think she was looking for his attention. Instead, Janet gathered up a basket of goodies and the things she'd promised Gertty for later and took them over instead of having Gertty come to her place for any dinner.

"Here's the things I promised you. I thought I'd save you the walk over and bring them to you myself." Janet offered Gertty the basket of food. "I'm just not up to having company for dinner tonight."

"I was just going to come by your place, Janet, and talk to you about the dinner. My feet just would not carry me. I'm very sore from gardening. I could also see Armani outdoors by you mowing and wanted to speak to him too. I just could not get there." Being as it was, Gertty was grateful Janet went out of her way to come by with the basket when she had.

"Seems you already talked to him today," Janet said in an offensive manner. "I'm sorry. I didn't mean anything by that. Maybe I did? Armani told me that you told him about Dean having been over to my place for dinner. It was no secret, but Armani was sure pissed off with me. He is already pissed off about other things. I'm not even sure if he is pissed off more that I had a sheriff over for dinner or if he is just jealous of Dean."

Janet seemed to be off on tangents, speaking her thoughts aloud again. It was best for her to be taking her medication regularly when behaving in this manner, but she hadn't been taking it. She wasn't normally a pill popper and only liked to take the anti-anxiety med when she felt she really needed it at bedtime. Disconnected thoughts and a rapid tongue were personality traits she'd displayed when not on medication.

"You know, Janet, your mind isn't right on this matter. I've known Armani a long time, and it's not my business to stick my nose in his where it doesn't belong. He knew Dean had been over and had kissed you before I ever engaged him in conversation. In any case, I didn't know there was any secret in that. If there are any secrets to be kept, Armani has plenty of them, I'm sure. They are for you to discover on your own or for him to tell you. Armani has known Dean many years, and Armani was not happy with Dean today. I'm sure he has multiple reasons for not being happy with him, and you are likely just a small part of it. None of this is any of my business, and I quickly ended that conversation with him. I may have a big nose, but I know better than to stick it in a shit mess." Gertty zipped her lips with her fingers. "I never even got a chance to speak with him about what I needed to talk to him about, Janet. He was in a bad, foul mood and stormed off without me asking him."

"You are right, Gertty. I don't know you that well to be burdening you with details. Getting you involved and caught in the middle isn't nice. It's hard to be new and fitting in here, I guess. So many changes. I meant to come to Antioch to relax and enjoy myself. Instead, I'm getting involved with everyone and everything. Don't mind me if I lay low for a little while. I just need some me time, and it just now hit me. You actually saved me a fortune. I would have been spending a lot more seeing that psychiatrist I know. The gin I brought by earlier and this basket was a bargain price to pay for your advice and truth." Janet laughed.

Gertty was pleased too. "Again, thanks for all these goodies as well, Janet. Glad our talk helped."

"The raw deer meat was frozen and may still be defrosting," Janet informed her. "I wrapped it in aluminum foil because it was becoming bloody in the package. I guess Steven didn't have them wrapped all that well before freezing. But you just gave me another thought. I don't know where Steven had that deer cleaned and wrapped. He was obviously in town and staying someplace to have had time to have done that. I wonder if wherever he was staying then is where he is at right now. Gertty, you are truly thought-provoking and inspirational."

Gertty again looked pleased. "Keep it up, kid. You'll catch on fast enough around these parts and be a regular in no time."

While Janet wanted to discuss the death of Eli, she wasn't sure if she should. Dean was still working on the case, and Janet did not know what was confidential and what wasn't. It might have been wise to have asked Dean if she was at liberty to discuss his death to everyone. It was then she had realized that she had not even appropriately discussed it with Armani. Armani and Eli had been friends. Her own well-being had taken precedence and had monopolized the conversation she'd had with him. Although maybe, it was not something she should be discussing with people, she thought. That served as her justification for now for her not to be a gossip.

Excitedly, Janet left Gertty's and could not wait to phone Dean to mention her revelation. She got his voice mail and left a message. "I'm curious where Steven had been staying prior to showing up at my place. I was thinking about the deer meat he put in my freezer. Obviously, he had the time to clean and wrap it or to get it done someplace. I just think that means he had to be in town someplace rather locally before he ever arrived at my place. Maybe he is currently back where he was? I just thought I'd mention it to you. I'll speak to my father very soon about the symbols. My parent's answering machine picked up when I called him. Give me a call if you come up with anything. I'll call you after I reach my dad. I know you are busy. Goodbye!"

Armani had finished the small lawn. Janet restrained herself from going outside and speaking to him about Eli since she had not reached Dean for permission. As soon as Armani departed, Janet finally felt at ease putting on her bikini and sunbathing on her pier. Had she been facing the house, she may have been able to notice the curtain in her window move aside and the dark figure standing behind it. Lost in thought and without care, she didn't realize she never locked the doors after she got home. That was probably in part to her new attitude of wanting to be alone. She did not want to give a thought to anyone or think anyone existed at all. That was why she moved here. That mentality suited her just fine.

It was so relaxing on the pier. Her phone played meditative music and lulled her into a dozing sleep. It lulled her deeper and deeper until her phone rang. Startled by the ringtone, it was best it had awakened her. How terrible it would have been had she burned out in the blistering sun. "Hi! Janet? It's your suburban friends. You know us. The ones you left behind for an independent life of luxury. You are probably lounging around right now while we are stuck in boring, old suburbia." Two female voices spoke in tandem.

Janet was excited to hear from her girlfriends in Prospect Heights. "I didn't think I'd hear from you so soon. What's new in suburbia?"

"Gloria and I were going to come up tonight. That is, if you aren't too busy with your new swinging lifestyle and new friends. We'd love to get some sun and play for a few days. If you are too busy with just moving in and all, we understand. Just be that way."

"No, Julie. I'm not that way at all. I could use some old friendships here to break up all the work. I need a rest." Janet knew some fun time with friends was just what she needed.

The other voice jumped into the conversation. "Hi, Janet, this is Gloria! I'm on speakerphone here with Julie. We look forward to seeing you. How about later this evening? We know you are outside right now taking in some of that terrific sunshine and getting vitamin D. Your pasty white ass needs it, girlfriend. We can hear boats in the background. You probably already have a tan. We're so jealous."

"Don't be jealous. I've been working too hard to play. Anytime is fine though. Tonight is great! You guys pick up a pizza for us on your way." Janet was so happy.

Inside the house, Janet washed off her suntan lotion and made every attempt to make the house look 100 percent presentable given the status of everything. Then she phoned her parents again. She was certain they would be home by now.

"Hi, Mom! I have been calling and calling." That was Janet's little white lie. It would get her off the hook for not calling as much as she should. "So much has been going on here; but, Mom, can I ask Dad a question first?"

"Sure, dear. Wes! She wants to ask you something. I was at the beauty parlor. And your father and I had some shopping to do, and we just walked in the door. Here's your father." Peggy talked back and forth between Wes and Janet for a moment and then handed the phone to Wes.

Wes got on the line, and Janet questioned him about the symbols. "Years ago, you took me to the center of the lake to that sandbar island or whatever it is now called. We saw trees with symbols on them. Steven had pictures of trees, and I recall seeing the pictures a few times over the years. You told me those symbols were put there by a long-gone tribe of Indians. You told me they were a curse to people who trespassed or desecrated their burial ground there. How cliché for a horror story that sounds. I'm curious if that's what those symbols really are or if you just made that up to scare me as a kid."

"Don't tell me you believe in curses?" Her father asked with a loud laugh. "You got a curse on you, do you, Sweetheart? It's the story as I read it years ago. I don't recall what I told you at the time, but I don't recall making anything up regarding that. You know how legends and tales are around there.

"The story is in an old book about Antioch Indians and settlers. If you look hard enough, you might find the book on the bookshelf in the living room. Your mom and I didn't usually throw those things out in case people wanted to read something while vacationing. The book isn't a best seller by any means. It was just some book or booklet by a local author. I got it many years ago at a mom-and-pop bookstore that was once there. That store has been closed a long time. What memories! You might recall the shop as you'd pick out children's books there when you were a young girl. They kept you pre-occupied by the hours when the adults were busy. Check good enough around that old house and you might find that book. What prompted that memory, Sweetheart?"

"An old acquaintance here brought the symbols up and looked at me like I was from another planet when I mentioned curses and the like. Then I told him my father told me them when I was a little girl, and we had a good laugh. It just made me curious where you heard about this stuff. Fond memories. I have lots of time here to reminisce with myself over old, fond memories. Thanks, Father. Before I forget, do you have any suggestions for removing this wall-paper border Mom put up in the kitchen?"

Her father laughed again. "That's going to be a chore for you. Your mother didn't know anything about installing wallpaper. She used regular glue paste. The kind you kids played with. You'll end up taking the plaster off with it."

"It's not that bad in most spots, Dad. I just hit a very tough patch and thought you might have a suggestion. You can put Mom back on. Love you!" Janet was happy her father knew about the Indian symbols. But she would have hoped the wallpaper would finish coming down more easily. At least she now knew why it wasn't.

"You take care, Honey. Your mom is right here. She's been anxious to speak with you and keeps trying to grab the phone." Wes was playing "keep away" with the handset until he eventually let Peggy have it. Wes and Peggy were playfully laughing at Wes's childish antics.

Wanting to tell her mother everything, Janet selected the words and details carefully. "Hello again. I heard you were at the beauty salon when I called earlier. Are you beautiful now?" Janet joked but also wanted to seriously know.

"I am. Simply stunning, Dear. Your father can hardly keep his hands off me now." Peggy didn't usually discuss sexual topics but would, keeping such topics to a minimum.

"Oh! Mom! I've had some things to tell you. Some things I can hardly believe. First of all, Steven showed up the other day and left without telling me he was leaving. I wanted to tell you all about it, but he said he wanted to discuss everything with you and it was his business. I told him that I would give him a day to do it, but I'm going to assume he never did. It seems he got to Illinois earlier than I realized and didn't tell me where he had been. It also seems he got himself into some trouble with the law. I don't know all the details. Sheriff Dean mentioned it to me. You might recall the headline in the newspaper about that Kim Kinski woman who is missing? Seems Steven had met her, knew her, or something to that effect. Sheriff Dean wants to speak to Steven if we hear from him again. I'm hoping Steven had nothing to do with that Kim woman. Being that he took off so abruptly and all, I hope he doesn't think he's in any trouble. I just don't know more details at this time."

Janet sat quietly while Peggy responded. Then Janet stated, "I have some sad news for you. It seems Eli Charter is dead. They found him in one of his boats. Some sort of accident, I assume. That's news that I don't think has even been released yet. It just so happened that Sheriff Dean was here to ask about Steven, and I got wind of Eli through him and his police business. Sheriff Dean and I have seen each other over the last few days regarding Irwin and Steven. I don't know if you remember him from his younger days when he hung around with guys we know here. He sends his best to you and Dad." Janet knew it was best not to tell Peggy about the patrolman found dead outside his car. Too many details, and Peggy would know there was trouble in the area. Distracting from negativity, Janet went on to say, "I do have some good news to report. Julie and Gloria are on their way up here right now. They are going to stay a couple days. So I'll have company and may not get to call you too often until I get more alone time. You know how much work entertaining people at this house can be. Whatever we do, just assume we are having fun!"

Aside from the responses one would expect from anyone having been told what Janet said on the phone, Janet had avoided any panic out of Peggy. When done speaking, Janet was happy with herself and the way she had handled the call. She always had to be on her toes when it came to handling conversations with her parents. There had been just enough dialect to convey the messages without having said too much for now. Peggy would hear more details another day, no doubt. For now, Peggy knew all she needed to without later being angry with Janet for not having said anything about Dean, Steven, or Eli. Strange, Janet thought, that she had put Dean's name first in her thinking. After thinking about it, she didn't even mention Armani. Was that a subliminal closure between her and Armani's relationship?

Chapter 15

Following the phone call to her mother, Janet checked the bookshelves in the living room for the local tribal book of which her father had spoken. If not for careful checking, she would have missed it pressed between the hardcovers of two much-larger novels. She felt fortunate that it was there. Bound in a thin, inexpensive paper cover, it was obvious this was a book written by a novice author and produced inexpensively. The book had been written by a man who once owned the local newspaper, and he had reproduced it in his own print shop, according to an inside page. Her fingers fumbled through the pages of easily read enlarged print, sophomoric drawings, and reproduced photographs. The pictures she had hoped to find within the book were easy to spot. Not many photographs existed from when the Indians had actually predominantly occupied Antioch, and what photos the book contained were few and far between. She was sure the drawings and photographs of symbols on the trees were identical to those Dean had inquired about.

Excited to contact Dean immediately with her find, she felt letdown when his voice mail answered her call. "I'm sure I have found what you are looking for with regards to those symbols. They are depicted here in an old book I have in my possession. Come by when you can, and I'll give you a photocopy of what you need. I'd like to hold onto the book because it is a part of Antioch history, and I don't think finding another copy of it would be too easy to come across. I should be around for a while. Friends of mine from Prospect Heights are due here anytime now, and they'll be staying with me a couple days." Janet completed her call just as someone knocked at her door.

Gloria and Julie had arrived earlier than expected. Janet was, however, prepared for their arrival. They had been to the vacation home many times over the years but hadn't been in several years. This time, it was different because it wasn't a parent-owned vacation house anymore. They were not going to have to share it with Steven, Peggy, Wes, or any of the other relatives or friends. They would not need to abide by Janet's parents' rules of the house. This time, it was the first time the girls had been there as women.

"How cool is this?" Julie appreciated the house and the situation. "It's been a few years since your family has had me up here. Not much has changed."

"Pretty cool," Janet replied. "Not much has changed here since I started coming here. It's about time for it. This place is in need of so much work. It could use a good change."

"Just *pretty cool*? What's wrong with you, Janet? This is far-out, totally cool."

Gloria appreciated it too. What she would not give to be in Janet's shoes. Like Julie, not much had changed in her life since college. She still lived at home with her own parents in quiet suburbia where nothing ever seemed to happen. Feeling trapped in life, Gloria longed for a way out.

Janet did not want to burden the girls with stories, but she had so much information to share with them. They were friends who shared almost every detail in life. Janet knew they'd be totally interested in all her stories. However, she did not want to creep them out with too much weird stuff right away. She'd speak to them in due time. Gloria and Julie got settled and lit a joint while Janet served chilled beers in a bottle and kept conversation light. Janet stuck to discussing stories about the title transfer of the home and every detail of moving day.

Julie giggled. "This, ladies, is so cool. Remember how we always had to take walks in the woods and get bitten up by bugs just to smoke a joint away from everyone? Now you own the house, and we can light up anytime. And it's legal! Times sure have changed. It figures recreational pot is now legal here after all these years."

"My mom and dad still wouldn't have allowed us to smoke pot around here even it had been legal," Janet said. She could just imagine what they would have said. The girls laughed.

"But at least they kept a stocked bar at all times!" Julie joked.

"I recall the last time," Gloria reminisced. "Janet, you fell asleep. Julie and I went out for a walk to light up, and we ran into Dan from that boat shop next door with your neighbor, Armani. Julie ended up banging them both in Armani's garage."

"Julie! The last time you both were here, you were underage. I recall it was the week before your eighteenth birthday because you almost could not make it due to a family gathering your mom wanted to have in honor of it. What the hell?" Janet thought about the years. "Armani was much older, and you were jailbait. Unless it happened during some break in their relationship. He was seeing Marissa, I believe."

"I was almost eighteen and horny is what I was, Janet, and Dan was really hot. He pounded me like a wild bison. Armani was kind of weird though. But I was very stoned, and maybe I just was a bit too much so and started feeling paranoid. Ah! Memories," Julie remarked.

"Weird how?" Janet was curious.

"He kept wanting to move me to a certain part of the garage while banging on me. I was trying to stay where I was comfortable. He was dragging me around like some sort of blow-up sex doll," Julie described the scenario.

Gloria laughed. "You could have floated away like one had you been any higher that night.

Knowing how you used to get, you were so trashed that he probably had to carry you."

"How come you two never told me any of this?" Janet definitely wanted to know all the details and more. Anything she learned would be used against Armani at the appropriate time.

"What did you want me to say, Janet? Thanks for letting me stay here! By the way, I fucked the neighbors?" Gloria again laughed at Julie's response. "Does Armani come around these days?" Julie asked unknowingly.

"Yes," Janet replied. "In fact, it just so happens I also fucked Armani. We also did it in his garage, too, just the other day. What is it with him and garages?" All the girls laughed.

Gloria then remarked about Julie to Janet, "I'm not sure why she never told you. She told me about every guy she went with since we started high school. That also included the neighboring school's wrestling team. I don't know what's funny: was she just a loose woman, or is this just great weed?" Gloria sputtered out between giggles and coughs.

"Janet, you are telling us that you never were with that man in all the years you came around here? You move here, and you just suddenly got an urge to give him a try?"

Janet laughed in response. "You got that right! That about sums it up."

"You didn't need to buy the house to get yourself some dick, Jan darling. You could have just got some good weed like Julie did."

"You all are just getting silly now," Janet replied. Janet started laughing and could not stop. "But I never screwed Dan," Janet clarified.

"From what Julie says, you should have done Dan and Armani at the same time. Two heads are better than one! So what was it like for you?" Gloria continued with the questioning.

"Shut up!" Janet became embarrassed.

"Seriously, Janet, I know what Julie said about Armani, but what do you have to say about him? That was your virginity, I believe." Gloria did know.

Janet didn't answer. She hoped that was not a question she needed to answer.

"Wait a minute, Janet. Get out! Is there something more than just a lay between you and Armani? There is! I can see it on your face plain as day. Janet and Armani are an item? Do tell, Janet! Do tell!" Gloria found it fascinating. She loved hearing of other people's sex lives as hers was nothing to speak of.

"No!" Janet seriously said. "I should not have done it with him. It really complicated our relationship as friends and took my virginity that I really was saving for my future husband. I thought he felt the same. Before there are any misconceptions, I lost my virginity in a bed like normal people should. The garage was the second time. I don't want to discuss him now, and there is so much other stuff to talk about. We can talk about all the men in my life later. He's just one of the few."

"Twice? And what about Dan? How is Dan doing these days? Since you haven't screwed him, I assume he is an open topic for discussion?" Julie wanted to know.

"Not great," Janet replied. "He's fine. He lost his best friend to an accident very, very recently, and I would assume he's not taking it well. You might recall his friend Eli Charter." They all became instantly saddened with Janet's news.

"Well, aren't you just the buzzkill, Janet. What happened to Eli? Of course, we remember him." Gloria was stunned by the news, and the level of happiness quickly diminished within the room.

"I only just found out about Eli myself, and I don't even know any details. They found him in his boat outside at the boat shop after I had had gotten here. I'm waiting to hear more." Janet left out the details.

"Is there anything we can talk about that isn't sad or off the table?" Gloria asked.

"Pizza. We can talk about the pizza!" Janet opened the topic for discussion "What kind did you get?" Janet's tummy rumbled with hunger as she brought it up. She hoped they remembered she likes extra sausage and extra cheese best.

Julie answered, "Fattening food now? I can't wait until I can get into my swimsuit and catch some sun tomorrow. The last thing I need is to slip into my swimsuit with the fat of pizza bulging out. I'm sure there are plenty of hot men on the lake who will be checking me out. Can we take the boat out tomorrow and lay out in the sun? Just look at how pasty I am this summer. I need sun! By the way, it's extra sausage and extra cheese. Do you think we forgot?"

The doorbell rang and interrupted their conversation. It was Dean. Janet had forgotten she told him to stop by. Fortunately, she had already made copies of the book pages he had come for.

"Who is that?" Julie asked while waving a gray-ish waft of smoke away from her face. "Is that a cop?"

"Don't worry girls," Janet said. "He's not here to arrest you for any one of the immoral, indecent, and illegal acts either one of you has committed over the years, unless you stole the pizza? That's just another one of my men. I'd introduce you, but I don't think your current stoned condition and you reeking from pot would make the best impression. I'll quickly send him on his way. He's just picking something up." Janet would have liked to spend time with Dean but was certain he would not approve of their current girl's night behavior.

Dean yelled from outside. "Hey! It's me!"

Janet answered the door. "I saw you coming up the walk. My girlfriends are here, and we were just having fun. Sorry it took so long for me to answer."

"I can smell the fun." The marijuana scent had followed her and was easily discernible. "I came by because you asked me to." Dean waited for Janet to say something.

"First of all, I do have what you came for right here, Dean." Janet carried the copied papers to Dean outside on the porch. She did not think Dean would want his clothes picking up the pot smell inside the house. "See the images? This is what I was telling you about. They look the same, don't they?"

Dean was very happy to receive the papers. "You have no idea how many people have been trying to figure these out and for how long they have tried. I guess it pays to advertise. I'm glad I asked you about them. You have been such a big help that I could just kiss you." Dean grabbed Janet and planted a wet kiss right on the lips. It was longer and harder than that of any sign of appreciation or friendship.

Julie and Gloria could be heard laughing from inside the house. It was clear they had been eavesdropping. They found it quite amusing. Neither could recall ever having seen a guy kiss Janet. Not the Ms. Goody Two Shoes they knew.

"That's just the girls inside having too good of a time," Janet explained. "I want to introduce you, but they are a bit wild right now. I don't want you to get the wrong impression of them. They lead very dull lives in Prospect Heights and came here to let loose this weekend. They are going all out and letting their hair down here." Janet was a bit embarrassed and was wondering what Dean must think of them. Now she was thinking like her mother.

"I can understand them wanting to do that," Dean said. "I'm a bit reserved on the outside because of my job. On the inside, I totally get it. I'd like to let my hair down once in a while, too, but being the sheriff, I need to always be the responsible one. It gets old though if you know what I mean?" Dean didn't mind people having fun as long as it didn't get out of control and his department members had to break it up.

Janet was more at ease after Dean spoke. "Want to meet them now?" Dean did. He had no expectations of them. From a professional standpoint, Dean wanted to know who was around. Janet called for the girls, and they came to the door. "This is Gloria, and this is Julie," Janet said with an introduction. "He wants to arrest us for having a good time without him. He is willing to forget about the charges if we agree to have an orgy with him. He has a fantasy of being with three nymphs."

"Janet!" Dean blushed and chuckled. "Hi, ladies. Glad you are here watching out for Janet."

The girls were still laughing, and Julie said, "I think we can accommodate that orgy. I just love a man in uniform. Are you single?"

Again, Dean blushed. "It's complicated. You girls be very safe this weekend. I'm sure Janet has filled you in on things that have been happening around here. The last thing any of us wants is any trouble." Dean had turned to look at Janet and had become serious. "No word from Steven?"

"No, Dean," Janet replied. "I was just filling the girls in on some of the things going on here. They only just arrived, and I'll fill them in on everything and more as we get the time to speak. As you arrived, we were talking about a boat ride and keeping conversation mellow," Janet added.

"You are going to drive a motorboat while stoned?" Dean replied, expressing his concern. "I didn't just hear that. Just so you know, Janet, I can't save you from the water patrol."

"I'm not stoned, Sweetie… Julie and Gloria are stoned," Janet replied. "Just look at them, red-eyed and with those goofy looks on their faces. Oh! Wait! They always look like that!" Janet said with humorous, insulting intent. "Anyway, Dean, I'm talking about a boat ride tomorrow. They want to get some sun on the lake, and I'd invite you along. But I know you are working."

Dean was actually thrilled over the invitation because it gave him an idea. "I would like to go with. I'd even rather enjoy driving the boat and letting you girls just relax and have fun. I only say that because I really should go to the island and see what I can find there. Maybe we can find a way for me to do that tomorrow while you ladies hang out?"

That, in turn, gave Janet an idea. "I'll tell you what… I've got an idea that I think will work. Can you girls stay here for a moment while Dean and I run by Gertty's next door? We will be right back."

"Go ahead! It will give Julie and me some time to finish unpacking and freshen up. Promise you will not be too long!" Gloria answered, assuming Julie would agree with her.

On their way to Gertty's house, Dean asked, "I was wondering if that orgy idea was on the table? It's got me thinking."

Janet hit him on the back. "I doubt it!"

Dean was quick to reply, "Hey! That's strik-
ing an officer of the law, and I could handcuff you
for that!" And so their joking continued until they
approached Gertty's.

The idea Janet had paid off. Gertty had a small
rowboat on the side of her house, which sat there
unused, and she was happy to lend it to them for as
long as they needed. She and Dean hauled the light-
weight piece of aluminum back to her place. Janet
had figured they could tow the rowboat near to the
island and the girls could anchor and tan while Dean
rowed to the island for an investigation.

As Dean departed, he said, "I have a question I
almost forgot to ask. When I got to your house, you
said, 'First of all,' and you never mentioned a 'Second
of all.' What was second?"

"We covered everything for one evening, Dean,"
Janet replied, not recalling what it was. If there was
anything else, it isn't important now. I've already forgotten." Janet was trying to answer through her pant-
ing from carrying the boat.

"Let me remind you, Janet… There is one more
thing." Dean leaned in and gave Janet a soft kiss.
"That is, to wish you a good night."

After reconnecting with her friends inside the
house, Janet found she was on a different plane of
mentality. Gloria and Julie were very high and had
started drinking. At least for now, her friends had the
munchies, and Janet was absolutely famished. Pizza
was just the thing they all craved. It had always been
their guilty pleasure when having sleepovers together.

Janet told the girls about Dean. In doing so, she realized she knew little about him as a person. She managed to hold their interest with what she could tell them. As Janet often had been doing, she kept the exact details to a minimum—just the basics.

"I have known him from around town for years. I had been on a walk the other day, and he was in the neighborhood on a call. He knows the neighbors, and we ran into each other. He asked about my family, and I told him about a book I have here. He was interested in it, and I told him to stop by this evening for some information on it. And one thing led to another. I've only been here a few days, and it's not like we are getting married or anything. So don't kid me about him. I'm just keeping my options open."

Conversation went on like that until the guests became so relaxed that they seemed to be zoning out and in their own mind places. Janet expressed how sleepy she was from all the excitement and was going to retire to bed very early. She wanted everyone to have a good night with plenty of sleep so the next day could be enjoyed by all. She knew she would sleep very well, and they all knew that a day of sun and water would be exhausting. It's not all as restful as one might expect.

The next day, Dean arrived while Janet and her guests were assembling supplies to bring with them on their day adventure. Janet realized she and Dean had forgotten to take the boat oars from Gertty's garage and excused herself while she went with Dean back to Gertty's home to obtain them. The oars were obtained without difficulty. It was a good thing Gertty was usually always at home to be of service. Janet assisted Dean with carrying the oars and setting them into the boat along with assisting him with a huge backpack of professional gear from his car, which he had brought with him.

"What is in this backpack you brought along? The wooden oars were heavier than I thought they'd be and this backpack is just as heavy. Do you really need all this stuff?" Janet was inquisitive. Dean was well prepared.

"There is everything I might need in there. There is some mountain-climbing gear to be of help in case the ground is not firm and steady. I've got some test kits in case I want to take some samples. There is some food, drink, towel, tools, and camera equipment. I wanted to make sure I have everything and am prepared. I don't want to not complete my mission today and need to go back there because I forgot something."

The guests had prepared well for the day too. Janet looked over the items packed and made a comment they had done a great job gathering everything.

"It's not our first outing," Julie reminded Janet. "By the way, Janet, you had a visitor looking for you or your parents," Julie said. "He did not mention Steven… Just you and your parents. He kind of startled me. I came out from the bedroom, and there he was. He said he was a friend. His name is Fox, but his name did not suit him. He was no fox at all," Julie expressed her opinion.

"Where was he?" Janet wanted to confirm what she thought Julie had said.

"Right there," Julie seemed unfazed while pointing. "In the kitchen, Janet."

"You mean a strange man claiming to be Fox just let himself into my home?" Janet had a look of panic.

"Gloria and I did not think anything about it," Julie responded. Whenever we've been here, unfamiliar people were always walking in and out. Gloria and I just assumed it was not out of the question for him to let himself in. He may have knocked, and we did not hear it. But the main door was open, and the screen unlocked too. Gloria and I would have just walked in," Julie stated.

"I don't know, Julie. It is just strange. Then where did he go to after he left?" Janet wanted some answers before she decided how to decide upon a reaction.

"He asked about Wes and Peggy, and I told him they were not here. He then asked, 'Is Janet here?'" Julie continued to explain…"I told him you are in town but stepped next door for a moment. I told him you would be right back. Then Gloria came into the room, and I introduced her to Fox. He said to tell all of you that he stopped by. Then he apologized for inconveniencing us and startling me. Aside from him startling me when I first saw him, I didn't think anything was unusual. Is something the matter?" Julie was now becoming even more concerned something was wrong.

"I don't know!" Again, Janet did not want to worry the girls. Janet continued to say, "It's just that this kind of unusual stuff has been going on around here, and I'm not used to it. This is my home now. I don't know any Fox guy, and him walking right in is rather disturbing to me. Of course, here in the country, people do walk in when they see an open door. It's the trusting, neighborly way. With times changing, strange things going on, and me here alone most of the time, I may need to address that behavior around here. I don't think I like it. It never bothered me before, but it does now. What did Fox look like?"

Julie replied, "I didn't really pay much attention. I have kind of almost forgotten. Must be the pot."

Gloria jumped into the conversation and answered in great detail…"He's a typical Indian man. Older, probably seventies or even older. He had on a fishing cap, so I didn't get a good look at his hair. But his hair was black hair with gray. His skin was leathery with wrinkles, old acne pockmarks, and big pores. He must sweat a lot. He had on a flannel shirt and jeans. I'd say he stood six feet and probably weighed 220. That's about all there is to say about him."

"An Indian man was in my house talking to you two, and Julie could not identify what he looked like? That's funny! Good description, Gloria. Thank you!" Janet was dumbfounded.

"No, I don't notice old men," Julie answered. "I'm not that much of a slut. I only check out the cute, young, virile of the species. Or are you saying I should have noticed his looks more so because he wasn't White? Prejudice much? I'm asking again if his being here is a problem or not. We didn't let him in. Don't shoot the messengers." Julie was starting to feel offended.

"You didn't do anything wrong. I would have locked the door when I left had I anticipated strangers would be coming and going," Janet declared. "However, I was asking my father about Indians earlier. That was partly why Dean was here last night to gather some information about them from an old book. I wonder if my father sent this Fox guy over to speak to me. Why do you suppose Fox didn't wait for me to get back? Dean and I were only gone for twenty-five minutes, tops!"

"If it's any consolation, Janet, Fox seemed a bit rattled that Julie and I were here," Gloria supposed. "Seeing me in a bikini probably got him overheated. Julie probably startled the old geezer when she confronted him. Seeing her in that outdated swimsuit with those saddlebags and love handles is enough to scare off anyone!" Gloria playfully pinched Julie's ass. "Seriously, Julie, did you buy that suit at some 1920s vintage clothing shop? Geez," Gloria playfully enunciated.

"Anyway, Janet, Fox insisted he'd wait around outside," Julie responded while slapping the hand of Gloria. "I'm not fat, Gloria! I'm voluptuous! Any man would love to get his hands on this bevy of beauty. As for my swimsuit, I'll have you know, it is the latest in retro garb. I'm high fashion!" Truthfully speaking, that was her own opinion.

The girls were laughing again, and Janet didn't want to ruin their good time. She'd be sure to remember to mention the visitor to her parents when next she'd speak to them. The incident was just one of many that disturbed her a bit these days. Just the fact that someone walked into her home uninvited bothered her now when it never had before. Her family always had an open-door policy, and it was a good-time party house. That was then, and it wasn't anymore. It was her home now. Janet's disapproval with that overly neighborly behavior was compounded by the concern that she did not recall anyone by that name. She would have been more at ease had she recalled knowing the man or been expecting his visit.

Chapter 16

Tiny waves rippled out from under the motorboat as it tugged the small rowboat in tow. Not due to any reason in particular, but other lake activity was rather quiet at this time. The sun was heating things up, and the day was wearing on to a point when most small craft boaters had left. Definitely, it was not as busy as on a weekend. It was rather quiet, and conversation among the boat party changed from one topic to another as each person spoke freely. At times, everyone was talking at once and comprehending multiple conversations.

Julie wanted to know more about Dean without implication she was hitting on a man Janet had an obvious romantic interest in. The friends knew Janet had a connection to Dean, which was growing into more than a friendship. Janet did not address the attraction and even tried to deny it at times. In a way, Janet pretended to be oblivious and would have insisted she and Dean were just friends had anyone stated more.

Gloria took in the breathtaking surrounding beauty of nature. From the yellow of the sun, to the blue of the sky, and even in the green-blue color of the water… Color exploded with vibrancy much more than it seemed to in the Chicago suburbs. Every home was unique and not like the rows of mass-produced dwellings in Prospect Heights. A beautiful lake was in place of what would be parking lots or strip malls back home. The air even seemed different. It was lighter and fresher without the smog. She found herself repeatedly saying, "Look at that! Isn't that nice? Look over there! That's so pretty! What type of plant is that? What type of bird is that?" She spoke nonstop like a small child in need of attention.

Janet mentioned to Dean about her conversation with Julie and Gloria regarding the uninvited stranger who had appeared in her home while they had been at Gertty's. She insisted no big deal be made out of it until she had an opportunity to speak to her parents. It was possible that Fox was a friend of the family and had just stopped by after noticing cars outside. The only reason for mentioning Fox to Dean at this time was because she had hoped her father had sent him regarding the conversation she'd had with Dean about local Indians. It would be just like her father to do something like that. She probably had reminded her dad of an old Indian friend he has and had not talked to in a while. Her dad was the type to call old friends and acquaintances after ages had passed solely for the sake of reminiscing. Even had he not talked to someone in years, he had a gift for picking up conversations where he had last left off with them. Her dad seemed to know everyone and everyone knew him. He was not antisocial in the least.

Janet was more interested in asking Dean some personal questions about his life. They never had a chance to talk much the night he had come over for dinner, and she wanted to know more about him. "Why did you become a cop? How long ago did you join the police force? How did that lead to you becoming Sheriff Dean?" She normally didn't want to encourage so much career talk but knew Dean was probably only with them today to inspect the island for business reasons. His mind was likely already on his work. Janet knew his mind had to be because straight guys would not be as otherwise distracted while being on a boat with three young, pretty ladies in swimsuits.

Dean answered by explaining that his father had been a police officer. His father's cops-and-robbers stories and gun had always intrigued him. It seemed to be in his blood to become a policeman, and he never thought of being anything else. Moving up the ladder of success to becoming a sheriff in what he called "a one-horse town" had just been a matter of waiting for the previous sheriff to retire. The girls knew there had to be more intellect involved than just waiting for his turn to be the sheriff. Dean was just being modest. He blushed easily, which made his modesty a dead giveaway. Now Janet could tell that Dean didn't really like talking about himself much when it came to being proud of his accomplishments. Was it a dull story, or was there an interesting story behind it that he was not opening up about? Janet knew she'd find out the truth one day.

Getting close to the island proximity, Dean shut off the motor. "Well, ladies, looks like this is as far as we go. We'll drop anchor here, and I'll take the rowboat out the rest of the way. If I'm not back in an hour or so, send the dogs out after me. Seriously! I'll try to be quick about it... Just accomplish what I must and get back. This island looks much larger up close here than it does from Jan's house. It even looks much bigger than the last time I had seen it from a closer distance. The papers Janet gave me said they call it Na'wa Kwa. It means 'Island Forest' in the language of the old local Indian tribe."

"You know more than I do," Janet said, having learned something. "It could actually be larger if the water levels are down." Janet offered warnings... "Be safe. Some of that is just swampland, and the ground is not solid. You need to be very careful where you are stepping. Even large rocks can shift with ease if you push or step on them. They sink right into the water-saturated sand. The trees you seek start growing just inside from the outer perimeter. I think the Indians wanted to warn people before trespassers ventured inland too far. Their burial area is more at the center."

"Burial area?" Julie asked with wide eyes of intrigue. Gloria found that to be exciting and wished they were all going ashore.

Dean was already in the rowboat and about to shove off when Janet stopped him for a moment. She whispered to him. "I just wanted to say that the cocktails I've had and the pot smoking... That's not really my style. I've only been trying to celebrate my independence here, and those activities are not a part of my normal routine. I just wanted you to know that because I may care just a tiny bit what you think of me." She whispered it because she didn't want the girls to think it mattered what Dean thought. If they had thought it mattered to her what Dean thought, they would tease her about it. They would think they knew there was more to their bonding than a just new friendship forming. In any case, Janet did care what people thought of her. She was self-conscious that way. As Dean left, she waved. Again she reiterated her warning, "Please be careful out there!"

Janet returned her attention back to her guests who were rubbing each other down with lotion and passing around a soda can. "The island is no place for us," she said to the ladies. "Too many bugs and too muddy. Just be glad we aren't going there with him this time. Maybe, another day, we can plan an excursion there. Besides, one of you would break a nail, and we'd be listening to you gripe through your entire visit here.

"In answer to your earlier question," Janet continued…"Dean is working on a police case. He thinks this island may contain some information he's been researching. I showed him an old book that stated that Indians may have buried their dead on this island many years ago because they believed the water here had some magical ability to resurrect the dead. That was long before British people settled in this area. That island was once a much bigger landmass apparently. It's possible this entire area wasn't even a body of water at one time. Perhaps it was once all underwater a million years ago. I haven't studied that much about the geology here," Janet confessed. She continued speaking..."All the lakes around here connect to Lake Michigan through water channels and rivers. As the water levels became higher, more and more land eroded. Eventually, water had filled in low territories, which are now the waterway channels and lakes. That tiny island has definitely shrunk over the years from what I have myself witnessed. It is said that ancient Indian graves are surrounded by carvings on trees. Dean went to see the carvings and maybe even find something else he is looking for... Something which ties into a case or cases he is working on. He doesn't share a lot of information with me because police investigations are confidential, or so he says." Janet ended her conversation with a claim that indicated she didn't believe his excuse entirely.

Gloria was particularly entertained by stories of the area. "I recall stories of Indians here, Janet, but I thought talk of burial grounds and all that stuff your father and brother told us was made up to scare us when we were kids? Remember the late-night summer walks we would take with your family, and they would tell ghost stories? I mean, who would bury their dead on a small patch of sinking swampland?"

"I don't know, Gloria. They claim that mass of land at one time had mystical powers. Their ways are different from our own. It's sometimes difficult to tell where the fine line between fact and fiction is drawn around here. This is Dean's interest. Who knows? Perhaps he will even discover a fountain of youth there. Someday, we all may need it!" Janet had no real interest in any of the folklore. If she were into that kind of magical mumbo jumbo, she'd have been poking around out there long ago.

Time on the boat was serene. A gentle rocking of the boat and a faint humming of distant boat motors had calmed the ladies. All of them were sprawled out, covered in oil. All of them, eyes closed under dark designer sunglasses and resting peacefully to the sound of soft jazz music on a CD. It was enough to sedate even the most severe insomniac. They all felt like babies being rocked in a cradle to the sound of a lullaby.

All at once, Janet and her friends jumped up when a loud thud banged against the boat. It was just Dean returning. "Find what you were looking for?" Janet asked Dean as she helped him onto the motorboat and assisted with attaching the rowboat to it with a rope. "What's it like there?"

Dean replied, "Swampy and creepy that it also played on my own paranoia. I imagined an alligator was stalking me and I was trapped on a deserted island surrounded by an ocean of man-eating sharks. We all know there are no gators in these parts. Then again, one never knows what nutjob let something dangerous loose in the wild. A person doesn't realize how separated from civilization they are until they are out there alone. Anyway, I saw the trees I was looking for. They are there. I just don't know what they could mean at this point. I took some pictures. Can we head back to your place? I don't mean to rush you ladies, but I would like to get these pictures to the station. I've still got lots of work to accomplish today. Besides, I feel kind of dirty after rowing in the sun and having been stomping around in muck."

"Well, ladies, what do you think?" Janet asked. "Should we drop Dean off and take a bathroom break? You don't want to burn too much on your first outing here, and there is plenty of daytime left for us to get back out here. A break might do us good." Janet wanted to go home for a few minutes anyway because she needed to pee.

Both girls nodded with approval and started packing up their towels, lotion, and gear. Their skin was looking a darker pink. The summer sun did not take long to do skin damage, and the lake water attracted and reflected the sun's rays even more than elsewhere in town.

Dean drove the boat back at an accelerated pace. His boat-driving skills impressed Janet as she knew he did not have much experience on the lake. She wasn't even sure he had a boating license. It was just assumed that if he didn't and was stopped by water patrol, he must have an in with them. So she asked him, "Are you licensed to drive a boat, or do you have an in with water patrol? You seem to handle my boat quite well. You told me you did not get on the water often, but you drive like a pro."

Dean winked, saying, "I've got many talents. Let's just say that I know the motion of the ocean."

"This isn't an ocean, Dean, and you haven't answered my question." Janet still wanted to know.

"I got a boat license ages ago, Janet, and just keep renewing it. There are so many lakes around here, and I never know when I might need it. I always wanted a boat but just never invested in one. Driving one comes naturally. I like to race cars when I can, and it's all pretty much the same. Just careful handling and awareness. That's all."

"Dean, a race-car driver?" Julie asked, wanting to partake in the conversation. "Where did you do that?"

"My relatives own farmland, and the family men are all into drift cars. We just drive wildly on a track they created there for family and friends. It was a hobby that I later shared with my brothers. I learned about handling the cars at high speed and have been behind the wheel since I was five years old when my dad would let me sit on his lap and steer. My dad and brothers built me a go-cart that I learned to drive. As soon as I could touch the peddles in a car, I was on my own. I've known people who have owned boats I've been allowed to drive, and I've taken many water-safety courses." Dean knew how to operate most machinery well, having grown up on a farm.

"Brothers?" Janet inquired. "We haven't had much time to talk about your family. Maybe we can discuss them next time you come back for that makeup dinner we discussed?" Janet wanted to learn all she could about Dean and took a genuine interest.

She had known of him from the past but never knew of brothers. She could not recall ever having seen or met any of his family members.

It felt later than it really was—high noon. Dean and the ladies returned the equipment to Gertty before Dean said goodbyes and headed on his way back to work. The ladies returned to Janet's home and utilized the facilities before discussing their afternoon agenda. Not much of one—just whooping it up on the boat and lake. Gloria wanted to water-ski, Julie wanted to suntan, Janet wanted to fish, and they had plenty of time to do it all.

Chapter 17

Janet's guests could not have asked more from her. She showed them a marvelous day, and it was more fun than any of them had had in a long time—exhausting but fun. Looking forward to the rest of it, they still had the evening to enjoy and discussed dinner plans. Each had a taste for something different. Fortunately, Janet knew of a restaurant that would deliver what each of them desired, and they'd happily share in the selections. Gloria called in the order and provided payment to cover the bill as a way of thanking Janet for her hospitality. A smorgasbord of various dishes to feed them was on the way.

"On the subject of dinner, what is this makeup dinner you mentioned to Dean?" Julie had caught that part of the conversation Janet had with Dean earlier. "Did you two have a fight of some sort, and did our just being here interrupt a dinner date? What gives?" Julie inquired while having helped herself to a drink from the bar.

"No, Julie," Janet divulged. "Nothing like that. I did not mean to say the word *makeup* in a way to mean that I was apologizing to Dean… It's just a part of what has been going on around here. Let me start at the beginning, which goes back to when I moved in. There is so much to tell." Janet was trying to organize chronological events in her mind while figuring out the best words to intertwine all her tales.

Gloria and Julie sank into the oversized sofa in the living room and made themselves comfortable until Janet felt comfortable speaking to them. They knew how Janet liked to organize thoughts in her mind before speaking when she had a lot to say.

"It's a long story," Janet said as she started her tale. "I got here and introduced myself to Gertty next door. She is very nice and not as messed up as I was led to believe by others over the years. Also, I talked with Armani and mentioned I may be needing help with chores around here. In fact, I had Armani help with installing new door locks for me. He and I spent some time together. One thing led to another, and we fooled around, as you already know. Gertty and I took a walk to check on her other neighbor's home, and we found the old man who lives there dead! It appears he fell down his basement stairs, and the situation was gruesome. Dean arrived on the scene with emergency crews after I called 911. As one would expect, Dean and I started talking. We did know of each other from the past. I didn't know him well but knew of him.

"It is complicated because Armani began avoiding me after he took my virginity, and I didn't know where things stood," Janet said with sadness. "I hadn't yet asked him what our time together meant to him.

You know how some people can be...'*Wham! Bam! Thank you, Ma'am!*' And all that sort of stuff.

"On another subject," Janet added, "Armani told me things about my brother that I never knew. Steven was apparently the town pervert. He was peeping in bedroom windows years ago and taking pictures of naked men. Armani found the pictures here while working, and that caused distancing between him and Steven. While Dean was here discussing Irwin and other things, Steven just showed up! I had no idea Steven was coming here or that he was even in town. He said he just got to Illinois and wanted to see me while he's in the area on personal business. Well, Steven shot daggers from his eyes at Dean while they were here together. It was an uncomfortable situation."

Janet changed subjects again, but the ladies felt it best to let her vent before interrupting her train of thought. "Unsettling as it may seem," Janet said, "I later learned from Dean that Steven had not just arrived in town and was being questioned in the case of a missing local woman. It is unclear to me what connection he could possibly have to her.

"There is more," Janet said as she began to cry softly. "Eli was found dead. I just saw him alive, and he was so nice." Janet attempted to voice some details while choking back tears. "He was found in his boat with symbols painted in blood. The symbols apparently match symbols they found on other dead bodies, and I thought of the Indian symbols Dean was looking at on the island.

"Then," Janet added, "if that's not enough, there is even more. There have been reports of missing people from the campsite across the lake and cults gathering. Dean put a patrol vehicle in my area because he was concerned about me and the things that have been happening. The patrol guy was found dead outside his car while supposedly taking a bathroom break. They haven't determined what killed him yet, at least not that I know of. His death seemed to be due to natural causes, but Dean thinks these events are not coincidental and may all be tied together." Janet was finally concluding her thought. "You know those spooky stories we heard as kids?" Janet said, "Well, they are apparently not all made up. It's not always the quiet-and-safe hamlet around here we thought it was."

"That's incredible," said Gloria. She couldn't believe her ears. "What the hell is going on around here? What kind of place is this and your parents let you move here? That doesn't sound like the Peggy and Wes I know."

Julie shook her head in disbelief. "That does not sound like the Steven I know. All of this is just too much, Janet."

"I know, right? Wait, there is more I can now tell you," Janet went on to say. "I gave Armani a key to my house when he changed the locks. Maybe, I thought, our relationship was on the fast-track after all these years. Then I thought he would need it to do chores around here as he always did. I also thought it would be nice to know someone had a spare key just in case of an emergency. But then Steven showed up, and I gave him a key to use. He told me he was going to be staying here while visiting. Problems started when items around the house began to become displaced or were disappearing altogether. I would sometimes see a shadow or what I thought was a person in the house, but there wasn't anyone here that I could find when I looked around.

"It made me start to wonder," Janet said. "Maybe one or all the guys were playing gags on me? Maybe I am sleepwalking or imagining things again? Maybe nothing is really going on? Maybe something is going on, and it involves me? Maybe something is going on and doesn't involve me? Maybe the place is haunted…if you believe in that stuff, and I am not discounting any reasoning at this point. So I started taking my old meds and went to the doctor for a refill, thinking I was becoming neurotic again. Maybe I am delusional at times and am experiencing side effects from my medication?"

Janet then stated she thought she could dismiss some of the explanations. She said, "I was chalking it up to my own imagination until Dean came for dinner one night and to talk. He hoped I could help him with any information pertaining to Steven or anything going on. Dean and I took a boat ride, and that's when a very strange thing happened. He inadvertently left his keys here in the house while the house was locked up tight. When we got back, we discovered his keys were in the trunk keyhole of his vehicle, and his uniform had been taken from the trunk. Dean was upset and concerned. Naturally, our evening dinner and discussions were cut short."

"So that is what your makeup dinner is all about," Julie jumped in. "That's a lot for you to have weighing on your mind. Especially for a mind that is usually so empty!" Julie tapped Janet on the head and turned to humor, not knowing what else she could say at the moment.

Julie's reaction did cause Janet to break a smile for a moment before she spoke next. "You understand that I discussed with Dean that Steven and Armani have keys to the house? When I next saw Armani, he was insulted that anyone would think he would do such a thing. His feelings were hurt, but I never said he had anything to do with it. Armani said he had been away from here at that time and was going to explain to Dean that he could not possibly have done it." Then Janet thought of Steven. "Steven was already gone from here without notification. I assumed Steven would be back, but he's never come back."

Gloria had now moved over next to Janet and was hugging her for emotional support. "I see how all this has turned into a mess for you," Gloria said with sympathetic support. "Be strong, and it will be okay. It definitely sounds like a rough adjustment." Gloria hugged Janet tighter and gave a look of shock to Julie behind Janet's back.

Janet felt that Armani was mad at her for so many things. "I made such a mess of things with him and have yet to patch things up," Janet told Gloria and Julie. "I have barely had a chance to speak with my parents about any of this, and then you girls called and came over. You know, I have been very careful now about what I do tell my parents or anyone at all. It's so nice you are here with me. Nothing makes sense when I try to think. It scares me that people come and go, and I have no clue who is doing what or when. Things just happen, and all while I am trying to get myself moved in and situated here. You understand what I mean?" Janet asked, not expecting an answer. "It's all so emotional for me. Sometimes I'm so happy like I am with you here, then I'm so scared of the unknown. At other times, I'm so sad for people, and some days, I'm so confused." Janet continued, "Sometimes, I'm so busy that my mind takes me away from others, and I get so emotional and cry, laugh, or talk to myself and don't know why I am doing it. It's not as calming here as I would have anticipated. I am one hot mess, am I not?"

Gloria and Julie could very much understand what Janet was conveying to them with regard to her emotions. Not that they had even experienced so much, but less would have pushed them over the edge mentally. Neither had ever had anything even remotely as interesting happen to them.

"Obviously, I don't want to worry my parents," Janet told her friends. "I can't talk to Steven, Armani, Gertty, Dan, or Dean like I talk to you two. They wouldn't get me like you girls do. We've been through so much over the years, and you know me. It's just not the same with the people here."

"There, there," Gloria said, consoling Janet. "I'm sure I speak for Julie when I say that we understand how you must feel."

Janet continued to vent, "They are all great, but you know what I am referring to. They may know what is happening in the world around me, but they don't get me. They could not possibly understand how I feel about all this and know all the details." Janet almost felt bad for herself that she let things get so far out of hand that she could not handle them. "I haven't talked to you since I left Prospect Heights, and I feel my life is in the crapper after just a few days apart. It's crazy!"

Janet wanted her friends to understand. "That's why I became so concerned when you told me that Fox guy had been in the house. I honestly don't know who he is. I'll say it again that Fox could be someone sent here as a prank. You know how Steven and the guys are! Maybe Steven isn't even a part of the Kinski case, and they are pulling my leg about that too. Those guys can be such pricks when it comes to their jokes. If Fox being here wasn't a prank, my parents may have asked him to stop by."

"You are not neurotic, Janet," Gloria declared. "Even though we've only just arrived, I can tell by the time I've spent with you that you will be okay." Then Gloria said, "Now you call your parents immediately and ask about this Fox guy. Maybe they know him and can put your mind at ease somewhat. While you may not be able to control everything, there are things we could be doing to help put your mind at ease a bit. Julie and I are only here for a short time, but we will try to help comfort you," Gloria said bluntly, including Julie in her promise. "We are happy to help any friend in trouble. Aren't we, Julie?"

Julie nodded while sipping her drink and rushed to swallow.

"Also, if you need a roommate to help look after you, Janet, I'm available… if you are interested," Gloria said, wanting to lighten the mood. She succeeded in doing as much. Gloria grabbed her own phone and dialed Janet's parents. Handing Janet the phone, she said, "I've dialed your parents for you. Speak to them about Fox."

Their answering machine answered, and Janet announced as much to her friends. Then she spoke into the phone, "Hi, you two. It's your lovely daughter. Julie and Gloria are here, and we all wanted to say good evening. I stepped out today to go next door by Gertty's, and the girls said an Indian man came by asking about you two and myself. Fox was the name he gave. I was just wondering if, by any chance, you know him? I had asked Dad about Indians in the area and thought maybe our conversation prompted Dad to reach out to someone regarding the matter. The girls and I have been out this afternoon ever since he had come by, and I don't think he had returned. If he did, I missed him. The girls didn't get any other information from him." Janet concluded the message…"Call me! Love you both! Bye!"

"Now tell us all about your feelings toward Dean and Armani, Janet," Julie asked. "Are there any other men we have not met yet? You promised we could talk about men later, and it's later." Julie always seemed to have men on her mind.

"Ladies, I don't know. If you two were not here right now, I'd probably go check on Armani. I guess I could call him." Janet hoped they would not mind.

"Go right ahead," Gloria offered permission. She wanted Janet to call him. "We insist."

"Ya! We insist," Julie reiterated Gloria's words.

Janet searched for her phone and had trouble locating it. "Would one of you call my phone? I need it to ring so I can find it. I'd use one of your phones, but I don't know the number by heart."

Gloria reached for her own phone and dialed Janet's phone. "Your phone is ringing. It's still ringing. It's still ringing. It just went to voice mail. Let me dial again."

"I don't hear it," Janet said quietly as she listened. "Do either of you hear it? I don't hear it. Do you hear it, Gloria?" Julie questioned Gloria.

"Neither Julie nor I hear it, Janet. Did you leave it on the boat earlier?" Gloria thought that seemed like a logical conclusion, being as though they had not been anywhere else.

"I might have," Janet said, regretting the thought of having done so. "This is what I mean around here... things are always out of place, and I'm so scatterbrained. Misplacing it is my own fault," Janet said admittedly.

"The sun is going down quickly," Gloria stated with obviousness. "We best find it soon before it gets dark. We should all go and help look together," Gloria suggested. Gloria dialed Janet's number repeatedly during the search.

After searching the boat over and over, Janet was concerned it was not there. She was trying to recall the last time she had used it or had even seen it. Janet did not know if the ringer was even on. "I'm sure I would have had it with me on the boat when we got back on this afternoon. I don't recall putting it any-where special when we were suntanning. It should have been in my purse. On second thought, I don't recall actually seeing it since this morning when I put it in my purse. It has to be somewhere. Gloria, could you dial it again?"

"I'll try one more time. Look! My phone states I've called it six times already. I'm sure we'd hear it if the ringer is on. Who could miss that ridiculous bugle call ringtone you have it set on? It is still set on that, isn't it?"

"Yes," said Janet. "It's the loudest ringtone there is, and it makes it easier for me to hear. Apparently, it still isn't loud enough for the three of us to hear on a quiet evening. I may have the ringer off." That was the only thing to which Janet could attribute her lack of locating it. "I'm sure it's not out here, or the three of us would have found it by now." Janet thought and then said, "It must be wrapped up in something we brought in earlier when we unloaded our stuff. Maybe the sound is muffled in a towel or something. I had thrown the dirty towels and our clothing from today down the basement steps for washing. It might be down there wrapped up in something. I'll go put the stuff in the wash and check through everything as I do."

Inspection of the dirty laundry and putting it in the washer was fruitless. No phone was discovered, and it was bothering Janet. Immediately upon joining her friends in the living room, she excused herself to take some time to continue looking for it around the house. She even looked in the refrigerator to be certain she didn't slip it in there with sodas they had returned with from boating. No phone. She checked her bedroom. No phone. She checked the back porch. No phone. No matter where she checked, there was no phone to be found.

Gloria wanted to know how the search was coming along. "We assume you did not find it, or you would have said something. If only you could remember if you had it on you earlier. Could it have slipped down between the sofa cushions?"

"Anything is possible at this point, Ladies. I feel like I am ruining our evening together. Let's just give it a rest for a while," Janet stated. She wanted to spend time with Julie and Gloria while the night was still young.

The threesome talked until all hours of the night. They discussed everything they could think of until each was going hoarse. When together, the three of them could always find something to gossip about. Much of their gossip always seemed to include a lot of laughter and kidding around. Janet liked that and needed such a break from her current emotional status.

Janet and Gloria eventually retired to their beds. Julie, alert and wide awake, didn't feel the least bit sleepy at all. She decided to take a walk in the yard and vape. THC was the type of vape pen she usually used to help her fall asleep on nights when she frequently had this issue.

Stepping outside, Julie saw a very small light up in the apartment above the garage and climbed the stairs cautiously in the dark to have a look. Expecting to just see a small night-light illuminating an empty apartment she'd not been up to in many years, she was surprised to see Steven reading something under a small lamp. Tapping on the windowpane set within the apartment's main door, she was gentle with her touch so as not to startle him too badly.

Steven came to the door. "I knew you were here at the house," Steven said. "I saw your car outside, and I did not want to impose upon or disturb you all when I got here. It is so late." He spoke to Julie in a hush and placed his finger by his lips to imply he wanted them to speak quietly.

"Yes. It is late," Julie replied. "Janet has been telling us about so much of the goings-on around here. She and Dean both want to speak to you as soon as possible." Julie always liked Steven a lot and was happy to see him. "I haven't seen you in so long, and Gloria and I are worried about what has been going on. Are you okay?"

"I'm fine" Steven answered. "But I need a favor from you. Don't tell anyone I am here. I'll let Janet know when I can." He begged, "Please, for me?" Steven hoped he could count on Julie and knew she'd do anything he asked. He, too, had been a friend for as long as Janet had been. Just not as close because of age and sex differences, but here was still a loving bond. Julie loved Steven more than her own brothers. Julie even loved Janet's whole family more than she cared for her own.

Julie agreed to abide by Steven's request. "Sorry to bother you so late. I didn't know you were here when I saw a light on and thought I'd take a look. Just as long as you are okay. As for your sister, she is so confused that she doesn't know if things are pranks you guys are pulling or if there is real trouble. She's is becoming very emotionally bothered and has been to see her psychiatrist."

"I'll tell you what I know, Julie," he agreed, feeling relieved to finally speak to a nonpartisan friend. "You must promise me not to tell Janet anything for the time being. Do you swear to me that everything will be our secret for now?" Steve made Julie swear, and she crossed her heart. Then he invited her in while they spoke.

Down the steps and across the yard, Julie made her way by the light of the illustrious moon. She slowly strolled while taking breaks in her steps to enjoy her vape. Veering off a path to the main house, she decided to head down to the pier to get a glimpse of the moon in its full lunar glory shining in the dark night onto the blackened lake water. Her attention was grabbed midway by the faint sound of a bugle horn in a nearby bush beyond some trees. She was sure that sound was the ringtone coming from Janet's phone, and she quickly went to locate the source of the sound. It had come from over in the direction of Gertty's house. Julie made an assumption that Janet had dropped it when they were returning the boat and oars. As the moon glowed and showed her a path, she made her way into an area of trees.

From behind a tall oak, gloved hands reached around and grabbed Julie's frail neck. They strangled her throat with all their powerful might. Julie fought with her own hands and legs, but her petite, girlish figure seemed no match for the strength she fought against. Then her neck snapped in a violent twist, and the last breath Julie would ever breathe expelled from her tender, balm-coated, ruby lips. Her dead body fell limp from the grip of the unknown beast as a trickle of thick blood began to ooze from her mouth.

Chapter 18

High noon neared, and Janet knocked on Gloria's bedroom door. "Good morning, Sunshine. I hope I'm not disturbing you?" Janet said as she slowly opened the heavy, solid door. "I just got myself up and noticed the time. It is almost lunchtime. Did you sleep well?"

"Almost noon?" Gloria replied. "I didn't mean to sleep this late. The day is half over. Is Julie up?" Gloria appeared to have had a wonderful slumber.

"She is," Janet assured her. "I don't know where she is though. Her bedroom door was open, and she is not around here that I have seen. She got up earlier than I did and took a walk or went somewhere. Maybe she is in the basement taking the wash out of the dryer—someplace I didn't look yet. I saw she wasn't in her bedroom and immediately came to your room. However, the back door is open, and she may be outside. She is probably out there smoking something." Thinking Julie may be getting the laundry from downstairs was just wishful thinking on Janet's part. "What's it like to visit here and now have a room to yourself without all of us crowding together in one bed, taking the floor?" Memories of past family gatherings always put a huge smile on Janet's face.

"Nice! The best! I slept this late, didn't I? Don't think I'd have slept that long in a sleeping bag on the floor. My body is getting too old for that. I never knew this bed was so comfortable. They don't make them like this anymore." Gloria was sitting up and pushing her hands up and down into the fine goose down feather mattress, appreciating the vintage quality.

"Should I make lunch for us, or do you want to go out? I'd like to get dressed, but I don't know what you and Julie wanted to do to know what to dress for." Janet hoped her quests already had some plan discussed between them. "It might be nice for us to go into town and go out to eat. I'll buy. I want to check the mobile phone store on Main Street and see what I can do about getting a replacement cell phone. I just can't imagine where my phone went. Before I forget to tell you, my mom had the landline here disconnected. If you ever had that number, you may want to delete it. Maybe I should just have the landline reconnected? I hate all these decisions I need to make around here all the time. It's just one after another."

"Would you mind making coffee while we discuss it?" Gloria requested. A cup always helped her think more clearly and get her day started. "I can take a look around for Julie while you make some. Can't make plans without her. That is, unless we just outvote her." Gloria smiled at Janet.

Janet made her way into the kitchen, shuffling her feet in pink fuzzy slippers. After starting coffee, she went into the room where Julie had slept and began making the bed. It was not a chore Janet appreciated doing, but she did not expect her guests to do chores. It was also not a chore she did particularly well. As long as a bed was presentable, it was acceptable. Waving the blanket into the air, a shiny object caught her attention. There, she found her phone. In the bedroom designated to Julie. In the bed where Julie had laid. Under the blanket Julie had used. Why would it be there?

Calling out the names of Julie and Gloria, nobody answered Janet. Gloria was evidently out looking for Julie, and Julie apparently wasn't in the house either. She could hardly wait for them to return and hear what Julie had to say about the phone.

Janet sat at the kitchen table and heard the screen door open and close. She reached for the coffeepot and poured some into a couple cups for her friends. But Gloria walked into the kitchen alone. Julie was not with her.

"Couldn't find her anywhere," Gloria told Janet. I looked up and down the street and on the pier. I walked around the house. She's just not in plain sight out there. I assume you haven't seen her either while I was out?" Gloria knew the answer.

"No. I did find my cell phone in Julie's bed. It was under the blanket when I went in there to make her bed. She obviously found it before she went back out. Her own phone is by her purse on the dresser.

No use in trying to call her. Although we can assume she probably would not have gone far without it."

"She probably took a walk to get high and ending up tricking with one of your neighbors," Gloria said jokingly, but with a hint of real possibility in her thought. "I don't want to waste my day worrying about her. This is so typical." Gloria was on the verge of becoming agitated. "Do you remember that time she took us to the Chicago festival and left us stranded because she took off with a guy she met in the beer garden? I just don't bother keeping track of her these days. She should be somewhat more adult-like. She has no concept of reliability. I guess it's not all her fault though. It runs in her family. It's the way she was raised."

"I see there were some calls on my phone from yesterday," Janet said, changing the subject of discussion. "My parents had called back. Look! Steven called! Dean called too!" Janet showed Gloria the phone. "Why don't you get dressed and then we can go to lunch in town? We'll take my car and leave notes on the doors for Julie if she isn't back by the time we leave. She can either catch up with us or wait here until we get back. While you are getting ready, I want to return these calls."

Janet returned calls in the order, which she felt was most logical. Steven first, although he only phoned and never left her any message. If she reached him, she could relay any information he'd give her to Dean and her parents. Annoyingly, she got Steven's voice mail again when she tried calling him. She, of course, left a return message. The issue of him not answering his phone at all was very much annoying her.

"You called, and I was unable to find my phone, Steven. I so want to hear from you. I see that you did not leave a message for me. I just noticed your number is on the incoming call list from last night. Looking at it, it would have been a while after I went to bed anyway. That was so late, but I've not have minded. In fact, it was almost morning when you called. I guess you know that. You know you can call anytime you need to. I hope you are okay. Please call back. I'll make sure I keep my phone with me and the ringer on."

Next, she called her parents. She got their answering machine. "Hi! I misplaced my phone yesterday and missed your call. Julie found my phone for me, and I just got it back. It makes me think I should have the landline hooked up in case of emergencies. You did not leave much of a message, and I am still curious about that Fox guy. I just want to know if he is anyone of concern. We are going out to lunch shortly and will be leaving. I'll have my cell phone with me, and I'll talk to you later. Bye!"

Finally, Janet called Dean. He answered. "Hello! I have been making calls, and you are the only person I have been able to reach in person. Don't people pick up the phones these days?" Janet asked, knowing she, too, had not answered her phone since sometime yesterday. "I know!" Janet said, "I didn't answer when you called. I'm a bit of a hypocrite. I could not find my phone, and I just found it. The girls and I are just getting up here, and I was just discussing lunch plans with Gloria." Janet listened to Dean speak on the other end for awhile. "Well, we stayed up so late last night. The sleep did me good. I was able to sleep better after talking to the girls last night. They are the best therapists if you ever need someone to talk to!"

Dean was always happy to hear her voice. "I was up late too, but I'm still very tired today," Dean said in response to Janet. "I was hoping to make some headway with all the data I want to review. It looks like I won't. I have so much other bullshit here to deal with." Dean's disgust for the tedious paperwork he had to complete was something Janet could understand. "I did pass on the information from yesterday pertaining to the carvings," Dean said with some excitement. "Unfortunately, it seems as if nobody thought it was as much of a break as I hoped it would be. That's probably because we don't know what the carvings would have to do with anything much at this point. It just means someone saw carvings in a book or on the island and duplicated them at murder scenes. Who knows where else those carving images might be found?" Dean wondered, and Janet would not know. "I did learn Sylvester had drugs in his system at the time of death. It's been brought to my attention that it could have been an overdose. I can't believe that though. I'd have known if he were capable of that. They've not released any reports to me stating what the drugs were or how they played a part in his death." Dean hated to admit he may have been wrong, but he had some news on Irwin. "As for Irwin, it appears his death was due to the fall. They found nothing suspicious. He was notably old and feeble and had taken a terrible tumble. The fall would have been enough to kill anyone." After stating the facts, Dean added his personal opinion. "Personally, I'm not totally convinced of the findings. No reason, except I'm always a disbeliever looking at things from multiple angles. The office political system wants everything to be black and white, and I know very few things are that simple."

Janet had nothing to report of any value to Dean. She did mention that Steven had dialed her number late last night after she'd gone to bed, but no message had been left. She mentioned her parents but also said they had not left any return message of importance. In general, there was nothing important she could inform Dean of at this time. "If you want to join us for lunch, I can give you a call when we get into town. My treat!"

Dean had to decline. "I really am buried in work here. I'm always happy to accept a rain check. Call me if you hear anything or think of anything. And, Janet, thank you! Thank you for just being you."

"Well, thank you for just being you too, Dean. I'll allow you to take a rain check. Don't forget… We still have a dinner to make up too. I'll let you know in the meantime if something comes up. You do the same. Have a good day, and don't work too hard." Janet hung up and set her phone down on the kitchen table. She was aware of how blissful she felt after talking to Dean.

"Gloria? Are you about ready?" Janet yelled. "It won't take me long to get ready myself." Janet could not hear Gloria's response. Leaving her phone on the kitchen table, Janet stepped away from it only briefly to go to Gloria. Within that minute of being away, Janet's phone had briefly rung. The ringer was set low, and Janet missed the call. It was Steven's number who had called, and the call went to her voice mail before she could grab it. "Damn! I missed a call from Steven." She snatched up the phone in her palm and dialed him back. His voice mail answered. "This is ridiculous," she said in a message being left. "You just phoned me seconds ago. It stopped before I could pick it up. I know you must be having a phone problem, or you'd be talking to me. Bad reception? Where you are? Call me!" Janet ended her message with frustration.

Hoping Gloria would not be ready and waiting for her, Janet prepared herself for town as quickly as she could. Phone by her side, to her disappointment, it never rang during this time. She decided it was time to express less interest in callbacks.

Gloria met Janet by the back door, and Janet vented her frustrations. "I don't know where my parents are. They are probably out working in their yard on a nice day such as this. It bothers me that Steven calls and is not leaving messages. I'm assuming it is because he is somewhere here in the countryside and has no phone reception. He really should look into a better phone service. Dean had nothing to concern you with when he and I spoke. I told him we were going to lunch and invited him along. He said he was too busy with work to join us today. I have not heard from Armani at all."

"Do you think that maybe you are making too much out of nothing much?" Gloria asked Janet. "What I mean is, you just moved here, and you are inquisitive about everything and everyone. Before you got here, you never cared what your parents were doing. You had not heard from your brother in ages. Armani, Dean, and Gertty were definitely not people who were ever on your mind that I knew of except for Armani and your pent-up sexual fantasies." Gloria thought and spoke her mind. "It seems as if you are dwelling on everyone and concerned with what they are up to at all times. It also seems to me that you are letting your wonderment of them interfere with your own life in the here and now. I'm here now!" Gloria proclaimed. "Do you think you can let the other adults lead their lives without you meddling for a while? Enjoy your life for a couple days while I'm still here. You'll have plenty of time after I leave to be alone and worry about everyone if that's the way you choose to live your life. You do have choices, and they are yours alone to make." Gloria was honest because she cared. "By the way, have you been taking your medication? I worry about you."

Janet knew Gloria had a right to speak up. Everything only seemed to be of concern because Janet was making it her concern. "I haven't taken my medication. We had drinks last night, and I didn't want to mix the two. I take it at bedtime." As Janet considered her thoughts further, she said, "For the record, I worry about myself too. I worry about you. I worry about Julie. That's why I have these notes here to leave for her. We can put them on the front and back doors. Then I'll leave a spare key with Gertty. Gertty is always home, and Julie can pick up the key from her if she needs to get in."

Gloria smiled kindly. "If you ever find that you are worrying too much and feel alone, call me. If it gets really bad, I can always move in and help take care of you." Gloria would do that if Janet ever asked.

"I'm just concerned about people," Janet assured Gloria. "I'm really not a total mental case!" Laughing, Janet knew she could always count on Gloria for whatever she needed.

Notes were posted on the doors for Julie and a house key left with Gertty. Truth be told, Janet was hesitant to entrust yet another person or two with a key to her house. Julie had left her with no alternative. Surely, Gertty could be trusted. Couldn't she? If not, Janet could always have a locksmith come out and change the key locks another time after her guests left. Janet knew Gloria certainly would not want to hear about more paranoia issues Janet was bouncing around in her brain with regard to keys and locks. Janet decided to keep the key concern to herself. She already felt guilty enough for leaving without concern for where Julie had gone. Julie was like that and always came back around when Julie was good and ready. It would have been pointless for Janet to expect any more or less out of a person like Julie was.

Putting any worries behind them, Gloria and Janet had a lovely lunch. Since Julie had not called to say she'd be joining them, they strolled Main Street and browsed shops. Gloria even recognized some of the shop employees and stopped long enough to engage in casual conversation just like Janet enjoyed doing. It did Janet good to see Gloria having fun. If only Julie were with them, appreciation for the day would have seemed more complete.

Returning home, Janet and Gloria saw that Julie's car was no longer parked outside. "Where do you think she went to now?" Janet asked Gloria, who again, would not have had the slightest idea.

"You know her," Gloria said. "If she had wings, that woman flies around the world in a day." Gloria knew Julie all too well. Janet did too.

Both girls immediately reached for their phones to see if they had inadvertently missed any calls. Gloria's phone had a missed call notification from Julie's phone. No message was left. "Why doesn't anyone leave messages anymore?" Gloria asked Janet who, again, would have not had the slightest idea why.

"If she couldn't reach you, why wouldn't she have tried to reach me?" Janet asked Gloria, who would not have had the slightest notion on that either.

The main door to the house was ajar. That did not sit well with Janet. Gloria even knew how that would upset Janet. "I'm glad I have screens on this house," Janet stated. "Why is my door open, and where is that girl? Gloria, I need to use the bathroom right away." Janet's words echoed behind her in the sparsely appointed entry room as Janet turned into a hallway, rushing to the commode.

As fast as her legs could carry her, Janet ran to the toilet to relieve herself. The pressure had been building inside of her from three glasses of soda at lunch, and she could not hold it in a moment longer. A loud flatulence could be heard down the hallway into the bedroom where Julie had been staying. Gloria was in Julie's bedroom, looking around.

"Nice one, Janet!" Gloria laughed aloud. "Say, Julie's stuff is all gone." Gloria looked around some more. "And it looks like your house key is in here on her nightstand. Why do you suppose she left it here instead of returning it to Gertty or taking it with her?"

"She better have a really good explanation when I see her!" Janet yelled from her perch on top of the powder pink porcelain throne. "I'm not happy. I know she is carefree and careless, but she knows how I feel about the security of my house. She knows what I have been going through. We are not kids anymore, and I would think she would respect my property and belongings. Not to mention, I'm still pissed off she did not even leave a note or leave a phone message. Who does that except my brother?" That made Janet think about Steven.

Gloria knew how Janet thought about certain things. She knew how Julie was prone to acting but did not necessarily ever agree with Julie. "Do you think Steven came back, Janet? Do you think they are together? Do you think they are just playing games with us?" Those possibilities caused Gloria to think about it and understand better what Janet had been going through lately when Janet tossed ideas around in her mind.

"They could be together," Janet answered. "I just don't think Steven would be playing games right now. He's made it clear to me that he can't stay in town long, and I am sure he'd be here with me if he could be." Janet thought some more. "If anything, Gloria, I think Steven may be in trouble with the police, and Julie is now trying to help him. Steven was persuasive when he didn't want me to tell anyone he was here. I'm sure Julie would do the same for him if he asked her. Maybe calling and not leaving a message is their way of signaling us?" Janet smiled. "Do you see what I mean, Gloria? This is the kind of stuff that goes on around here, and I try to wrap my mind around all of it. What do you think we should do about it?" Janet was puzzled.

"Nothing," said Gloria. "You do nothing. Their calls obviously do mean they are thinking enough of you to signal you that they are okay. They are adults. If they want you or me to be involved in whatever he, she, or they are up to, they'll let us know." Gloria agreed with something Janet had said…"If they are playing a game, the joke will be on them when we don't join in." Gloria did not like mind games. "Janet, I want to go lay on the pier and get some sun today before another day passes us by again. We had already slept half of it away. Then we were downtown long enough that peak sunning hours are already gone." Gloria wanted Janet to firmly understand. "I'm not going to let Julie's immature actions spoil this trip for me. Leaving here the way she has is not right. Leaving your door ajar was not right. While I am not supporting her actions, fortunately, no harm was done."

"Of course!" Janet agreed. "Let's get our swimsuits on and go outside." With some jest, Janet added, "However, don't think I am not wondering what everyone is up to. I do want to call my parents later if I don't hear back from them again. First thing, before I join you in the sun, I want to go over to see Gertty and ask if Julie mentioned anything in particular to her. I'll meet you at the pier shortly."

Chapter 19

Gertty was happy as always to see Janet. "I hope you enjoyed your trip into town, Jan sweetheart."

"It was great, Gertty. Gloria and I always have fun. Listen, I just wanted to know if Julie said anything to you when she picked up the key? Anything at all?" Janet was sure Julie would have.

"Julie never picked up the key. I have it right here if you want it now?" Gertty grabbed the key from off a small table inside her door and extended it to Janet in her hand.

"I guess you just keep it at this point," Janet said. "I should have numbered these keys to keep track of them!" Janet said with a laugh. "Just promise me, Gertty, you will not use it unless I know you are going to or there is some critical life-threatening emergency. I have enough unannounced people coming and going the way it is, and I can't keep track of them."

Janet left Gertty's and thought long and hard about the key. Had Armani let Julie in and returned a key? Had Steven met up with Julie and let her in? The only logical thing to do was to ask Armani. To

Armani's house she went immediately to satisfy her curiosity.

Armani was home. He was happy to see her. Greeting her with a big hug, Janet felt comforted in his strong, well-defined, muscular arms. "I'm sorry things got a bit tense between you and me," Armani said with a sympathetic tone and not his stern, masculine self. "I have had a lot on my mind lately. I'm sure the death of Irwin and other problems have been affecting me more than I care to admit. I've been giving you some space with your friends being here."

Janet was appreciative of all the things Armani had to say. It comforted her greatly. He was being blatantly sincere, and she knew it must be hard for a man, such as he was, to open up about his pain and problems. "It is wonderful you've said all these things." Janet had another issue on her mind. "I have a question for you, and I do not want it to imply anything bad in any way," Janet posed the conversation to be as polite as she could. "Nothing is wrong. Please don't get angry at me for thinking this. Julie went out this morning before I could give her a key to my house. Gloria and I left to go have lunch, and Julie was to pick up a key I left earlier with Gertty. But Julie never picked it up from Gertty. Julie apparently came back for her things and left a key on her nightstand. I was wondering if you saw Julie and let her in with the key you have? Was that your key on her nightstand? Because it definitely wasn't the one I had left with Gertty."

"I didn't let her in, Janet," Armani responded. "I haven't seen her." Thankfully, Armani didn't mind the question Janet had asked.

"That means Steven was here," Janet deduced. She knew that it must have been him. "Did you see him around my place today?"

"No," Armani replied. "I haven't seen him either." Armani thought for a moment before saying, "If you care, I did see Dean drive by. There was also some Indian guy walking by who stopped in the road and took a long look at your house, but he kept on walking without going near the house. At least, not that I noticed. You know me. I've been coming and going myself, taking care of business and staying busy as always. You know how busy I get this time of year with lawns and all." At least Armani told her what he could.

"Thanks! That's something to go on, I guess," Janet thought with a bit more clarity.

Janet gave him a kiss on the cheek. In doing so, she noticed Armani lacked his usual passion when he didn't reciprocate. Yet it did not bother her. It was almost comforting not to have every moment be sexual or tense when she was around him. She saw the old Armani she used to relate to in him... the man she'd known before they had taken their relationship to the next level. It pleased her to have a normal, friendly interaction between two adults without all the relationship pressure.

Chapter 20

As Gloria laid upon the pier, gentle waves struck the metal support posts, making a slight splashing sound beneath her. Sun drenched her suntan oil-soaked body, and the warmth soothed her to the bone. Earplugs filled her ears with the sound of the music and drowned out almost all external noise. Singing along to her favorite music, she didn't realize how loud her voice was or how far it was carrying. The boat gently banged against the pier followed by a lesser, more gentle tapping below the slatted wood she laid upon.

Beneath Gloria, several inches under the surface of the water, was the corpse of Julie. Her hands had been tied to one of the pier support posts, and her feet bound to another. Her lungs had not fully bloated with water as she had been dead from strangulation before ever being placed in the watery grave site under the pier. She had been precariously placed just deep enough under the water surface that she'd never be noticeable in lower tide even if the shadows from the pier were not shading and concealing her from any view. If only Gloria knew of the death that was bobbing with eyes wide open only a short distance from her own face as water ripples whirled about. Unknowingly, Gloria enjoyed herself, sprawled facedown on a beach towel atop the boards just above her dear, dead friend.

While Gloria relaxed, Janet took a look above the garage. It was evident Steven had been there. However, there was no indication he was still staying there or would ever be coming back. Any indication of him having been there was no indication as to how long it had been since he was there or how much time had lapsed since he had left. Nothing of his remained except some trash. In the trash were burrito wrappers and a soda cup from his favorite Mexican restaurant in town. All of it was a sure sign it was Steven who had been staying there.

Gloria was happy to see Janet when Janet returned to her. It had been awhile since Janet had left, but neither of them had actually paid attention to how long Janet had been away. Gloria had been enjoying herself and was just glad Janet was back.

Apologizing for a lengthy absence, Janet said she was now of clearer mind. "Armani had not seen Julie around," Janet informed Gloria. "Steven had been here. He had been staying up in the apartment. He's gone now, I am sure, as his stuff is gone. He just left some garbage behind, and I know it belonged to him. It seems likely Julie is with him, and he let her into the house earlier. It still seems strange though. Steven didn't have a key for the new lock to the apartment. It's maddening that they were both here and they didn't tell us. A note is not that difficult to write, and they could have easily left one. While Steven and I know how cell phones sometimes work and sometimes don't in remote areas around here, a note left during his stay isn't too much for me to expect. Is it, Gloria?"

"I don't think so," Gloria answered. "In fact, I do think it is very rude Steven nor Julie have had the common sense to notify you of their whereabouts. They are guests within your home."

"Exactly my thoughts on the matter," Janet agreed. "Now I care even less about them. If they don't care enough to keep us informed, I'm definitely not going to worry myself any longer."

"Agreed," said Gloria. "One would think they would have matured a bit by now. I sometimes wonder if Julie will ever utilize common sense? I thought Steven had become more worldly and responsible by now having been on his own in California. I guess the world hasn't taught him much. Hmmm?"

Nodding in agreement, Janet did not answer the question with words. Instead, she changed the topic. "I do want to call my mom and dad again. If I know who Fox is, I will be able to clear my mind of any people concerns. Mind if I call them right now?"

"Go right ahead," Gloria said, supporting Janet's desire to call them. "I'll keep my earpieces in and won't even hear you at all over my music. You can tell me about the conversation when you are done. Listening in on only one side of any phone conversation drives me nuts anyway." Gloria put her earplugs back in.

Her mother answered Janet's call, and Peggy was glad to hear her voice. "I have been playing phone tag with so many people lately. I left a message earlier." Janet was stating the obvious.

"Your father and I were outside working in the yard. We accomplished so much out there and are beat! The work and the heat are too much for us old people. We are not as young as we used to be, I keep telling everyone. Time for a condo, I think. Anywho, we just came in and got washed up so we can relax a bit before we go to dinner. I don't think I will be cooking as much without you here, honey." Peggy sounded relaxed, but Janet knew it was partly exhaustion.

"Just as long as you cook before visiting me or when I come to visit there, Mom." Janet was joking. "By the way, your cake was a hit the other day! I shared it with everyone I could." Her mother was glad. "I'm mainly calling for Dad though, Mom. I wanted to ask him about a man who came by the house here. Perhaps you even know of him? I left you a message earlier. Do you know an Indian man around here named Fox?"

Her mom responded, "I don't. I mentioned your message regarding him to your father earlier, and he said he wants to speak to you. Apparently, he knows him. Honey, here is your father." Peggy handed Wes the phone. "What's happening? You asked about Fox?"

"Yes, Dad. Mom said she doesn't know him but you do?"

"Well, honey, I met him at one time. I had breakfast with him. You know that book you were asking about? He was a major contributor to the information in the book I told you about. I met him through the writer who was also the publisher. The writer was well-known in town, being that he owned the local paper and he was part of many social groups. He once brought Fox to a breakfast gathering I attended. That may have been around the time he was consulting with Fox on the book. If not, maybe just after the book was written. I don't know.

"Fox was extremely interesting and monopolized conversation that morning. Everyone was captivated with his stories and knowledge of the history of Antioch. After talking with you, I made a couple calls to my buddies telling them that you bought the house. I mentioned that you were asking questions about the local Indians, and I mentioned Fox's name to them. They remembered him well, but they assured me Fox is dead. In fact, dead for quite some time, they said. Maybe Fox is still alive, and one of my buddies passed on your information? They would know the house address, but not your personal phone number to reach you. Your mother tells me she had the house phone disconnected. It surprises me Fox would be alive and just stopped by like that though. That would be an honor for you if he does stop by again and you get to meet him. You be sure to treat him with respect. The man is a legend in his own time around Antioch. He's very much a local celebrity. Very highly regarded among the Indian community near and far."

"Okay, Dad," Janet said graciously. "I will do that. Thanks for trying to help." Janet was glad she cleared that up. "Gloria and I are just lounging by the lake. It's a nice day, and I am glad the recent rains have passed. It helps to have nice days when people are visiting. You know how it's better to enjoy the lake on a sunny day than be stuck inside on a rainy day playing Canasta. I'm just glad they are here. Scratch that. Gloria is here with me. Apparently, Steven came by while Gloria and I were out earlier and whisked Julie away someplace. We haven't heard from them since, and we all know how typical that is of them."

"I can't tell you how many times I had to pick you up somewhere because Julie or your brother left you someplace or forgot to bring you home," her father remarked. "I remember when you and Gloria went to Chicago with Julie for that fair, and Julie left you two there. I was so mad that I had to go pick you two up. You know how much I hate the big city and all that traffic. Not that I was mad at you, but I never trusted Julie after that. As for your brother, he has caused your mother and me no end of grief over the years when it came to scenarios just like that with Julie. We love him anyway," her father said, stating a fact Janet was already well aware of. "Listen, you girls take care. Your mother and I are going to be leaving soon to grab an early dinner out as she doesn't feel like cooking again and has worked hard in the yard all day."

"Yeah, I love you and Mom too! I'll talk to you another time. Bye!" Janet disconnected the call before having to speak to her mother again.

Gloria and Janet enjoyed the beautiful afternoon and relaxed quietly for what was left of it. Even much more conversation would have been appreciated by Janet, but Gloria seemed to mostly prefer to keep her ears filled with the sound of music. However, there had been so much talking the night prior and through lunch that Janet understood Gloria's desire to socially distance herself and relax her gums for awhile.

After taking a moment to breathe, it didn't take but a brief time before Janet felt guilty simply for relaxing. There were so many other things she could have been doing and getting accomplished around the house. Suddenly, she was fighting the jitters and urge to be productive. Such a feeling hadn't seemed so prominent in recent hours when she was conversing or moving about. Now Janet reflected upon the conversation Gloria had with her earlier, and she wondered if she really had been using the lives of other people around her to keep her entertained. It was a definite possibility she'd need to pay attention to.

Chapter 21

Evening hadn't started out to be much more eventful for Janet and Gloria. Gloria just enjoyed kicking back with Janet nearby, making that their plan for the night. Janet made popcorn, and they decided to watch a movie on disc. Both of them loved horror movies, and that was the subject matter Gloria had selected from Janet's vast array of movies for them to view. Summers were often spent at a drive-in movie theater in McHenry when they were growing up, and horror movies had been frequently shown there. So many different ones had been viewed by them that they were both immune to any disturbing violence they contained. For the most part, they both felt they could have written a better script than most of the modern movies utilized. That considered, they opted for an old black-and-white movie classic to watch instead.

Sitting quietly, they heard a repeating tap against the outside wall. It was a tap Janet had never noticed before. She did not think anything in particular was there to tap against that side of the house. Peeking out a window, Janet noticed it had become dark out. It was too dark to see anything at all.

"It's dark out," Janet announced. "Should I go see what the tapping noise is? I can't see out there from this window. Whatever it is will drive me up the wall if it continues."

"It's up to you, but I concur," Gloria said. "It will drive us both up the wall if it continues all evening." Gloria preferred that Janet try to cease the distraction, if at all possible. Although she didn't want to seem to be difficult to please.

The tapping stopped shortly after Janet stepped outside the door to go investigate. Time lapsed, and Gloria yelled out the nearby window, "Janet? Janet? Are you coming back in soon?" Gloria was starting to feel uneasy. There was a creepiness surrounding her, and the hair on the back of her neck stood on end. A noise came from the basement. Gloria went to the basement door and slowly opened it. "Janet? Are you down there?" She listened intently as the sound of silence only grew stronger. Hairs on her neck stood on end, and goose pimples covered her arms. Nervousness set in as she made the decision to go outside and look for Janet.

Outside, it was dark just as Janet had earlier proclaimed it was. Gloria turned on the only light switch she could find and illuminated the porch outside the door. She did not know if there were any other lights for the outside of the house, and she could not find any other switches if there were any. Using the flashlight feature on her cell phone, Gloria illuminated a path to the side of the house. Crickets chirped, and frogs and toads croaked; but they seemed to quiet within a short range around her as she impeded upon the territory they occupied. A couple of enormous orb weaver spider spun silken webs in the bushes lined the walkway Gloria was treading upon. Spiders gave her the heebie-jeebies. Goose pimples again sprouted on her skin. "Janet? Janet? Are you out here? I will scream as loud as I can for you if you don't answer me. *Janet?*"

There was no answer except the living creatures nearby quieting down even more. Gloria became very concerned. In the dark, the thought of spiders and creepy crawlies were freaking her out. Janet was nowhere to be seen. While warm out, her flesh reacted to the feeling of a chill. Then it happened. Janet jumped out from behind the bush with a loud "*Boo!*"

Gloria screamed. "You bitch, you have no idea how worried I was, do you? Why were you not answering me, and what was making the tapping noise?"

"I don't know what the noise was," Janet replied while laughing at Gloria's startled response to her scare. "There is nothing over there, and I don't hear any tapping out here at all," Janet said confidently. "I just hear crickets, bugs, frogs, and toads. I did enjoy jumping out to scare you though, and my jumping out made you scream louder and jump higher than any horror movie we have ever watched. Haha! I got you good, eh?"

"You are still a bitch, Janet," Gloria said with some relief. "I was worried, and I could not figure out where you had gone. And why you were not answering me? I forgive you though. I'll give you an extra point for your execution of the gag." Gloria tried to be a good sport even though her heart was still pounding.

"Crap, we left the door open and unattended again," Janet remarked as they were walking back to go inside the house. "I can just imagine what slithered in. You know what though? I don't want to live my life always in worry, fear, and concern for everything. The countryside was never the place to worry, and I loved coming here because I could leave my troubles behind in Prospect Heights. And now I feel I am just creating new worries here. It is time I started being a new me. Maybe I should become a real bitch. I can be anyone I want to be, right? Even the bugs and amphibians silence and cower in my presence. Anyone want to take me on? Come and get me!" Janet was proclaiming her feminine strength jokingly and fiercely.

Gloria supported her. "You go, Girl. Show the world who is boss!"

The two entered the house giggling and carrying on. Returning to the movie, the tapping on the wall began again as soon as the movie started. This time, it was slower and more methodical. They both screamed out loudly and simultaneously, "*Shut up!*" It did suddenly stop, but if only for a few moments. Then it started back up again.

"Could it be Julie, Steve, or Armani playing a gag on us?" Janet asked Gloria.

"I give up!" Gloria said with plausible explanation.

Janet concluded it was an animal scratching on the house perhaps. A raccoon scratching to dig a hole or trying to get in? "As long as it isn't a skunk!"

As the noise continued, Gloria eventually felt a need to make Janet uncomfortable for the gag Janet had played outside. "You probably have a rat or some animal behind the sectional sofa here. The noise is probably coming from within the house. You know how these unattended houses can become overrun with critters."

Janet began to panic. "Do you really think that's it? I didn't even think of that. There had been mouse-traps downstairs. I know things do get in. Should we pull the furniture back from the wall and inspect back there?"

"No, Janet," Gloria said with laughter. "I am only joking to get back at you for jumping out at me before. Besides, do I look like Hercules? I don't move furniture. It'll ruin my manicure. I'll let you go on worrying about a python on the loose back there." Gloria loved that Janet was seriously worried over her comment. "Don't be so lame, Janet!"

As the movie neared its ending, the tapping noise finally stopped entirely. "That was almost an hour of tapping," Gloria said while looking at her phone. "Would you look at my phone, Janet? I must have a hundred text messages here, but not one from Julie." Gloria considered the situation and stated, "You know, Janet, you'll need to take me home the day after tomorrow if Julie doesn't come back for me. That is, unless, you want me to just stay. I could move in. Are you sure you aren't looking for a room-mate who can work in lieu of shelter and food? I also give great massages!"

"Oh! Do you really think Julie just left and isn't coming back at all for you?" Janet said, just having been assuming Julie would be back before the end of their anticipated stay. "I'm sure I can drive you home, Gloria. If I end up doing so, I'll stop in and see my mom and dad."

"It wouldn't be the first time Julie has dumped me off somewhere and left me to fend for myself. Probably not even the fifth time," Gloria was trying to count. "I just assume that she isn't returning or she would not have taken her stuff and left the key." Gloria was now thinking she should have known better, and they should have taken her own car to Antioch. If not for Julie having the nicer car, they probably would have done that. "Why I always think she has changed is beyond me." Gloria wanted to kick herself.

"She did take all her stuff," Janet informed Gloria. "Even her swimsuit was taken from the clothes dryer. I've always known Julie to forget about people or ignore performing a task, but I've never known her to go away for days and not let us know where she is. I know I have said it before, but she bet-ter have a good reason for ditching us like this." Janet was now thinking that the idea of Julie not returning was a real possibility.

"You know, Janet, I've got a story to tell you about Julie," Gloria started to tell. "She'd fly off to another country and not say anything." Gloria was anxious to tell Janet something, and Janet listened intently. "One time, Julie called me from Arizona. She had done some heavy drugs and awakened with some guy in a hotel room. She could not even recall his name at the time, no less. I had to loan her money for a last-minute return flight home. She made me promise never to tell anyone that story, but screw that! I'm tired of this bullshit she pulls." Gloria was becoming even more pissed thinking about what Julie had done in the past. "If she dumped me here and doesn't come back to get me, it will be the last time. It may even be the last time I ever speak to her." Gloria seemed to be plotting some sort of retribution. "I just wanted a nice getaway, and now I feel as if she has screwed it up. But as long as I know you can drive me home, I won't care as much. I'm not going to let her get to me. It may not be the way I imagined it here with the three of us, but so what? We've been friends all our lives, and I would hate to end my friendship with her. If that's what it comes to, so be it. I can't deal with this bullshit though. It is bullshit! At least you are showing me a nice time, thank you! Thank you in advance if you need to take me home."

"It is bullshit," Janet agreed wholeheartedly. "Maybe she needs an intervention on how to treat people. If she returns, she will need to have a good talking to. Even if I let the issue go, I don't like seeing you treated in this manner. On the flip side, she is like a sister to us. We've known her all our lives and have been through so much together. Do you really think we may not all be friends anymore? With me here, I probably will not be seeing her as much anyway. She can stay friends with you, and you can deal with her. Ha!"

"I don't know." Gloria was upset and not thinking clearly. "I'm just venting and getting things off my chest. You have things to get off your chest, and I have things to get off mine. Julie's antics have a lot to do with most of things I have weighing heavily upon mine. If not for her, my chest would probably be two cup sizes smaller!" At least Gloria was trying to make light of a somewhat disturbing situation. "Julie gets me worked up. It's bad enough she does dumb things to me, but I let her keep doing them. She gets me all hyped for something such as this time together, and then she lets me down. It's like that little cartoon kid who gets set up to kick the football, and the girl pulls it away just as he goes to kick it. It happens over and over in the comics, and their life goes on together. They never really discuss the problem, and it never gets resolved. Nothing changes. Julie keeps pulling that football away from me. I don't think anyone can ever solve a problem like Julie."

What Gloria was talking about was all true. Everyone knew it. It wasn't just that Gloria and Julie had a personal problem between them only. Julie treated everyone the same. She even treated her own family the same, and nobody ever stood up to her.

They may have had words with her, but nothing ever changed at all. Julie had a rough family life and may even have been known to be a touch mentally unbalanced, which people often attributed her neurotic behavior. The taking of recreational drugs and drinking wasn't helping her personality any. Janet had known Julie occasionally smoked weed but had no idea she would use stronger street drugs or anything at all like that. Julie may have been somewhat different from other children when they were younger; but Janet and Gloria had grown up accepting Julie and her differences. Having turned twenty-one and drinking legally along with the legalization of pot even more so seemed to justify Julie's partying in Julie's mind. At least that had been becoming Julie's own defense should anyone have mentioned her habits to her. By now, she should have grown up to take on more responsibilities and should be more respectful of others. If not, Julie would likely someday be forced to face consequences. If Janet and Gloria could not help her, nobody could—or so Janet and Gloria thought and discussed.

"At least we know what we have to say to Julie when we see her." Janet had a lecture created in her head. "In the meantime, enjoy your stay. I'll do all I can to make it a nicer stay for you. I'll drive you home if it comes to that. Julie may not even be speaking to us after we lecture her. Although maybe she has a good reason this time, and we'll feel like heels for talking her down. Who knows?" Which was the case, but their poor friend Julie was not there to defend herself from her killer that took her life. "I'll likely be speaking to Steven about the same behavior too. The older people get, the less they like to be told. Of course, Steven did not dump you here." Janet thought about something else too. "As for desiring a roommate, I am not ready yet. I need my space after leaving my mother and father behind. It's my chance to grow as an individual. Not that I'm off to a great start!"

Chapter 22

Morning brought bright sunshine. Gloria and Janet awakened in cheery moods. Life seemed good.

Gloria went outside and sat in an old lounge chair while reading a magazine and sipping a glass of juice. She was relaxed and finally felt as if she was on a real vacation. The relaxation was agreeing with her, and she knew it had only taken most of her visit to feel this way. Janet stood at the kitchen sink, washing dishes. Being productive made her feel complete, and her energy level was up for it.

Without a doubt, Janet was sure she could see an Indian fitting the description of Fox standing across the way between a clump of trees and vegetation. She was sure he was looking at her house. His eyes seemed fixed on her, but there was no way he could see in her small kitchen window from any distance. Someone could see in at night with a light on in the kitchen…not during the day. Janet grabbed her dish towel and dried her hands as she headed through the house, out the door, and across the way where she had seen the man. He was not there. Nobody was anywhere around.

Dean called and stopped by. Janet sat inside, visiting with him. Dean had concerning news. "Officer Sylvester had been apparently murdered. He had been poisoned. There had been a needle mark directly into the heart. Before that, he had also apparently been hit over the head before poison was injected. Reports said he had likely been knocked unconscious while the poison was working, and he would not have experienced any pain. Fox is another mystery. The man Julie and Gloria claimed to have been here is, in fact, deceased. I know from the photocopies you gave to me that there is a picture of him in the book. I'd suggest you show the ladies his picture to see if they can identify him."

"Fox has not been back. Well, not exactly, and not on my property. Armani said he saw an Indian man looking at the house from the road. I know I just saw an Indian man across the street looking toward the house. You know I have not been around here much until now. I just can't recall ever seeing any Indian people in this neighborhood. My father said he spoke to friends about Fox and was sure one of them must have told him about my asking questions. However, my father also thought Fox was deceased. We can show Gloria his picture. Julie isn't here. That's another story, and Steven had been here and had been staying above the garage without me knowing. I found his trash, and I know it was his by the types of food wrappers he had left behind. Now he and Julie have apparently taken off together. They both have tried to call Gloria and me, but they never left any messages. That is typical of both of them. Steven has known Julie her whole life, and she'd do anything he asks. They have Julie's car. I've written down her personal and vehicle information here for you. Maybe one of your officers can spot them or the car someplace.

"One other thing: my missing key I told you about turned up on Julie's nightstand. We found it after we left. The day it went missing, I was sure the plant it was under was in my kitchen. Then I told you that I found the plant in the spare bedroom after Steven went out that day. He had said he had not moved it. I don't know. Maybe I did put it in the bedroom for some quirky, unmemorable reason. Perhaps the key had fallen on the floor and went unnoticed until Julie picked it up and put it on the nightstand? Armani nor Gertty had let Julie in after I asked them both. Steven would have had to let her in using another key. He may have even had spare keys made while he was in town one day. If it bothers me, I'll need to have the lock changed."

Dean nodded with comprehension. "I never could find out where Steven was staying in town prior to here. We've checked the local motels and hotels. They've not had anyone registered under his name. I have my suspicions that he was staying both here and at Irwin's home. He wanted to lay low. This was the address he gave to the police department when they questioned him about Kim. Who knows at this point?" Dean wished he knew.

"He may have been staying here prior to me moving in. He would have had a key to the apartment at that time. Strange thing about that though... Gertty nor Armani knew he had been around here. I would have thought they'd have seen him coming and going." Janet just had thrown the idea out there for consideration.

Reviewing the picture Janet and Dean had shown her in the book, Gloria could not positively identify Fox as having been the man who had been at the house. "Not to sound prejudice, but all old Indians look alike to me. Fox was the typical-looking old Indian you would think of when one would come to mind. He looked like that famous Indian who was against littering years ago. In that respect, this picture does look like him and any one of thousands of other men. It could be him." Gloria went on to say, "The man who was here did not have a feather headdress on like the man in this picture. Concise details of the man who was here are not very fresh in my mind. I would recall better had these been shown to me right after he left. I would also recall better if he had been a hot-looking man. This is just some gross, old man."

Janet understood what Gloria meant. "I can relate. I saw an Indian man in the distance this morning. I, too, would not be capable of positively identifying one old Indian from another in a lineup. Not after seeing one from a distance this morning. All the members of this tribe seem to have similar physical characteristics from what I see in this book. The man I saw definitely did not have a headdress on either. I have no doubt that the man I saw this morning from my kitchen window is the same man who was here though. Just a gut feeling… too many reports of an Indian near my place. There is still no way I could identify him from this book picture either. If it's not the same man coming around each time, why would I suddenly have Indians so interested in my home? Why are they coming around and then not staying to speak with me? There is just no reason for it."

"I'm guessing we are no further ahead with our Indian logic. You two girls need to be more aware of your surroundings and let me know if anything unusual is witnessed. Something is happening around here, and I need to know what it is. Irwin has been listed as an accidental casualty. Eli's murder may or may not have not been premeditated. My hunch is that it was premeditated because of the bloody symbols, which had been applied on previous occasions. We know the girls found in the big, empty house were murdered. We know Sylvester was murdered." Dean wanted answers and knew it was only a matter of time until something else that's tragic would be happening. Most likely, it would happen sooner and not later. He wanted to stop it before it did. And most likely, Janet and her neighbors could be in real danger. That worried Dean more than it would have had it been strangers. He knew these people, and it was personal. Also worrying him was the fact these incidents and deaths were not making him nor the police force look good.

"Who is Sylvester?" Gloria questioned. "What girls?"

"I'll fill you in after I show Dean out." Janet did not want Gloria to learn about it and then panic over any of the information Dean had been sharing. Janet had promised Gloria a nice visit. Too much had already been discussed with her to ruin it. Gloria had to only get through another twenty-four hours before she'd be leaving, and she knew all she needed to.

"I'll walk you around to your car, Dean," Janet said, leading him by the arm. On the way around the side of the house, Janet paused to look at where the tapping had been heard last night. "While it may be nothing, Dean, Gloria and I kept hearing a noise out here last night. I came out to look, and it stopped. We went back inside, and it started again. It was rhythmic and eerie. I'm sure it wasn't helping that we were watching a horror movie and trying to scare one another. It was probably just an animal."

"Do animals wear a larger-size men's shoes? Look! Footprints in the soil. I'd say they have not been here long with all the rain we had. Older prints would have been washed away. Have you asked any men to walk around your house in the last day or so?" Dean investigated the prints.

"No," Janet replied. "I was out here looking around last night, but those definitely are not my prints. Mine are over there." Janet pointed to where she had been.

"Do you mind if I look around a bit more before I leave? Can I see the apartment above the garage too?" Janet saw no reason not to show it to him.

"Gloria leaves tomorrow. I don't want to involve her in any more of this than I need to. Can we keep things quiet between us as far as Gloria is concerned?" Janet didn't want to worry Gloria.

"You mean you don't want her to find out about our hot and heavy romance? About all the wild, animalistic-style sex we engage in and the fiery, passionate love we share?" Dean blew a kiss in her direction.

"You wish!" Janet said, winking back at him.

"A wink, Janet? Did you just flirt with me, Young Lady? Because you know that turns me on?" He was hoping she had been flirting. He would have taken her right there on the apartment floor had Gloria not been around.

"What I was saying is that I don't want Gloria getting wrapped up in all your police business. If she suspects there is any reason to worry about me, it will only make matters worse. She may not want to leave, or worse, tell my parents and worry them. If she stays, she may only cause more problems for both of us. If there is any danger at all around this community, I don't want her here. Deal?" Janet knew Dean would not want Gloria involved either.

"I get it. I do need to tell you that she is involved until we find Julie. If Julie does not show up soon, I may need to list Julie as a missing person along with your brother too. There is an investigation in progress pertaining to the Kiniski case, and pressure is mounting to bring Steven back in for more questioning. With mounting questions surrounding the deaths of Eli and Sylvester, he could end up in a lot of trouble if I don't produce him very soon. Steven had been warned against leaving town without informing the police as to his whereabouts. He knew we would be wanting to speak with him again. If we are going to assume Julie is with Steven, there will be questions for Gloria. You two were the last to see Julie. If not for the car rental agent, you, Janet, were the last known to have seen Steven. I don't want to have you and Gloria pulled into the department's questioning and investigations if we can avoid it. If you are willing to admit that you are guilty, I can be of more benefit to you."

"Guilty? Guilty of what?" Janet was baffled and concerned at the same time.

"Guilty of finding me absolutely irresistible. Guilty of desiring a kiss from my flaming lips. Guilty of undressing me with your eyes. Guilty of falling in love with me. I could go on and on if you don't stifle my words with a quieting kiss from your lips." Dean was blushing but felt his words were worth a chance.

Janet yanked his head down and gave him a hard, fast kiss on his lips. "That was to shut you up. Don't let your head swell too large."

Dean didn't mind. "I'll take what I can get. If that was how Armani has been teaching you to kiss, I'll need to give you some lessons. We can practice anytime you'd like. As for any swelling, well, both heads are already swelling."

"Isn't that police harassment, Sheriff Dean?" Janet playfully commented. She knew she was teasing him and rather enjoyed the titillating toying with his emotions.

"No witnesses, Your Honor. Seriously, I should get back to work." Dean had a lot of work ahead of him.

Their stroll of the property had taken them around the house again while Dean continued looking around. Dean was a pro at snooping around and appeared to be very observant of all sorts of things Janet had not ever paid attention to before. He knew the name of fungus growing on the base of the house and told her how to put a stop to it. He showed her mushrooms and told her how to identify edible ones from poisonous ones growing in her yard. He showed her insect holes on the side of the house and a wasp nest teaming with wasps for which she'd best call in a professional. Janet definitely did not want any bugs around.

Dean then pointed out shoe prints from a man's shoes and what appeared to be footprints having belonged to a woman shuffling or struggling. "See how firmly embedded the man's prints are? Yet the smaller, delicate prints are not embedded so deeply. They are smeared around in the soil. Are you sure no man has been around here? What about any woman?"

"Maybe Armani may have been. He did mow my lawn. I haven't asked him to do anything else in particular in this area of trees and bushes. He was pruning in his trees and bushes the other day and may have been over here to pick up fallen clippings and branches. Aside from that, I don't know where Steven walked when he's been here." Janet knew nobody else should have been on her property.

From a few feet away, on the opposite side of the cyclone fence, Armani spoke from behind bushes. "Did I hear my name?"

It startled both Janet and Dean. Dean responded, "Yeah. You been hanging out around here? Got any unfinished chores?"

"Yes. I've been around. Just pruning bushes that have grown through the fence. So what?" Armani didn't mind the questions but minded Dean being there and being the one who was asking them.

"Just checking. Janet has been hearing noises outside at night, and we saw these footprints. Have you seen a woman over here? And what about on the other side of the house? Been pruning your bushes there too?" Dean was being a smart-ass.

"No!" said Armani. "I was there to disconnect my hose from the spigot. I had been using my own hose until I know if I'll be doing any more work by Janet or until I got around to telling Janet she should buy her own… Janet, you need your own hoses. There, you happy? What do you mean by asking if I know about any women over there? It's been like a pussy stampede lately, and I've been trying to give Janet her space with her friends being there. Obviously, Mr. Dean, you don't seem to be as respectful." Armani was playing it cool but was heated inside.

"There's the answer to your mysterious foot-prints." Dean turned and walked away on his own but then came back and still took pictures of the prints just in case he might need them at a later time. Once Dean finished taking pictures of the entire area, he started to walk away. Janet's feet remained planted for a moment.

"Did the great detective solve the mystery of your tonsils too?" Armani continued to speak with Janet. "I saw you kissing him. It's not the first time."

"It's not what you think," Janet tried to explain. Really, she didn't have an explanation Armani would be happy with, and no more of her words followed from her lips.

"It never is. Nothing is ever what we think, Janet. Remember that." Armani left the bushes, turn-ing his back on her.

Janet shook her head and went to catch up to Dean. "Anything else?" She wanted to know if Dean had more to discuss or any other places he wanted to look at.

"No." Dean could not think of anything else to spend time investigating there. "I have a lot to do at the station. Basic work is falling more and more behind each day, and time here is taking me away from the office. By the time I get back to the office, I'm sure I'll be called to report somewhere. There is always someplace to be or something Deputy David D. Dean can do! Supposedly, I have the day after tomorrow off. I may use part of it to catch up some.

I could make time for us in the evening if you desire me? We can start with that dinner."

"We'll see, Dean. Armani was pretty irritated that I kissed you again. He saw. I may need to drive Gloria back to Prospect Heights tomorrow and visit with my parents. I'll have a lot of catch up work after that. I'll call you. We'll get together really soon, and you can tell me what your middle initial stands for and tell me all about your family." Janet reached her hand up and gently patted him on the cheek. "I need to collect my thoughts after Gloria leaves me in peace. It's been chaotic and confusing since I arrived. I have a lot to catch up on. That doesn't mean I don't want you near. I'm growing more concerned over the events that have happened and those which may have yet to happen. I need your comfort and protection. Stay close by!"

Gloria was done sitting outside upon Janet's return and requested they take a boat ride. "I'll even take you to brunch at the boat-shop restaurant to make up for the lunch you treated me to yesterday." Gloria wanted to get away from the house for awhile. "You can even take me farther through the channels and around the other lakes. I'd like for you to show me more scenery. It is so breathtaking around here."

"You got it. Let's get ready, and we can go shortly!" Janet was anxious to go. Boating was her favorite activity, and it was more fun to enjoy it with someone. "Sounds like great fun!"

Chapter 23

Baskin's was a bit quiet for this time of the day. It was later than most people ventured in for breakfast and earlier than others ventured in for lunch. A perfect time of day to be there. Gloria walked ahead to grab an outside table near the water. Jan let her do so because she wanted a moment in private with Dan. She extended her sympathies to him on the loss of Eli and asked if there was anything she could do.

"Nothing at all." Dan was at a loss for words. "I can say it was the most unusual thing I have ever experienced. I'm at a loss for words, and he was my best bud!" Dan had tears forming in the corners of his seasoned gray eyes.

Janet agreed it most likely would have been a terrible loss. "I heard the details from Dean. It was brutal, and I'm sorry. I'm surprised you are at work and not grieving."

"It was as if Eli knew it was going to happen," Dan said. "He kept mentioning that things would catch up to us and we'd regret it. I honestly don't know what he meant. When I'd ask him what he was exactly trying to tell me, he would just look at me and stare strangely. When I'd question him again, he'd say that I knew what he meant, but I didn't know what he meant. It bothers me that he was trying to tell me something and I couldn't figure it out. I told him he was talking crazy and to knock it off. We had this same discussion in this same manner on more than one occasion and then just before it happened. They were the last words we had together. I still don't know what he meant by them." Dan broke down, heavily sobbing.

"I don't know what Eli was trying to tell you, Dan. If I think of anything, I will be sure to tell you." Now Janet was uncomfortable and wanted to join Gloria at the table so she excused herself. The walk to the table disturbed her as she could imagine images of Eli's boat covered in blood docked in his slip ahead of her. That particular boat had since been pulled from the water for investigation.

Gloria could see Dan from the table through the glass wall of the shop and saw Janet turn and make her way to her. "That looked to be sad and uncomfortable for you," Gloria had observed and commented as Janet reached the table.

"Yeah, he's pretty broken up about it. Eli said some things to Dan the last time they spoke, and Dan did not understand what Eli was talking about. Now Dan wishes he had paid closer attention. Dan is broken up, but there is nothing we can do for him though. I wish there was as it's so tragic."

"I will give him my sympathies on the way out," Gloria said. "I thought it best to give you two a moment alone. I know you have known Dan and

Eli much better than I have. Are you okay?" While remorseful for Eli and aware of how Dan must be feeling, Gloria was more concerned with Janet's handling of Eli's death.

"Fine. Let's just enjoy lunch. I don't want to seem as if I'm always burdening you with my worries and woes. There seems to be so many of them right now, and I should probably see my therapist and vent after you leave. You know… just to be sure I am not carrying around some hidden baggage, which will explode inside me at a later time. I don't think I am, but you know how we crazies get. Something might snap and cause me to go off the deep end." Janet made a crazy face, which cracked Gloria up.

"Look out there on that boat. The blue one out there!" Gloria kept pointing.

There were too many boats on the lake, and most seem to be blue on one part or another. Janet thought she saw the boat Gloria was referring to. She wasn't certain but agreed to seeing it just for the sake of being agreeable.

"It was an Indian, and he was looking at us through binoculars. He's far off, and I could be wrong. I'm sure that looked like that Indian Fox guy."

It was too late to tell. The man's back was to them, and the boat was now way off in the distance. There was no way for Janet to see anything clearly now.

"Now who is sounding neurotic?" Janet asked Gloria. "I'm sure there are many Indians in Antioch and more than one has been on a boat. Are you saying you could not positively then identify the picture of Fox as having been the man you met at my house but you can identify him from a nautical mile away on a boat when the sun is in our eyes?"

"I know. I'll see Indians everywhere I go now and think of Fox. Maybe I should go to your therapist with you, Janet? Think he has room for another patient? You know, patient referral discount or multifamily discount? Two loonies for the price of one multiple-party discount? First neurosis diagnoses on the house?" Gloria was being silly, just the way the girls enjoyed acting. At least it took their minds off Steven and Julie for the time being. Not completely. Just enough so that they did not come up in conversation. Neither name was to come up in conversation during their entire seated dining experience. "Who is Sylvester, and what girls were you and Dean speaking of back at the house?"

Janet dreaded those questions. "Sylvester was a police officer Armani knew from the force, and the two girls are just an open assignment he's working on. Remember, I said he keeps a lot secretive. Ongoing police matters he is not at liberty to discuss. I never really know all the details pertaining to anything." Janet would not know if she was being told everything, given it was police business.

The answers pacified Gloria. She had not recalled every topic she'd been told by Janet or overheard since being at the lake. She hadn't thought enough to connect the dots. Yet the topics were of interest to her. She found forensics and police work captivating. "Does he ever speak of any other cases in detail?"

Janet thought for a bit. "Not as of yet. Remember, I only just met him. I'm sure he will in time."

"I find it interesting."

As Gloria spoke to Dan after lunch, giving condolences, Janet sat outside for the waiter to bring them their leftovers in containers to go and bill. It was taking a while. Dan asked Gloria about Steven and Julie.

"Funny you should ask about both of them in the same inquiry," Gloria replied. "Seems they both went off together, and we have not seen them. They ditched us."

"That's not good." Dan seemed unnerved with Gloria speaking to him. "I saw Steven here earlier."

"A few questions for you," Gloria asked Dan. "What do you mean that's not good? If you saw Steven earlier, why are you asking about him now? Didn't you ask him how he is doing? Was Julie with him?"

Dan looked puzzled. "You sound like our Sheriff Dean. I only meant to imply that it doesn't sound good that they ditched you. It doesn't sound like a nice thing to do to people. That's all. As for the other question, no, I did not see Julie at all. Steven did not come here in a boat. He must have driven here by car and parked where I did not see his car nor Julie in it. He grabbed a few groceries and looked at the missing persons' board for a moment, but another clerk assisted him. I wanted to talk to him for awhile, only I had a delivery that arrived and was in over my ass with boxes. I told him to come by for lunch while he's in town and I'd comp his meal. I felt awful I couldn't spend some time chatting with him, but duty called. I just assumed he would mention Eli, and I wasn't in the mood to speak to yet another person about it. Everyone asks, and I just can't bear it." Dan concluded his answers with "I guess that's all I observed. Why the third degree?" He wondered.

Gloria answered, "I'm sorry if it came off as the third degree. Janet and I are pretty miffed at Julie. Could you not mention to Janet that Steven was by earlier? He was staying at the house and took off. He hasn't called her even though she had tried to reach him by leaving voice mail. Her justification is that he must be in a remote area where he is not getting phone reception to call her. If she knew for sure that he was around here and not returning her calls, she'd be crushed. It would ruin our fun today, and I'm the one who would need to console her. Capisce?"

Janet approached the counter where the others stood. "I hate to interrupt you two if you're not done talking yet. I'm good to go, or I can browse the shop and waste time if you'd like?"

"We are done." Gloria smiled at Janet. She then took Dan's hand and said, "I really am sorry. You take care of yourself. I'll pray for you."

Dan appreciated the feel of her hand on his. Was Gloria just being friendly, or had she meant something more by it? He wondered about it briefly. He undressed her with his eyes. Maybe someday, he'd work up the nerve to ask her out. There were not many local women who were his type and none he knew of who would go on a date with him. It might be fun to spend an evening with her when she is in town sometime. It was only a notion he entertained before getting back to business.

Events of the day saw the passing of time. Janet and Gloria finished their boating excursion. They laughed, played games, joked, and ordered dinner out. They then watched old black-and-white reruns on television from the golden era of Hollywood when they had real actors and actresses, not the junk reality star ones Hollywood puts out in mass quantities now with fake want-to-be celebrities. She grew up watching shows her grandparents and parents watched and was jaded by the exceptional of yesteryear versus mediocre-to-poor performances of today. It gave the girls much enjoyment.

Gloria was disappointed that she'd be leaving in the morning. Janet was somewhat relieved Gloria would be leaving in the morning, mainly because she wanted Gloria safe. Before bed, they both discussed having not heard from Steven and Julie. And so came the end of a nice day together.

Chapter 24

On the road to Prospect Heights, Janet was grumbling over Julia not having returned. Gloria was not happy about it either. The car ride did not bother Janet, and she was enjoying their time together and the anticipation of seeing her parents. While Janet was bursting to tell Gloria every detail she had ever left out of any conversations, she kept clammed up. It was mentioned to Gloria, however, that the police may want to question her with regard to Julie and Steven if Julie did not show up soon.

"Janet, I am sorry for something," Gloria had things to say. "I've been somewhat selfish, but I wanted to tell you that Dan had seen Steven at Baskin's yesterday morning. I asked Dan not to say anything to you. I just wanted you to relax and for me to enjoy my stay. I thought if you knew Steven had been in the area and had not contacted you, you'd be terribly upset about it. I didn't want you upset. Can you forgive me?"

Janet was not happy about that but knew she had kept her own secrets. Among other things, Janet had not told Gloria details of Sylvester's murder for the same reason. Janet felt obligated to reply, "I guess I knew. I guess I knew in my heart that Steven has been in the area. I just didn't want to admit it to myself. I also knew in my heart that Julie would not be back for you. I had hoped I would have been wrong. It seems many things are wrong, and I will need to face the facts at some point."

"I'm sorry. If you ever need to talk, you know you can always call me. I'm not as unreliable as some people we know. I meant what I joked about the other day. If you want a roommate, I'm available. I can cook and clean for rent." Gloria wanted to be serious but knew Janet wanted her space.

"You know, Gloria, I may take you up on that someday. I'd like to get so much done. With house remodeling, upkeep, my job, friends, and so much to do, it all takes up my time. I'll probably need help and an extra set of hands someday. For right now, I need to get my life settled down." Janet thought it might make for a good plan to consider Gloria as a housemate, just not now and while strange things and murders are occurring at the lake.

The girls finally arrived at Gloria's place, and Janet hugged Gloria in her driveway and walked Gloria to her door where the end of Gloria's visit was finalized; and she said goodbye. Gloria was sad to see Janet go as they were so close. Gloria realized she had never seen Janet leave prior to the move, and it didn't seem their parting was so permanent then. Now, seeing Janet off, she thought she may never see her again. She was so distanced even though Gloria could drive to visit Janet anytime. There also was always the phone to stay in contact. That was not the same as being able to walk to Janet's house and seeing her on nearly a daily basis. Janet had moved on with a new life ahead of her while her own life was stalled. Gloria waved goodbye.

Janet took off heading to her parents' home where she spent the majority of the day, which she found to be a tedious visit. Everything she spoke to her parents about required careful thought. Too much would spill the beans and worry and upset them. Too little, they'd know she was hiding things from them, and that would upset them and cause them to pry even more. Janet felt like she had been walking on eggshells the entire time.

Only one topic did make Janet extremely uncomfortable. Wes asked about Julie. Knowing she didn't have facts, Janet still felt the need to say, "Julie hooked up with Steven, and they took off to God knows where. Steven had been at Baskin's earlier yesterday, but Julie had not gone into the shop with him. Apparently, Steven had driven Julie's car there, and it appears she is spending time with him since Steven returned his rental car. Gloria told me that Dan said Julie was probably waiting in the car. I don't even know where they are staying. Neither has returned my call. You know how they are. They still act the same, and I'm not pleased with either of them. But what do I know? People have lives of their own, and I'm just the baby sister."

Peggy and Wes got the drift. They had always excluded Janet from family discussions that involved

Steven because she was just the baby sister. Janet now made her point loud and clear. She was laughing inside and wished she had worked that jab in before she had felt the need to discuss Steven. Too late. Now would it matter anyway, given the matter really did not concern her?

Peggy offered Janet some things to go as Janet exited the house to head home in the late afternoon. In return, Janet left behind a blue rotary-dial, table-top, landline telephone wrapped in newspaper. A part of Janet wanted to stay as it was the old home she'd grown up in. It felt unnatural leaving, knowing a day could come when she may never return to it. Peggy and Wes were aging, and the larger house on a half-acre manicured lot was a lot for an older couple to manage. It likely would not be long before empty-nest syndrome sent them packing to a small condominium. The other part of her was anxious to get home to her own place. She kissed her mom and dad and graciously accepted the gifts they were sending home with her. This visit, she knew, would mark the end of her being considered the baby sister of the family.

It turned out to be a perfect time to be on the road. Not too much traffic this time of day, and the hottest of the midday heat was subsiding. Her windows were down and blew in a wind through her hair. She could even tune into the music she wanted and play it as loudly as she wanted with nobody in the car to accommodate and entertain or anyone else to please. It was liberating.

Wanting to do just one more thing before leaving Prospect Heights, Janet drove around the block just for the sake of seeing if Julie's car was in her driveway. A few cars were there, but none were Julie's.

Janet went to the door and spoke with Julie's father. He was an unkempt, unshaven man with a dirty white tank-top undershirt and boxer shorts and was exuding the smell of beer and had not showered for a period of time. His look around the house had never changed over the years. She explained how Julie had ditched Gloria in one of her more common, classic moves and vented that she had to drive Gloria all the way home. When Julie returned home, Janet wanted to be sure Julie knew how mad everyone was with her for taking off like that. Julie's father was accustomed to Julie running away from home. He was a drunkard who really didn't care about people and now didn't interfere in the lives of his adult children. The whereabouts of any of his kin were of no interest. If he cared in the least for the moment, he was so drunk that he may not even recall having talked with Janet come his next awakening from his drunken binge. He looked away and said, "I'll let her know," in his hoarse voice before he closed the door. Janet knew he never would. He had never once, in all the years of knowing him, passed on any messages Janet had left for Julie. Their whole family was dysfunctional and was easily attributed to the alcoholic parents. They did their own thing and only thought about themselves. Their children took after them in every way possible. Julie was no exception. Little did

Janet know that Julie was trying to get her life back on track, which was ultimately why Julie went on the trip to ask Janet and Gloria for help. A sad situation for Julie indeed.

Janet continued her thought process in spite of not really knowing the true story of what happened to Julie. "No wonder Julie acts the way she does," Janet said to herself. She clearly saw the carefree attitude Julie possessed had obviously been inherited from her father. "I would not be surprised if Julie never returns to this place." Janet looked to the sky and said, "Take pity on her!"

Chapter 25

As Janet pulled down the long gravel street leading to her garage, an Indian man jumped out from behind trees. Janet slammed on her brakes to avoid hitting him. Luckily, she'd not been going all too fast anyway. The gravel kicked up from under her locked tires as the vehicle slammed to a halt. Janet jumped out of her car and addressed the man.

"You should be careful, White Woman," the Indian said with warning. "Your kith and kin hold many secrets, dear. Secrets that will bring about their doom."

"Hey, old man! Are you threatening me? Who are you? People have been telling me you are Fox, but Fox is dead."

Janet wanted answers immediately, but got none. Everything went black, and Janet fell to the gravel road, scraping her leg and arm. When she came to, there wasn't any old man to be seen. She knew she had seen him. She must have! What had happened, and how did she hit her head? Why did she fall, and why the hell did the old man leave her there? Maybe he went to get help?

Everything was extremely fuzzy to her. While she may not know why she had passed out, a big lump on her frontal noggin implied she had struck her head. Another on the back of her head indicated it had struck twice. Perhaps she had even hit her head in the car on the steering wheel and fell out of the car while trying to get out? Maybe the Indian man was a hallucination. Had she seen the man? Janet did not know. She just wanted to get home.

Washing off the dirt and gravel pieces embedded in her arm and leg from the fall, Janet tended to her wounds. They were no worse than when she had been a teenager skateboarding and fell, but irritating nonetheless. And still, she did not know how she really had come to getting them.

Realizing dinnertime was nearing, Janet was reminded of food. Not hungry today, she'd make do with whatever she could throw together later from morsels in her kitchen. She did, however, want to preplan her meals for the days to come and headed downstairs to her freezer. The light bulb she'd had previous issues with was again partly unscrewed and not lighting until she tightened it. The freezer was on the fritz and starting to defrost. Checking the plug, it had been partially pulled out of the socket. Plugging it back in, the freezer motor began to rumble as it kicked on. "Thank God! I can just imagine if all of this defrosted," she spoke aloud. Oddly, the freezer seemed more full. "My imagination? Must be."

Carrying the meat to the upstairs kitchen, Janet had an intuition that she was not alone. The feeling continued and nagged at her while she flitted around from one cabinet door to another, looking for a tray to set the meat in while it finished its defrost. She looked out the window to see if anyone was there looking in. Nobody was out there that she could see. She went outside and didn't find anyone and not inside the doorways to connecting rooms either.

Her doorbell chimed and scared the wits out of her. It was Dean. "I'm glad it's you. I just came home a short time ago, and the silence in the house was starting to disturb me. My imagination gets the best of me at times. I'm not completely used to being home alone yet and least not in this house. Say there… anyone ever call you Deputy Dean instead of Sheriff Dean? It has a better ring to it. Don't you think?" Janet smiled and brushed her finger over his name tag." She needed a hug and kiss from Dean to make her feel safe and secure.

"No. Not if they knew what's good for them." Dean thought Janet had already asked him that once before and was in a serious persona this time. "I have news for you. Nothing is over until it's over, but we think we caught the person responsible for the killings that have been happening around Antioch. We have not linked him to all of them yet, but he's a darn good suspect in those we haven't been able to pin on him. You'll not be completely happy to hear it. It's Dan from Baskin's." Dean had dreaded delivering that news, knowing Janet had been acquainted with Dan for such a long time.

"Oh! I don't believe that any more than I believed my brother had anything to do with the disappearance of Kim Kinski. What evidence do you have of any of this? It just isn't possible, and I'm not saying that because I am in denial. If you tell me I am in some sort of denial, I will slap you so hard. I don't care if you are an officer of the law." Janet demanded to know why Dan was suspected and had been placed under arrest. "Why Dan?"

"I can't tell you everything right now because it's confidential. You know how that goes. I'll tell you some things. Before I do, I want to ask you something. I think you once told me…but I couldn't quite recall. Where did you get your keys duplicated?" Sheriff Dean inquired of Janet.

"Why, Dan made them at Baskin's. Why do you ask me that?" Janet look puzzled.

Dean grabbed a huge ring of keys from a canvas backpack and asked if he could try them in her lock. "I'll tell you now that Dan had been making an extra copy of keys he was cutting for people and then using them to access the homes and vehicles of the said people. We did a raid on his place and found my stolen uniform along with the keys and other incriminating evidence. Most of the victims, if not all, were people Dan knew personally or people who had, at some time, visited Baskin's."

"I just can't believe that. If he had made extra keys without my knowledge, I guess I have no reason to trust him any longer." Janet felt a teardrop roll down her cheek. "It's just so, so difficult for me to believe. I've known that man. I've even consoled that man."

Dean tested key after key and eventually found a key on the ring that fit the lock to Janet's door. Dean looked at Janet and said, "I'm so sorry. I'm sure this will fit into the explanation for some of the issues you've been experiencing around here since you moved in. Come here. Let me give you a hug."

The hug was comforting. Janet opened her mouth to speak, but no words came out at first. Her brain was blank and numb. When she finally did speak, she said, "Dean, I have had the crazy feeling that someone had been in the house. Maybe it was Dan all along, and Julie is still missing. One of my keys was missing. The key I thought Julie left for me on the nightstand the day she went missing might have been Dan's calling card. Oh, Dean! Now more than ever, I want you to find Steven and Julie. Gloria had only just told me when I was taking her home to Prospect Heights that Dan told her Steven had been by Baskin's yesterday morning. What if Dan hurt him? What if Dan has hurt Julie? That weird Indian man jumped out in front of my car when I was coming home from my parents' earlier. When I got out, he issued me some sort of warning about the people I know being responsible for things. I can't even think clearly now. The next thing I knew, I was waking up on the gravel road as something had made me black out. I don't know if I saw the Indian and something came over my head or if I hit my head when I slammed on my brakes and only imagined seeing the

Indian. The gravel scraped me up, and I must have hit my head on the ground too. Afterward, I started thinking that I hit my head on the steering wheel while swerving to avoid something and fell out of the car while hallucinating. No. I'm sure I was outside of my car speaking to the Indian when a pain came over my head. Then I could not figure out why he didn't get me any help if I had collapsed and he had been there. If he had been there, he just left me lying on the ground in the middle of the road."

"There are parts of stories that I am not quite clear upon myself. The department is still working on some details. Fox had brothers, sons, and other male relatives. One son is called Small Fox. Another is Red Fox. Appears they are all named one thing or another with *Fox* in the name. Some sort of homage to him. It is possible one of them has been around here. Years ago, a female was water-skiing here out on Lake Marie. She was decapitated in a boating accident. Dan and Eli were on the water that day. I think Eli's death was, ah…well, we think someone in the Indian clan is responsible for his death. They may all have worked together for all I know. Although Dan still had motives I can't discuss. Dan is still tied to other murders. It is unclear why the Indians would have killed and left the symbols on two girls found a few doors down from your house though. And your brother? Well, he still isn't clear of the Kinski case until we have enough evidence to convict someone on charges. I want you to be vigilant until I wrap these cases up. I don't know if we ever will. Many crimes do go unsolved, and there are truths we may never learn. If we don't, God help us."

"I am sure you are doing your best. Dean, I am proud of you, and I respect you for the work you do. If Armani had not complicated things over the last week or so, I would gladly have been your girlfriend from the first moment I saw you." Janet wanted Dean to know how special he was to her.

"You like me! I knew you liked me! You'll come around. You wait and see!" Dean said, knowing how Janet felt all along, but it was nice for him to hear. He knew her better than she knew herself.

"Do you mind if I tell Armani the news? I should speak to him. I haven't talked to him since I kissed you in the garden, and I don't know where I stand with him." It was necessary for Janet to speak to Armani. "I'd like to tell Gloria too. She may be concerned about Julie. If I see Gertty, it will give me something to gossip with her about. May I speak to people about this?"

Dean assured Janet it would be okay for her to speak about what they had discussed. "I haven't told you anything in confidentiality at this point, Janet. There are things I can't tell you, but you can share whatever I have told you. I'll try to never keep secrets between you and me about those you care about. Until any trial or trials, I may need to stay tight-lipped on some business though. I don't want to be. It's just the way the law works. We can't interfere with justice, got it?"

Dean left the premises, and Janet phoned Gloria right away. They shared their thoughts, and Gloria thought it best she contact Julie's parents and tell them just in case they wanted to talk to the police. Janet agreed.

After the phone conversation, Janet went to tell Gertty the news. Gertty could not believe it. She had known Dan since he was born and had even been to his baptism. "He was an infant of God," Gertty proclaimed. "I am shocked. I feel I can't trust people these days." Gertty was crying, and Janet stayed as long as she felt necessary to comfort her. Their gossip session hadn't quite gone as cordially as Janet had expected, and Gertty had taken the news much worse than Janet would have suspected she would. Janet had not known Gertty had been so close to Dan aside from knowing him as the guy at the boat shop.

Then Janet went to see Armani. He did not seem the least bit surprised at the news. If anything, he was happy that Janet now trusted him regarding the key situation, and he took comfort in her knowledge. More than anything else, he wanted to know about their relationship. Janet assured him that her kisses shared with Dean were just those of friendship at this point and had been nothing more. She was not a slut. Although she was not sure how she felt about a bolder relationship with either man at this given minute. Janet wanted more time to explore both of them, and for the time being, both of them would need to accept that. If that was "playing the field," then she would "play the field." She deserved the opportunity to date and allow her relationships to nurture respectfully. It had only been just a week and a half since either relationship had blossomed, and so much had happened during that time. Good and bad. She needed to think about and experience love naturally.

Armani grabbed Janet and planted a passionate kiss upon her ruby-tinted lips. Janet felt the passion, but the kiss still felt a bit awkward and caught her off guard. Janet's mind was wondering how Dean would feel if he saw Armani kiss her like that. In that moment, Janet knew it meant so much that she would be thinking of Dean's feelings. She pulled away, excused herself, and departed, not looking back. While she desired the passion and manly inter-action Armani provided her, something felt askew when she was with him. It was a gut feeling of lacking trust. That disturbed her being as though Armani had always been so respected. She needed time to fig-ure out what was eating at her. Maybe it was just a way of pushing Armani away to allow Dean into her life. Again, she needed time to think about it.

Janet returned home and felt exhausted. Returning to her kitchen, she attempted to figure out where she had left off when Dean had distracted her earlier. For no reason except to continue function-ing in the kitchen, Janet pulled out the tray of veni-son packages and decided to see how much they had thawed in the unplugged freezer downstairs. It made her ponder, "Who took the plug out of the wall?

Who unscrews the bulb? Was it Dan? Why would he?" It could have been Steven.

The packages of meat seemed soft to the touch, and Janet unwrapped the first. She let out a stuttered, terrifying scream. The package was not venison. It was a hand. A severed human, female hand with a tattoo. Lifeless. Drained of blood. Graying in color and shriveling in size. Opening the second package, Janet saw that it was a hunk of flesh. Human flesh of a stomach with a belly button. Then Janet realized that the meat she last ate with Dean more closely resembled this human flesh and not the deer meat at all. It made her project vomit several feet from where she stood. The room spun, and she blacked out.

Regaining consciousness, Janet cleaned the vomit spewed on herself and on the floor, cabinets, and counter. She wondered why she had blacked out. Had she blacked out in the street? Had she been having similar blackouts and not realizing it? Was it just the stress? She did not know and may never learn. She would speak to the doctor, but later. Now she had to figure out what to do, and calling Dean was at the forefront of her mind.

Before Janet could do anything else, the doorbell rang again, and she was afraid to answer it. She was sure it would not be Dean calling upon her again so soon. She had just seen Gertty and Armani. This wasn't the moment to entertain anyone else she could think of. If it was the Indian man, the thought scared her. Disheveled, she made her way cautiously to the door with a kitchen knife in her hand for protection.

What she needed protection from, she did not know. She only knew that what she didn't know was usually something bad. This felt bad to her. Arriving at the door while the doorbell chimes continued, Janet was relieved. It was only her brother.

Janet grabbed Steven and pulled him inside quickly and shut the door. "Do you have any idea what is going on around here?" Her voice was stern and shaky while she gritted her teeth in madness. "You are wanted by the police as a possible murder suspect, and there are packages of human body parts in my kitchen right now as we speak. You know as well as I do where they came from. They came from the freezer downstairs where you put your venison. They are even in the same wrap. What is going on around here?"

Steven was about to explain his part in what had been going on when Armani stepped out into Janet's hallway from her bedroom. He had just come from the closet where he had hidden many times before. As he joined Janet and Steven, he held a small handgun, which was mostly concealed within his hand and by his shirt. Before anyone could say more, Sheriff Dean knocked at the back screen door. "Invite him in, Janet," Armani instructed. "The more the merrier. You, Steven, get against the wall over there where I can see you at all times. Don't make any sudden moves. This gun is loaded, and I am prepared to use it if you leave me no options."

Dean entered, not seeing Armani's gun in hand. "I figured Steven made his way here. I was in the

317

area and thought I had seen him head this way on foot through the woods. Thought I'd check it out. Everything okay, Janet?"

"Not really." Janet was rattled to the bone. "I don't even know what is happening right now, and I'm scared. Look at Armani. Armani has a gun. Why do you have a gun, Armani?"

Armani had Dean lock the door behind him and then put his hands up in the air. "All of you, put your hands where I can see them at all times. Then let's all stroll calmly, single file, into the living room and sit and chat for a while. Shall we? We are going to have a bit of a party here. It's not my intent to hurt any of you, nor will any of you leave here until we sit down and talk this all out." Armani waved his gun about and spoke in a controlling voice. "Let's tell some stories as it seems some of you are playing games. As for games, nobody seems to want to play by my rules these days." They all walked into the living room and took a seat with their hands in the air. "I know Dean has a gun on him. He always does. I don't know about you two. Steven? Janet? No? Okay. Dean… Don't reach for your gun, and everything should be just fine."

"Janet, Baby Sister, I didn't do what you think I did. I never took pictures of men. I never peeked in a window in my life. I never killed anyone." Steven sounded honest and sincere. He was clearly upset.

"Then what is this messy situation about, and how did you become involved?" Janet was frightened. "Armani, did you put human body parts in my freezer? You did have a key to get in and do so."

"I didn't know anything about body parts until Steven got here. That's what scared me into coming out. I have seen people coming and going from your home with sacks of stuff. I didn't know what was in them, and I really didn't care until now." Armani really had not known. "I was here and heard you talking to Steven about it. I knew the police would be coming if you reported it, and I became concerned. I came out of the other room. I didn't want to be caught hiding here. It would have been very awkward. Not that this isn't. I would have been gone if Steven hadn't shown up. Then Dean showed up."

Steven needed to speak and didn't know if Armani would give him the chance to do so. Armani did give him the opportunity and was happy to give him the floor. "Armani never found any pictures under my bed. He had planted some pictures in my suitcase I brought home from here years ago. When we got home to Prospect Heights, Mom unpacked the clothes in it for washing. She found the photos Armani had planted. I got blamed for having them," Steven spoke up.

"But why? Why did he plant pictures on you? You were his friend." Janet was even more confused, and she knew she'd not like the answer.

With great silence, Gertty cautiously entered the room with a handgun in her hand and poised it to shoot. She aimed it at Armani, knowing he had a gun exposed. Although he was not going to be singled out if the time came to use hers. Gertty had never actually fired the gun. She had never fired any gun. Today, she was ready to fire if the time would be right. "I saw you all come here. The lot of you," Gertty said. "I knew there was trouble. I used a key Janet left with me in case of emergencies to let myself in and listened in the other room for long enough. I was sure this was an emergency and Janet wouldn't mind. Put that gun down, Armani. *Armani! Put that gun down!*"

Armani lowered his gun but held it in hand. It's not that he wasn't happy to see Gertty, but he did not expect to ever see a gun in her hand. Armani spoke again to Steven, saying, "I believe you had the floor. So speak now, or forever hold your peace."

"As I said, Janet, I didn't take those pictures. I didn't even own a camera back then. This all started years ago. Armani is the shutterbug. He had been blackmailing me for years. I'm sorry to tell you this, Gertrude. When May died, I was there, and I was scared. I wanted to give May a kiss on the cheek while we were on the pier at her birthday party. I thought nobody was around, and I'd just steal a little kiss. I loved May. She pulled away from me and slipped. I didn't realize Armani was there with his camera, spying on us. It all happened so fast. I tried to reach for May and save her from the fall. He snapped a picture without me noticing. He was thinking he'd get one of me kissing your daughter, but his camera shot the picture too late. I reached for May to save her, and it appeared in the photo that I had pushed her and caused her fall. Before he even developed the picture, he told me he was going to tell people I had pushed her if I didn't do what he wanted. I was such a scared kid and did what he asked for a while. We didn't tell anyone. Then one day, he had the picture developed, and it sure did look as if I pushed May. I became even more threatened by Armani once he convinced me the picture was further evidence. I continued doing whatever he asked of me—stupid little stuff.

"The situation started to consume me emotionally, and I told Armani I was going to come clean with the truth. That is when Armani showed me the pictures he'd taken of naked men through their windows and said he'd tell my parents that he found them in my mattress. I was dealing with being gay, and nobody would have believed Mr. Macho would have actually been the one to have taken those pictures of men. Everyone already suspected I was gay, and they'd have blamed me for sure. He was blackmailing me every chance he could. When I protested, Armani planted some of the nude pictures in my suitcase for me to find as a reminder I'd be forever indebted to him. What happened instead is that Mom found the pictures by mistake when she unpacked my luggage. While Mom and Dad had words with me and Armani used the excuse they were under my mattress, it wasn't enough for Armani. He then learned the power those pictures had over me and used them against me to a greater extent. He showed them to other people, and Dean's dad became aware at least one existed. Armani told me he would get rid of all the pictures if I agreed to make one sex film in his garage. He kept film cameras in his garage and would film his sexual encounters in there. To prove to me that he would not make an issue of the film, he was going to be in it as well. There would be two girls with us. His instructions were simple. He wanted the two girls and me to worship only him in the movie. That way, I'd still be displayed as the fag. By doing those things to him on film, he thought I would not say anything. He was right. I did not want that video made public.

"The nightmare just kept snowballing out of control. He began hitting me up for money until I could not afford to pay him. That's one of the reasons I came to town was to put a stop to it all with Armani and come clean. Then the Kinski case opened, and other problems in life that don't concern any of you became more important for me to deal with."

"The two girls in the movie with you… by any chance, were they the girls found dead a few doors down?" Janet assumed she knew.

Armani assumed he knew too. "Irwin was a pimp. He'd occasionally exchange sexual favors provided by his women in exchange for labor around his house. The two girls in the movie were a couple of his prostitutes. Dean came around asking questions at the time the girls were murdered. I didn't want to get involved and didn't speak up. I'm pretty sure they were the same girls. I'm not 100-percent positive. You all should know that I don't agree with Steven's story. We were all consenting, and he wanted to service me. He wanted me, and it was the only way I'd let him touch me. All the other crap he told you is just that—a bunch of crap. I never took those pictures. I did find those pictures under his mattress. I had a suspicion. If Steven really did not take them, Irwin had. I think Steven had other business with Irwin he is not sharing with us. He's talking about other business… Do any of you know what that is about? I think Steven and Irwin were a bit chummy. Once the pictures came into my possession, Steven and I had our discussions. And I'm not saying he didn't push May. There's no proof his story isn't fabricated. You need to decide for yourselves."

"Well, what about my story?" Gertty spoke up next. "Armani was blackmailing me, too, if you put it that way. I grew sick of it. My husband had been molesting my little May. Armani had pictures, which had been taken through our window. I don't know who took the pictures. They showed my husband doing unspeakable things. I didn't know until after my son-of-a-bitch of a husband left. He left me! Can you imagine? I guess I wasn't scum enough for him. Maybe he, too, was being blackmailed and took off. Maybe it was just that younger woman he left with who convinced him to go. I was on an emotional roller coaster. At first, I couldn't figure why he'd left me, and I blamed myself. Then Armani showed me the pictures, and I didn't care about the man after that. He could burn in hell for all I care! I didn't care about anything, which is why I ended up drinking to deal with the pain. Armani didn't come right out and ask me for money. Instead, he said he wanted to do my chores and console me and I'd pay him. I paid him all right! I paid him over and over and more and more until I couldn't afford him anymore. I was only trying to protect my little girl's dignity…any dignity my family had. Armani took every penny I had over the years. He left me totally penniless."

Armani defended himself again. "Again, there's no proof this story isn't exaggerated. Maybe I showed her the pictures I found under Steven's mattress so she'd know what had been going on between her husband and May. Maybe Gertty was appreciative enough to hire me as a way of thanking me. You decide. Maybe Gertty and Steven were out to get me for a totally different reason, Dean and Janet. Again, you decide. Our dear sheriff may like to say something?"

"Because I was caught and blackmailed by you too, Armani? You know that decapitated skier out on the lake? Dan, Eli, and I were in the boat that caused the accident. We were very young, and Dan took some beer from his dad's store. We had one of Eli's dad's charter boats. I was older than they were. I just appreciated the beer and boat ride. Eli was driving the boat. We were all underage, drunk, and careless. Armani had proof of what happened. He held it over us. He taunted us every chance he could. He'd hide a fake head for one of us to find or throw some kind of animal blood all over one of the charter boats for Eli to find. It was always something different and upsetting. He reveled in the taunting of us. He knew how much trouble I'd be in if and when my father's department found out I was involved. I couldn't risk being dragged into that scene. He knew how much we'd all be in trouble with our parents if they found out. I only just learned that skier was a relative of Fox and part of their band of Indians. Not only that, Armani also had some other things he was holding over my head. As an example, he had a nude picture of me he had snapped in the high-school gym locker room at school. He would threaten to show it to the girls at school. Armani and I didn't stay friends for obvious reasons. We drifted apart. Taking pictures is something Armani does, and he blackmails anyway he can. However, we did find many pictures at Irwin's following his death and a camera. It was the same film as the picture Armani had of me. Someone was printing those pictures, and it was Irwin. He had a film-developing room in his home. No matter who was taking pictures, I think Irwin was happy to develop them. He had countless photographs of naked men and women."

Armani defended himself again. "I didn't take that picture of Dean. Steven moved his hiding spot for pictures here at the house, and I found them a second time. They were in the garage rafters. Maybe I did taunt you with pranks and that photo. So what? I was only having fun. It's all been so much fun. You all acted like you want my game to end? Maybe I don't want it to end. Maybe I enjoy pranks. Maybe I appreciate the work Gertty had me perform. If she feels she overpaid me, this is the first I've heard of it. And

Steven…almost like the brother I never had. Maybe the guy enjoyed satisfying me by doing whatever I asked of him. Maybe Dean helped me a few times when he didn't really need to because he wanted to be my friend or didn't want to get in trouble with his piggy cop of a daddy. Anyone who knew Dean's daddy knew he was the most corrupt officer this town has ever seen. Sorry to be the one to tell you Dean… Irwin's whores and your daddy were very close. Irwin and your daddy had an arrangement. You knew that but just kept it quiet. Just like you keep a lot of secrets. Pictures from Irwin's prove it."

Janet's head was reeling. "I loved you, Armani. I made love to you and gave my virginity away to you and showed how much I cared about you."

"That I can't defend." Armani was blunt. "Come now, Janet. You are a naive young woman who was potentially being set up for the games people play around here. I just could not go through with it. You know the sex we had? I admit, I filmed it all without you knowing. I admit it clearly. You're just another opportunity to make money! While on this subject, Marissa left because she wanted out of the business. From the start, Janet, I knew you'd not want people seeing videos containing you doing some of the sexual acts you performed with me.

"Unlike other women I filmed and sold online or wherever, with you, I didn't sell. I thought I'd leave you up to chance. A chance that maybe you would fall in love with me, which you did. I could marry you for that nice inheritance your grandparents handed down to you and get out of the business Irwin helped me start. If not, I had the movies. I could sell them and make a lot of dough if I wanted. You'd never have even known about them probably.

"Just the overseas markets alone are lucrative and away from anyone locally from finding out. I know people would say that if you pissed me off, I could produce the movies and make a lot of money off your film footage. While blackmail could have been an option, I didn't do that. Just as I didn't blackmail Gertty or anyone else. I never did anything to really hurt any of you. I did not leak the picture Steven is talking about to the police. I never sank Dean's career. I never hurt Gertty. She is like a mom to me. Don't you all see? You all allowed your own flaws as human beings to control you. You all were in a panic over thinking about what I might do to you that you allowed yourselves to go above and beyond, looking out for me. Don't think I never appreciated it. You all made me into what I was. Think about that.

"With Janet, I thought I almost screwed up too soon a couple times. An example is when I led Janet to her bedroom the night I took her virginity... I didn't think until afterward that she might have wondered how I knew she had now claimed a different bedroom for herself. You see, I had cameras installed in this home, at the request of Wes, long before you moved in. I even put some extra cameras in some obscure areas for kicks. They were not intended to be permanent. I assume Wes had forgotten he had asked me to install them. Maybe he didn't know I had installed them since I never submitted the bill to him. Those cameras caught some interesting activity. Steven had been creeping around the house. He had me wondering. Why was he creeping around your home? Huh, Steven? Why were you? And later, Dan was? And an Indian? Julie and Gloria gave me some great undressing scenes. As did you, Janet. They could always go public. The internet eats them up. Want to be a star, Janet?"

"I came back to town to deal with you, Armani," Steven was willing to admit. "I had some other business as well. I was staying in the apartment above the garage when I was around. At times, I stayed at Irwin's and in the house here to remain undetected. Just for a short time. My first problem was that I made the mistake of talking to Kim Kinski at a bar. I didn't know her exactly. What I did know about her was that she was one of Irwin's girls. She had since disappeared, and I am a suspect because I was the last seen talking to her. After that, I didn't want anyone to see me here. I didn't know how to break the news to Janet and my family, and I knew Janet was so happy to be moving in here. I didn't want to spoil her joy. When I did figure I'd make the announcement I was here, I wanted to surprise Janet. I was waiting for the right moment and way to tell Janet I was here and explain why I did not want anyone to know, worry, or become involved at that point.

"I wasn't sure how I would approach you, Armani, but I knew I was prepared to do whatever I needed to do to end all of this. I snuck in early one morning to surprise Janet. I accidentally went into the wrong bedroom, not knowing Janet had switched rooms she was sleeping in. She awakened before at an awkward moment. As she awakened, I had seen someone I could not identify leaving the house. He was dressed all in black with his face obstructed within a hoodie jacket. I still have no idea who it was. Definitely a man. I thought it was some burglar. Had he stolen anything, I thought Janet might think I had taken it. I hadn't actually been invited into the home that time, and the element of surprise had become very awkward. Janet had awakened as someone slipped out of the house, and I couldn't follow the person without Janet seeing me leave too. I panicked. I was stupid, and I hid until I could figure out what was going on. I continued to hang around the area to observe for a short time. It was soon obvious that Janet had not been robbed. I thought she might be in trouble. It was you in the house, Armani, wasn't it? It was you dressed in black? You were checking out your camera devices, I assume?" Steven was only drawing conclusions.

"You are right. I was around here at times, checking on the cameras. Sometimes adjusting their angles. I never dressed all in black though. I saw that black figure on film, but that wasn't me, Steven. I even saw that you were in the house that morning. I was wondering why you were lurking about. I did not know about any Kim Kinski investigation. It has since been determined that Dan at Baskin's had a key to the house and may have been coming around.

Janet told me that much." Armani wanted to clear himself of any misconceptions. "If you check with your father, I'm sure he will tell you that he ordered me to install cameras for security. Yes, I even put one in each of the bedrooms without his knowledge. In my defense, he didn't specify where to put any of them. Imagine if I tell your father that I got some of the cameras up and running and saw people creeping around. Now they are storing dead bodies here? That should go over well. And daddy's little girl having sex with the hired help. That should go over well too. The sin in this home is almost too much!" Armani thought he had the upper hand.

Steven justified matters. "See, Armani is the one who takes pictures of people in bedrooms! I tried to tell you. Won't you all believe me? I'm sure my father did not order cameras for the bedrooms. He kept them a secret." Steven thought he had drawn an intelligent conclusion, which would persuade the thinking of everyone in the room.

"What cameras? You go see if you can find any cameras now in the bedrooms," Armani said, knowing he had already just removed them. That's why he had been in the house in the first place. That's all he had wanted to do: to collect the cameras and get out. Circumstances had prevented that. "Maybe, Steven, you should explain to Janet what you have been doing in her closet? Was she ever naked while you looked on? Did you watch us the evening we made love? Did you get off on watching your sister doing it with the hot Italian guy next door you have been lusting over? Tell her the truth right now. I know the truth. She deserves to know, and she deserves to hear it from you." Armani knew the truth from what the cameras had shown him.

It was true. Steven had been in her closet that night. Only because he had been staying in the house and became trapped in there when Janet and Armani came in earlier than expected. He could not get out undetected. But Steven didn't watch them that night and kept his face hidden in his hands through the entire sexual event. He did not know all the evidence Armani had on him, and he didn't want to know. Steven was not about to push his luck. Armani's gun was still within perfect shot of Sheriff Dean or anyone, and he, himself, had no weapon of defense. Steven did not want to go into detail. He commented by only saying, "I was trapped in the house that night. It's true. I had not wanted to confront Armani and Janet during the intimacy. I figured if I stayed put and quiet, nobody would ever know. It was not something I enjoyed as Armani is leading you all to believe."

Gertty's gun remained pointed at Armani, but she had settled down since speaking her mind. After hearing what had been being said, Gertty had second thoughts about everything Armani had been saying. He had charged her for chores. What if what Armani had said was true about Steven, or what if Steven's story was the correct version? Would she ever really know? Would it make a difference to her? Probably not, and she knew that.

"Don't believe Armani." Sheriff Dean was about explain something more. "Armani has been holding that lake accident over my head for a long time. We found some proof that Irwin had been blackmailed by someone when we examined his home. What I haven't told anyone is that authorities do have some proof linking Irwin to deaths around here. That includes the two girls next door to him and the campers. Dan is not the only suspect. We think he is attached to the missing persons' Kim Kinski case, but it's difficult to tell without Kim's body. I never told anyone here, but Kim had been reportedly involved in sex-for-hire situations, which you all know. It confused me why Steven would care about a female prostitute. There have been details I was not at liberty to discuss, but the guns in the room are my excuse for talking now. Also, think about this… If Armani was doing these things to us, I'm sure he was manipulating other people as well."

"You have no right to accuse me of that. Nobody has ever approached me with an issue of how I treat them until here and now. Dean, I appreciate that as an officer of the law, you need to keep an open mind, but you are very offensive to people. You speak your mind a little too much. I'm not the only one in town who believes that about you. Mind your mouth!"

"Dean, did Kim have a tattoo on her hand?" Janet felt she knew the answer to that question too.

"Yes. Why?" Dean was curious how Janet would know that.

"There are the body parts in my house. I just found them as you all arrived. There is a hand that was wrapped in a meat package in my kitchen. Also, part of a human stomach in another package. I'm sure there must be more parts in the freezer downstairs, from where I removed the packages. I thought the freezer looked exceptionally full when I was last down there." Janet didn't dare explain to Dean that she was certain the meat they had consumed at the dinner the night she cooked for him had most likely been human. She did not want to mention that meat given to anyone may have also been. As it was appearing, evidently, meat from Kim's corpse. "I also knew someone was here by the light bulb in the basement. I knew it was screwed in tightly and working, and then it was loose and not working at a later time. Another time, the plug on the freezer had been partly pulled out of the socket, and the freezer was defrosting."

"I loosened the light bulb," Steven admitted to having done as much. "I wanted to leave you a sign that someone had been around here. I didn't want you to know I had been around, but I wanted you to know someone unidentified has been coming and going without you knowing. I felt as if someone had been planting evidence around and leading police to think I killed Kim Kinski. I had to figure out who it was. If they had known I was onto them, they'd not have come around. As for the body parts in the freezer... I didn't put those there. More evidence planted? Just more evidence that was meant to discredit me and put the police on my tail. The only one I could assume would do that would be Armani. I never suspected Dan. Now it could have been Irwin earlier. Did anyone here kill Irwin, or was it an accident? Were you and Irwin at odds, Armani?"

"Don't you try and pin that on me," Armani protested convincingly. "Maybe you were trying to dispose of the body parts when Janet happened upon them? Maybe any number of things happened. Don't you pin it on me. You were the one holding the bag, so to say—that is, until Dan came into the picture." Armani was defensive. "I had never met Kim and have never been to the bar. If I need one, I have an alibi for the night she disappeared. That's my business and not yours. That is, unless you are booking me, Dean?" At least, that was what Armani was saying.

Steven replied, "I just wanted to add that I had not been back down to the freezer. Although I did sleep down there. If the appliance was unplugged, I didn't do it. I never put anything more into the freezer after the deer the first night. I got the wrap from Irwin's garage. That's where he and I prepared the deer meat. He has rolls and rolls of butcher wrap there. He was a hunter."

"Steven's last comments are true. Also, Armani could be telling the truth with regard to his last statement," said Dean. "I have something more to add… The corpse of Kim Kinski could be in this house. It's also true Steven is still a suspect in her disappearance. He had been in the bar the night Kim went missing. It's also true that Armani didn't have any known connection to Kim, and there was no evidence he had ever been a patron of the pub. This is your house, Janet. If the police department does not piece together Dan's or Irwin's involvement, Steven could still likely be blamed. We know he is not to blame. The department could think otherwise. I'm sorry, Steven."

"Don't be sorry. I'm just glad you caught Dan and are putting pieces together with Irwin and previous murders. Maybe I didn't handle matters as I should have, but I am happy things are coming out into the open." Steven knew how lucky he was, or would be, to be cleared in the disappearance of Kim. He was confident he would be.

"My theory at this time is that Irwin had committed murders," Dean said. "Dan had a copy of the key to Irwin's house, and I have verified that. I suspect Dan had used it at times. Maybe Dan even knew what Irwin had been doing. It's possible Irwin caught Dan in his house and an altercation led to Irwin falling down the stairs. We'll never know unless Dan admits to anything. Being that Armani seems to be so good at becoming a borderline blackmailer, maybe Dan learned a few tricks from him. I don't think we can ever prove everything unless someone admits guilt or sheds light on some clue we've overlooked. Can we put the guns down and go look in the kitchen? I can't believe any of us would shoot another person in this room despite your soap-opera issues. All I care about right now is finding out what happened to Kim Kinski. She was a person, you know? Let's try to show some respect. If it's not Kim who has been cut up in pieces, we should be thinking about who was. Other people are missing. Also, who did it?" Dean wanted to move on with the inspection of evidence.

"My gun is relaxed. I'll put it down if you two put your guns down too. I mean Gertty and the one you are carrying, Dean. We can all set them in the center table at once. Agreed?" Armani was willing.

"I can't do that, Armani. Mine is a police-issued gun. I need to go into the kitchen. If I walk away from my gun and someone gets a hold of it, it would be my neck. I can't have that. Just put your gun down at your side like Armani, Gertty, and we can all be happy for the time being."

Guns down at their sides, they walked into the kitchen. It was the hand of Kim as far as Dean could tell. It no longer looked like the hand of a living human, but it was likely her hand. As for the other package, that would take forensics to determine. Nobody knew what to say. The group was simply grossed out and mortified. Gertty did not want to take a look at all.

Sheriff Dean spoke up again, "Listen, everyone, I am going to need to call the department. I'm sure Janet doesn't want porn tapes of her made public, Armani. Since nobody else has seen those movies, why don't you and Janet just drop the subject, or else we can all see to it that Armani is brought up on blackmail charges whether he thinks he deserves them or not? Don't think we can't, Armani. Gertrude, your husband's actions with your daughter were not your fault. I think we all know May's death was an accident, and Steven was not intentionally responsible for it. Irwin is dead, and the department will likely reopen his case in lieu of circumstances. Eli was driving the boat the day that water-skier died. It was an irresponsible accident that Eli lived with his whole, short life. Officials will continue looking into his death. Dan is paying the price, and he'll be all right in the hands of the courts if charged with anything. Armani has been making me pay a price ever since that boating accident, and I wasn't even driving the boat that day. It was an awful event I will never forget. Armani claims he was out on the lake filming the day the skier died. I know he saw the accident, and he claims to have film of the accident. He has been holding that over Eli, Dan, and me for long enough. It still is not cool with me, but it's time to let it go. Enough!

"I think we all suspect who is telling the truth about the nude photos Steven had. Who cares? Nobody who knows about them cares to discuss them at all. I can help Janet and Steven by discussing it with her parents. I'll tell them that I have proof those pictures were planted by an anonymous source as a joke that got out of hand and that source is now deceased. Steven and Armani, consider your feud ended now. What if we just drop everything now and put the past behind us? No more accusations, jokes, gags, blackmailing, or guilty consciences. There is no reason to hold onto these memories. Let's just ignore everything and stop this madness. We can leave Eli's death and all the others to the police department to deal with. Irwin could have put Kim Kinski's body in the basement here. Dan most likely did. Irwin did have one of the old keys Janet's parents had given to him, and Dan had a new one. It's just potential theorizing. Police can figure out the timing the parts were placed in Janet's house and could coincide it with the timing of Irwin's death. Maybe they'll even find some fingerprints. Also, if Armani has any tapes of someone in black creeping around, maybe Janet can surrender them as evidence. They can try to match the clothes of the intruder and see if they match those belonging to Dan, Irwin, or some Indian? Any other ideas?"

Gertty nodded and agreed to everything. "Let's let Dean do his job with regard to the murders. Whatever you decide, Dean. You know best. We need to stick together and help one another through this. Steven, I know you liked May, and you would not have hurt her. I'm sorry you carried that baggage with you through life. You are not a killer."

"I have a couple questions I need to ask," Janet asked as she raised her hand as if she was in a classroom. "We'll need to explain why we've all been here so long talking should it ever come up. Shall we say I invited you all over for a party? I opened the meat to cook and found the body parts while you were all here? It would make more sense. Otherwise, the question of what we have been talking about so long before calling authorities may come up. Also, Steven, how were you getting into the apartment to stay there? I had those locks changed with the others after I moved in."

Steven stated that he had changed the lock on that door the day Janet gave him the key to put supplies away up there. "It only takes a few minutes and a screwdriver. When I came in, I gave you the new key. I admit to snooping around your house again after that. I was looking for your stash of extra keys so I could replace the spare. I never found them. If you ever went to use the extra key, it would not have worked. Here is the spare new one. I don't have any other copies. I promise." Steven handed Janet the key.

"I think Janet's idea was a good one about keeping this all private." Dean knew everyone would be in agreement. "Agreed?" It was unanimous.

Armani had something to say, but it was not what anyone expected. "I've known all of you my whole life. I don't know how I allowed things between us to get off track, but I'm sorry. I was wrong, and it's time I change. Janet, I do love you and would be so appreciative if you'd give me a chance to show you I can change. You are the most incredible young lady I've ever known. I'm so sorry this all came about. I envisioned you and I would be the perfect couple, and I could put my sexual escapades behind us without you ever finding out. I'd never really hurt any of you. I become scared at times. I am alone in this world except for all of you. I have nobody. The truth is that nobody ever really taught me much growing up. Mom died early, and Dad was bedridden. And I grew up on my own. I loved Steven like a brother. His gay lifestyle and mannerisms affected me if others saw us associating. Dean, I'm sorry you and I went our own ways. Perhaps we can be friends again someday. Just so you all know, the loss of Irwin and news about Dan have very much disturbed me. I'm sorry to all of you." For the first time he could ever recall, he shed a tear in front of others.

Janet was in agreement with most of what had been said. "I care about you, Armani. I care about you as any sister cares about her brother. In my eyes, I'd regret ever being the one who ever has to judge you. If you do anything to hurt my family or friends again, you will regret it. As you see now, they are all capable of banding together against you, and you'd regret it. Mark my words. Do you understand?" Janet walked over to Armani and gave him a kiss on the cheek. "Make me proud to be your neighbor and friend. You do know you are not the man for me, don't you?"

Then Janet had a thought she'd not considered. "What about my friend Julie? Where is she?" That was a question nobody could answer. Maybe she would be a piece of the missing persons' puzzle nobody ever would complete. Her body would likely wither and deteriorate as fish nibbled at the flesh until the bones fell loose from their binding and dropped to the bottom of the lake, never to be seen again.

Armani knew Janet would not accept him as her man and was heartbroken. He had hoped things would have turned out differently but knew he was way too mischievous for someone as innocent as Janet. He would always love her in his own way. He'd always have her next door. He'd always have copies of film footage of them together stored online.

Janet walked to Dean and gave him the greatest kiss she'd ever given anyone. In her heart, she knew Dean was the man for her. She was not happy that his career path put his life in jeopardy at times. That was just something she would deal with. She also knew that her own life may have been in jeopardy at times and there was nothing she could have done to prevent that. If anyone could protect her, Dean could and would.

Chapter 26

Within a month, Janet was settled in her house, and her life was as normal as it could be. The apartment was just the way she needed it to perform her career tasks. Money was coming in consistently. Renovations on the main house were underway and would continue through the fall and winter. Her health had improved. Primary physician tests uncovered that she had diabetes, and medications resolved any dizziness and symptom issues. Mental concerns no longer plagued her.

Armani was hired by Janet to work around the house at a reasonable rate. He even appeared to ignore the comings and goings of Dean and apparently respected any bonds anyone had with Dean. Armani never even batted an eyelash when Dean would coddle Janet in front of him. He even apparently began to consider Dean a friend once more.

One day, on the pier, Armani approached Janet with a question. He had been curious if there was more reasoning behind why she had forgiven him at all. It had all seemed too easy for him. She answered, "Yes. What Dean said resonated with me. He said we may never learn the whole truth and some crimes go unsolved. Years ago, I was searching obscure places within my parents' Prospect Heights home. I was snooping for my birthday presents when I came upon my brother's hooch stash. Along with his stash hidden in attic rafters, there were pictures. Steven told us all that he did not have a camera. I know he did. He had taken pictures out on the island. Pictures of trees he kept in an album. The pictures I found with his stash were not of scenery. They were photos he had taken through an open window. They were of a naked guy. Not just taken at one time... taken over a period of time. The pictures were of you. It was evident you didn't know they were being taken. Steven loved you. I knew that. We all loved you. You were like family to all of us. But Steven loved you differently in his own way. I'll never profess to understand one man's feeling for another. Anyway, I knew Steven was telling us all some lies, but it wasn't worth getting into. He wasn't out to hurt anyone. The finding of those pictures was when I learned my brother was gay and he liked to drink. I just didn't know other people knew, and I never told anyone. Had I, things might have turned out very differently for him. I didn't want to interfere in his life. When I came here and learned other people did know, I wasn't comfortable with that. I'm over it now. I just wanted to impress everyone when I came here and wanted everything to be picture-perfect. Excuse the pun. You know, you all aren't worth impressing. I thought those pictures made you the victim. You, Armani, are no victim. I still care about all of you very deeply."

Julie was not to be found but was always near. She was always near in heart, body, and spirit. Janet could feel she was near and thought of her often. Never a day went by that Janet did not speak of her. Janet feared the worst as Julie would have never taken off and disappeared in the manner in which she had. Yet hope remained that she may one day be found alive and well. That seemed unlikely since her car had been found in a desolate cornfield in Wisconsin. She never would have willingly abandoned her automobile and fled. Given the life she led at home, she may have fled as a possibility. Where would she have gone? And with whom?

Dan was facing a trial, and Janet would be called to testify. It didn't worry her. It upset her to think that Dan was capable of any murder, and it upset her that he had been making the keys and trespassing; but Janet could not have been in any control of any of that. She hoped to visit him in jail someday and show her compassion and support in hopes Dan would somehow be cleared of murder charges and end any nightmare he was living. He still had not admitted any guilt. That would be at the trial if he chose to plead any. There was always hope charges would be lessened or dropped entirely. Knowing he had made an extra copy of her key meant that he'd never be completely innocent, as she saw it. Yet she could forgive him. He had long been loved and respected by his family, friends, and people in the community. Now he had a tough road ahead of him even if his record ever was to be cleared of any crimes.

Gloria would be coming to visit soon. She was happy Janet had settled in and was hoping for a less complicated visit this time. While never having been provided all details of what had transpired as Janet knew them, she knew enough to make sense and understand that the situations were not to be worried over. She was happy Janet was safe and had a sheriff in her life to protect her. She, herself, had a new man in her life and could not wait to introduce him to Janet. It was someone Janet and Gloria knew from high school. However, he was not someone they had associated with, and they could not recall who he was from back in the day. Janet could not wait to meet him again and find out the story of how they got together as a couple.

Gertty and Janet visited each other daily. They appreciated their time together. Janet understood why Gertty treated Armani like the son she never had. While they did not always agree, they were all like one big family—Dan included. Gertty treated Janet like her own daughter and once slipped and called her *May*. Their relationship was special. Very different from any other relationship Janet ever had. This was a first friendship for her with an older woman.

Dean worked hard at his job. He grew to love Janet more each day. Janet was proud of him and all the wonderful things he did for the community she had always cared about and loved. He worked hard to keep the community safe and keep citizens content. That was a hard job. And dangerous.

Janet sat on a beach towel on her pier and felt at one with the surroundings. She belonged and knew it was where her soul wanted to be. A new puppy and kitten snuggled next her. Closing her eyes, she took in a deep breath of the fresh country air. From within trees and bushes, on the side of the house, an old Indian stood watching her through the branches. She was unaware even as the pup looked in that direction and let out a tiny yip. At the very same time, the curtains in her four-seasons room window dropped back as a dark apparition who had been staring at her sank back into the house. Of that, she was also unaware.

About the Author

A. J. LeBergé is from the Chicago area but has spent most of his adult life in southern California. It is from spending summers at a lake house at Lake Marie that this book came to be. After having worked on the school newspaper in high school, he later had his own featured column in a Palm Springs magazine. This is his first novel in his nonfiction series, *The Left Bank of Time*. LeBargé is also a renowned interior designer, gallery quality canvas artist, and professional jewelry designer.

CPSIA information can be obtained
at www.ICGtesting.com
Printed in the USA
LVHW101542040422
R17259800001B/R172598PG714871LVX00001B/1